The Wedding

PAT NICHOLS

The Wedding by Pat Nichols
Published by Armchair Press
Copyright © 2024 by Pat Nichols
979-8-9860519-8-7
Cover Design by Elaina Lee
Edited by Sherri Stewart

Available in print from your local bookstore or online.
For more information on this book or the author visit:
https://patnicholsauthor.blog
Printed in the United States of America
The Wedding is a work of fiction. Names, characters, and incidents are all products of the author's imagination or are used for fictional purposes. Any mentioned brand names, places, and trademarks remain the property of their respective owners, bear no association with the author or publisher, and are used for fictional purposes only.
Library of Congress Cataloging-in Publication Data
Nichols, Pat.
The Wedding/ Pat Nichols

Books by
Pat Nichols

Women's Fiction

Blue Ridge Series

Blizzard at Blue Ridge Inn
The Inheritance
The Wedding
Christmas at Hilltop Inn (November 2024)
More titles in 2025

Butler Family Legacy Series

Big Secrets, Little Lies
Truth and Forgiveness
New Beginnings

Willow Falls Series

The Secret of Willow Inn
Trouble in Willow Falls
Starstruck in Willow Falls
Bridges, Books, and Bones

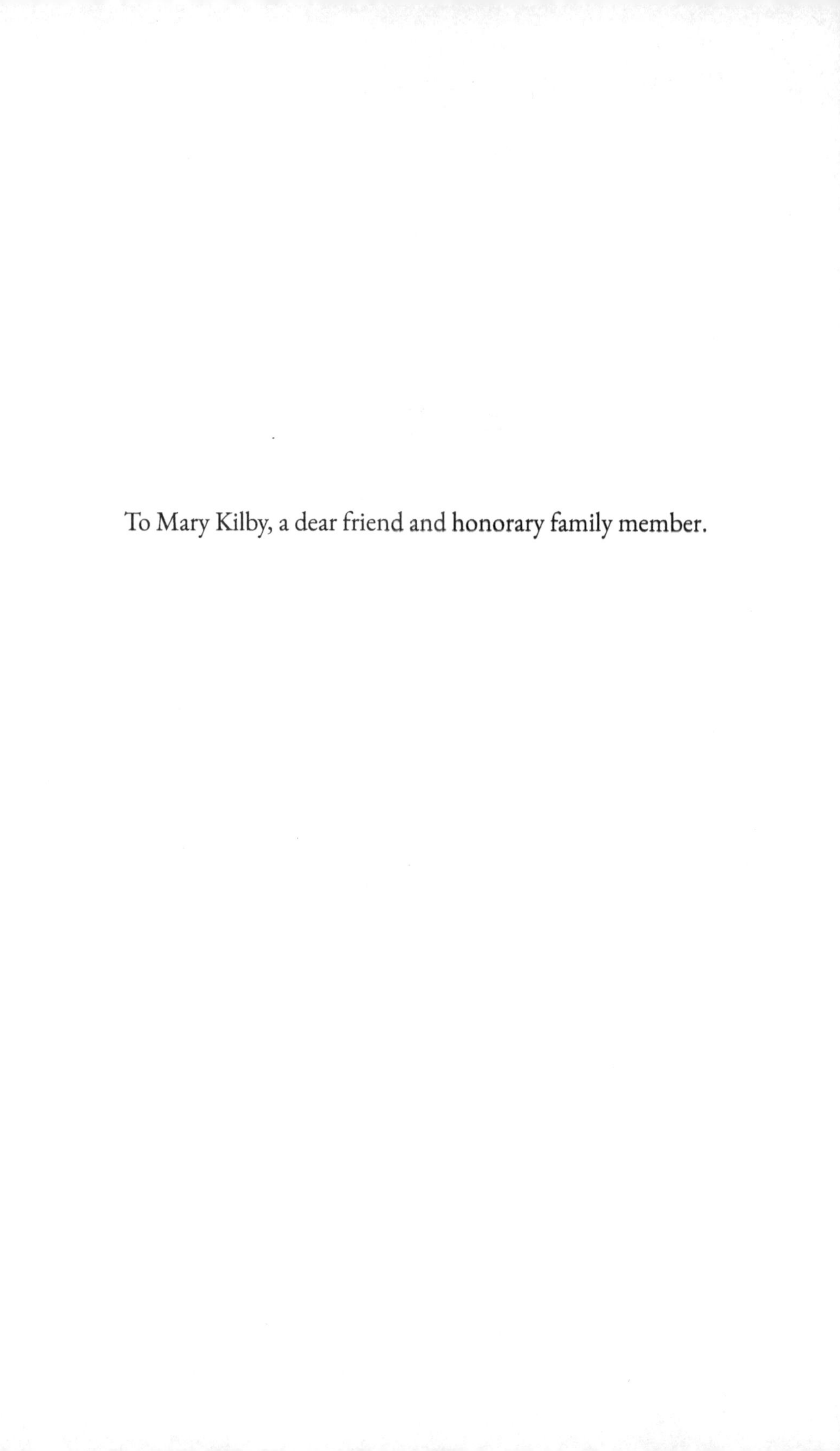

To Mary Kilby, a dear friend and honorary family member.

Chapter 1

As Wendy Thomason hiked down the ranch house driveway, the afternoon sun caressed her cheeks, its warmth mingling with memories from last night's date with Chris. Reliving his touch and the tender way he had kissed her in the moonlight warmed her heart and curled her lips into a smile. All seemed right with the world--until she reached the end of the driveway and opened the mailbox.

A jab of pain attacked the back of Wendy's throat as she removed a stack of mail and gaped at the top envelope. Maybe it was an illusion. She squeezed her eyes shut. Dare she look again? Her eyes fluttered open. It was all too real. Wendy's heart pounded against her ribs as she trudged back to the home she shared with her Awesam business partners. After tossing the other mail on the kitchen counter, she carried the dreaded envelope into the den and collapsed onto the sofa. Weeks had passed since she'd blocked calls from the Nevada prison. Now this.

Reality struck home as Wendy pressed her hand to her baby bulge and forced her eyes to focus on the envelope. The hope for a future free from her child's father vanished as she read *Wendy Peterson* written in the all-too-familiar handwriting. The name she'd known for three years suddenly tasted like acid on her tongue. Fighting the urge to rip the envelope to shreds, she slapped it face-down on the cushion beside her thigh. She peered over her shoulder at the sound of the back door opening followed by the clang of keys in the kitchen-counter bowl.

Erica Nelson strode into the den and tossed her purse on the coffee table. "Anything exciting happen while I was in class?"

Wendy eyed at the envelope. "You'd think by now he would've accepted the fact that I've ditched the name Peterson."

Erica dropped onto the sofa beside her. "He wrote to you, didn't he?"

Wendy tapped her finger on the envelope. "Since prisoners' phone calls are recorded, do you suppose their mail is inspected by a guard or some other official person?"

"Are you struggling with whether or not you should open the letter?"

"What would you do if *your* name was on the envelope?"

"I suppose—" Erica hesitated as if debating how to answer. "For my own peace of mind, I'd want to know what he's up to."

Wendy's bottom lip caught between her teeth as her focus shifted from the envelope to the still-life painting hanging above the fireplace mantel. Maybe Erica was right. Not knowing what was in the envelope would lead to all sorts of wild assumptions—none of them good. "I don't want to read it, but I need to know what he sent."

"Do you want me to open it for you?"

Wendy nodded.

Erica removed then unfolded a single sheet of lined paper. "It's a hand-written letter. What do you want me to do with it?"

Wendy's eyes remained laser focused on the painting. "Read it to me."

"Are you sure?"

"No, but go ahead anyway."

"He starts with, '*Dearest Wendy.*'"

"The same way he started that disgusting letter he wrote to the three of us." Wendy closed her eyes and let her mind drift to the day after she'd first met Chris in the Blue Ridge Inn dining room. The same day she'd accepted reality about the man she'd married three years earlier.

"Do you want me to stop or continue reading?"

Wendy opened her eyes. "Keep going."

"*I wasn't surprised when Erica and Amanda blocked my calls, but I was astounded that you had done the same. But then I realized how painful it must be for you to hear the voice of the man you love, knowing he's languishing behind bars as a falsely accused victim. Rest assured, I'm appealing the verdict.*"

Wendy's nostrils flared. "How could that man possibly believe I still love him after everything he's done to the three of us. Plus, every bit of evidence the district attorney presented proved that stabbing the life out of a loan shark couldn't possibly qualify as self-defense."

"Which is why his appeal will fail, and he'll spend at least the next decade in jail."

"Ten years isn't nearly long enough to pay for all of his crimes."

"If we're lucky he won't be paroled before serving his full twenty-five-year sentence." Erica's focus returned to the letter. "*As I write this, I'm remembering the day I first saw you—the beautiful young waitress whose long blonde hair, mesmerizing blue eyes, and smile intrigued me. Had I met you before I met Amanda and Erica, I would only have one wife. You.*"

Wendy scoffed. "In Amanda's words, what a load of monkey muck. I was only fourteen when he married Amanda. Not to mention the fact that when he met me, he'd already snagged a redhead, a brunette, and a silver-haired wife. He obviously wanted a blonde to complete his illegal wives club."

"At least the three of us ended up with the two houses he inherited from Eleanor Harrington, especially the one next door."

Wendy's muscles tensed. "If he finds out about us transforming the big house into the Hilltop Inn and Spa, he might try to steal it from us."

Erica shrugged. "Impossible, since he deeded both houses to us, and we paid all the back taxes to take possession."

"He conned the three of us into believing he was someone he wasn't, so I don't trust him one little bit." Wendy wrapped her arms around her baby bump.

"You don't have to worry because we have the law on our side. Besides, Chris is our attorney. He'll protect us from any illegal shenanigans that con man might try to pull."

"I suppose you're right. What else does the criminal have to say?"

Erica blinked. "*I have three photographs of you taped beside my bed. Those pictures brighten my cell and give me hope in this dreary place.*"

Wendy cringed at the thought of strange men convicted of all sorts of crimes gawking at her image. "That's way beyond creepy."

Erica brushed her fingers through her dark hair. "Are you sure you want me to continue?"

"No, but keep reading anyway."

"Okay. '*Since my wife is no longer alive, I am free to marry you and assume my role as the father of our child. If you give birth to a boy, he should share my name.*'" Erica's jaw clenched. "That man is the most disgusting narcissist on the face of the earth."

Wendy swallowed the bile erupting in her throat. "He'll never leave me alone, will he?"

"You have nothing to worry about." Erica reached across the cushion and touched Wendy's arm. "He has no claim on you or your son."

Wendy heaved a heavy sigh. "We both know that won't stop him from trying."

"He can try all he wants, but he won't succeed." Erica pulled her hand away and focused on the letter. "*Thank you for funding my account. If Amanda and Erica helped, thank them too.*"

Wendy gasped. "How could he possibly know?"

"Chris set that account up anonymously, so he's guessing. There's one more sentence. '*I'll eagerly await your response. All my love forever, Gunter.*' At least he signed his real name and not one of his aliases." Erica folded the letter and slid it back into the envelope, then laid it on the cushion. "Maybe you should talk to Chris—as your attorney—before you decide what to do."

"Seems I have a lot to think about." Conflicting emotions rattled Wendy's brain as she scooped the letter off the cushion and stood. Erica was right about her needing legal advice to avoid making a wrong move. She traipsed to her bedroom, closed the door, and laid the envelope on the dresser.

Cold fingers of fear inched up her spine as her gaze slid to Chris's photo wedged into the mirror frame below her baby's sonogram picture. He was already struggling with the idea of raising another man's son. Would Gunter Benson's interference in her life unravel their still fragile relationship and dash any hope of her becoming Wendy Armstrong? She curled up on her bed and closed her eyes, praying for the courage to make the right decision before their next date.

Chapter 2

Amanda Smith set the bottle of window cleaner aside and peered out the French doors at the professionally-designed backyard. Thanks to their cantankerous yet generous neighbor's offer to plan and fund the project, guests would soon stroll along the paths and enjoy the serenity and beauty of the country-style English garden. Her eyes drifted from the fountain to the gazebo featuring white wrought-iron panels between the pillars. How many couples would hold hands and kiss under the chandelier suspended from the cone-shaped roof? She imagined men and women sitting there, as much in love as she and Preston had been all those years ago—before that drunk driver sent him to his eternal home. Was it possible she, a forty-three-year-old who had been married twice—the second time illegally—would ever fall in love again?

Dismissing the notion as ridiculous, Amanda spun away from the view and eyed the curved traditional-style sectional sofa facing the fireplace. She ambled to the door to the left of the hearth and traced her finger over the plaque identifying the first-floor guest suite as the Rainbow Room. Transforming Eleanor and Warren Harrington's summer home into the Hilltop Inn and Spa had been a monumental task. Now the future hung in the balance, as did her integrity as a businesswoman.

Amanda pulled her ringing phone from her pocket and swiped her finger across the screen. "Are you finished?"

The tech guy responded, "Come on up and take a look."

"I'm on my way." Amanda climbed up the back staircase to the hallway spanning the full length of the second story.

"TVs are set up in all the bedrooms. Before I leave, make sure they're where you want them."

Amanda peeked into the six remaining guest suites. Pleased everything was exactly as Erica had requested, she returned to the hall. "Excellent work."

"That's my job." He stashed the last bit of packing material into a large plastic bag. "The way you've turned this old eyesore into a new business is impressive."

"We had a lot of help and more than a little luck." Thanks to the Harringtons' antique Cadillac she and her partners were able to sell to a collector for a small fortune. Amanda pulled a check from her pocket and handed it over.

"Thanks." The tech guy stuffed the payment in his pocket without checking the amount. "Every July, my sister and her sorority sisters book a couple of days at a different B&B to catch up. I'll tell her about this place."

Amanda's mouth curved into a smile. Their first referral. "We'd be delighted to host their next reunion. Tell your sister she can reserve rooms on our website."

"Will do." He tied the bag closed and hauled it toward the back stairs.

After taking one more glance in each room, Amanda descended the front staircase leading to the foyer. She opened the turret room's antique French doors Erica had found at a garage sale. Despite her preference to work independently, it had taken a team to pull off the transformation on time and on budget. Especially given the condition of the house after standing vacant and unattended for more than two decades. As her eyes drifted to the antique chandelier she had brought from New Orleans, one looming question remained. Could the three Awesam partners who had no innkeeping experience successfully manage a first-class vacation destination?

"The day Chris first showed us this house, Wendy said it looked like a haunted mansion inhabited by creepy ghosts."

Amanda spun toward Erica wandering in from the back with a folder tucked under her arm. "Turns out the inhabitants were well-fed spiders and four-legged critters."

"Five months ago, Gunter Benson threw three strangers' lives into unimaginable turmoil." Erica swept her arm in a wide arc. "Until we pulled together, did all this, and turned tragedy into triumph."

Amanda puffed her cheeks and blew out a long stream of air.

"Don't worry. We'll figure out how to transition from an unlikely team of fixer-uppers to three successful innkeepers."

Amanda shot Erica an incredulous look.

Erica looped her arm around her friend's elbow. "You're wondering how I know what's going on under all that red hair, aren't you?"

"The thought crossed my mind."

"First, I'm observant and second, your expressions are easy to read."

Amanda rolled her eyes. "Perhaps I need to master the art of putting on a poker face."

"Not worth the effort. Besides, as chief executive officer in charge of team building, I have to count on reading my partners' moods."

Awesam's cheerleader traipsed into the foyer clutching her laptop to her chest. Her dulled expression hinted that Gunter's letter continued to haunt her. "Sorry, I'm late."

Erica released Amanda and looped her arm around Wendy's elbow. "Your timing's perfect. Right, Ms. President?"

Taking the cue, Amanda pasted on her best smile. "Absolutely." She led the way across the living room to the formal dining room and pushed open the double-pocket doors, then sat at the end of the table in front of her laptop. Her eyes shifted from Erica settling on her left to Wendy dropping onto the chair to her right. Given their CFO's mood, she needed to kick off the meeting on a positive note. "Before we begin, I want to take a moment to reflect on everything we've accomplished since our first board meeting at the Blue Ridge Inn when we identified our roles."

"Actually—" Erica laid her folder on the table. "Our first board meeting happened at that Mexican restaurant in Asheville when Wendy came up with a name for our new company."

Amanda nodded. "I remember. Figuring out how to use the first letter in our names, plus Abby and Morgan's, was a stroke of genius."

Wendy's eyes shifted from Amanda to Erica, then back to Amanda. "You two can stop trying to cheer me up and get on with the meeting."

Amanda reached across the table and touched Wendy's arm. "You know if you want to talk—"

"I don't."

So much for trying to lift her mood. "Well, all right then." Amanda withdrew her hand. "We have several important details to iron out." She opened her laptop and tapped the keyboard. "This morning, I updated our website to announce our booking incentive—reserve one night and get the second night free. The offer begins Memorial Day weekend and runs through the second week in June."

"I'll update our social media pages with the new info." Wendy opened her computer. "We have enough money in our budget to run an ad in five small-town newspapers. One in Tennessee, one in South Carolina, and three in Georgia."

Erica gave Wendy a thumbs-up. "I'll write a press release for the local paper."

"Which brings us to the best timing for our open house." Amanda hesitated. "In my opinion, two Saturdays before the first guest arrives makes the most sense."

Erica's brows raised. "That's a little more than two weeks from now."

"Millie Cunningham already agreed to prepare the appetizers—"

"And Chris's mom emailed me names and addresses of influential people to invite." Wendy stood. "We can print invitations and mail them tomorrow. Right now I need a bladder break."

Amanda's eyes followed their CFO's dash across the living room. "Considering everything going on in Wendy's world, I don't know how much responsibility she can handle."

"We need to keep her busy without overwhelming her."

"There's a fine line between those two tasks."

"Wendy's demeanor will let us know when and if we cross it."

Amanda sighed. "I hope you're right."

"You can trust me to read her mood." Erica removed a drawing from her folder and pushed it to Amanda. "This is how I plan to decorate the converted garage."

"Turning that building into a spa was another brilliant move."

Their CFO returned with a bounce in her step. "I just came up with a cool idea."

Amanda chuckled at their young partner's ability to shift moods in an instant. "Maybe you should take more bladder breaks."

"Believe me, that's not a problem. Anyway, we're having our board meeting here instead of back at the ranch house, right?"

"What's your point?"

"We need to pitch the inn as the perfect place for a company retreat." Wendy plopped onto her chair. "Think about it. Fourteen people fit around this table, which makes our dining room the perfect place to hold an executive meeting."

"Good point." Amanda's brow pinched. "Except this is where we'll serve our guests breakfast—"

"From eight until ten. After that, the room's available."

"I love the idea." Erica eyed Amanda. "It could open our doors to a whole different clientele."

Two against one. Amanda faced Wendy. "With our grand opening happening at the beginning of peak tourist season, are you okay with waiting to promote the idea during slow periods?"

Wendy shrugged. "I suppose that makes the most sense. As long as you don't forget about my idea."

"I'm sure you'll remind us. Now, about our open house two weeks from today." After nailing down the details, Amanda pulled up a spreadsheet. "We need to discuss our innkeeping roles. Since we all live next door, we'll share check-in duties."

Wendy drew her lower lip between her teeth, a shift in mood already apparent.

Erica covered Wendy's hand with hers. "Don't worry. After your baby is born, Amanda and I will take over that role."

Grateful for their president's observation skills, Amanda smiled at their CFO. "When it comes to the inn's finances, you're our expert."

Wendy blinked then released her lip. "This morning I estimated our expenses and reviewed our competitors' rates." She tapped her laptop keyboard and turned her screen toward her partners. "This is what we should charge guests for a room each night. We'll start earning salaries after our two-for-one offer ends. Of course, we'll have to pay Millie and whoever we hire as our housekeeper."

Amanda stared at the twenty-three-year-old who had managed to transition from an immature shopaholic to a financial wizard.

Wendy's brows pinched. "What?"

"You continue to amaze me."

Wendy rolled her eyes. "When we first met, you didn't think I was smart enough to figure stuff out, did you?"

"I admit I had my doubts. Lucky for us, you've proved me wrong."

"Now that we've established our CFO's brilliance, let's talk staffing." Erica propped her elbows on the table and faced Amanda. "What's your opinion about hiring Abby as the inn's housekeeper, at least for the summer?"

"Is that your idea or your daughter's?"

"Hers. She wants to continue tutoring kids at the crisis center, but she also needs to earn money." Erica's focus shifted to Wendy. "Are you okay with the idea?"

"Why wouldn't I be?"

"No reason. Now about the day-to-day responsibilities, I'll manage the inn." Amanda caught Erica's eye. "In addition to managing the spa and serving as the inn's massage therapist, you're the best person to manage the staff."

"I agree," quickly added Wendy.

"Then it's settled." Amanda closed her laptop making it clear the discussion had come to an end.

Chapter 3

Erica pressed her lips tight to avoid objecting to her new role and slid the drawing back in the folder. After all, in addition to the demands of the inn, Wendy would soon face caring for a newborn, and the young woman was far more suited for cheerleading the team than supervising it. Given Amanda's stubborn streak and impatience with distracting people, she'd be more likely to wreak havoc than keep the peace. Even though conflict set her nerves on edge, Erica had to face reality. She was the partner best suited to manage people—especially their cranky chef who would be the first person to greet their guests every morning.

Wendy closed her laptop. "Do you remember the first day you and I trekked next door to meet Mildred Cunningham?"

Erica nodded. "She gave us such a cold shoulder I thought we were headed for another blizzard."

Amanda laughed. "Despite her temperament, Millie has become an important part of our team."

As if on cue, their cranky next-door neighbor with salt and pepper hair rushed in from the front porch. "Did I miss a meeting, or did everyone forget to invite me?"

"She's all yours, Ms. CEO," Wendy whispered seconds before dashing to the kitchen.

Amanda leaned toward Erica. "Your first assignment, bring our chef up to speed." She grabbed her laptop and followed Wendy.

Erica pulled in a deep breath then released the air through pursed lips and strode into the living room.

Millie held a notebook in her right hand and propped her left hand on her hip. "Even though I'm not a voting member of Awesam, I expect to know everything that's going on, so I can effectively fulfill my role as your chef."

"Absolutely. Which is why your timing is perfect."

"Because I interrupted your private meeting?" Millie's tone mocked.

Determined to create a pleasant working relationship, Erica pasted on her best smile and motioned toward the sofa. "We've decided on dates for our open house and grand opening." She sat beside Millie and shared the details.

"Lucky for you, I have both menus figured out." Millie opened her notebook and handed it over. "Will your approval do, or will Amanda also need to give me her okay?"

"My consent is all you need." Erica nodded as she read Millie's selections and her proposed budget. "Your creativity is impressive."

"That much I know. What I need is the go-ahead and a check from Wendy."

"In that case, you have my approval." Erica typed a text. Their CFO responded with a thumbs-up. "Wendy will bring the check over in a few minutes."

Millie peered around the room. "When I first learned about your plans to turn Eleanor's home into an inn, I thought she'd object to the idea." She leaned back and faced the fireplace. "Reading her journals changed my mind. Even though she didn't have overnight guests, she loved entertaining friends with fancy dinner parties."

"Dedicating your backyard masterpiece to Eleanor honors her memory in the best possible way."

"I still miss talking to her."

"At least you have a lot of happy memories of your time together."

"There is that." Millie paused. "Have you heard anything from Gunter?"

Erica hesitated while weighing her options. She could avoid answering or tell her no. Except Millie had perfected the art of wheedling information. With the inn's grand opening fast approaching, she couldn't risk angering their chef. Erica returned the notebook. "He sent Wendy a letter."

"Based on everything we know about him, I'm not surprised. What did he want?"

"He didn't write to me, so it isn't my place to share the details."

Millie remained silent for a long moment. "Maybe Eleanor didn't tell me much about Gunter because she was afraid I would call her foolish for marrying a much younger man."

"Would you have?"

"Called her foolish? No. Warned her? Definitely." Millie hugged her notebook to her chest. "I wonder if she ever had doubts about his motives?"

"Gunter's charm fooled a lot of innocent people. Little did Eleanor know she was the original member of her husband's private wives club."

"An exclusive wives club, mind you." Wendy ambled in from the foyer and handed their chef a check. "I'll leave you two alone—"

Millie grabbed her arm. "Wait. I want your opinion on my menus."

Wendy exchanged a quick glance with Erica, then hiked her hip on the sofa arm. "Okay."

Millie released Wendy's arm then opened the notebook and handed it over. "Except for my homemade cinnamon buns, I have a different breakfast menu for every day of the week."

Wendy ran her finger down the list. "They all look mouth-watering delicious." She returned the notebook.

"How are you feeling, now that you're getting closer to your due date?"

"Fat and overcharged with hormones."

"I bet he's kicking a lot."

Wendy crossed her arms over her baby bump. "You asked me to stay because you're dying to find out what Gunter wrote, didn't you?"

Millie's eyes narrowed. "What makes you think that?"

Erica tapped their chef's arm. "The text I sent to her."

"Well, in that case." Millie faced Wendy. "Are you gonna tell me or keep me in suspense?"

"Would you believe the creep wants to marry me? Only this time legally."

"As if he had one chance in a million that would ever happen. Unless—" Millie's brows arched. "You're not going to, are you?"

Wendy glared at her. "Do you actually believe I'd do something that insane?"

"How would I know?

Wendy scoffed. "Not if Gunter Benson was the last man on earth."

"Have you told him?"

"Not yet."

"That man's in for a real shocker." Millie slid the check into her notebook then stood. "Thank you for trusting me with the news."

Wendy shrugged. "Why wouldn't I? You're an important part of our team."

"Everyone says that, but I'm obviously not important enough to be invited to your private board meetings." Millie whipped away and took three steps, then halted and glanced over her shoulder. "You promised I could be the first guest to spend the night here. So make sure Eleanor's suite is ready for me tomorrow night." Millie marched straight to the foyer and out the front door.

Wendy rolled her eyes. "Managing her will take tons of patience."

"At least we can trust her discretion." Erica's phone pinged a text. "Abby's home and wants to talk."

"I'll walk with you." After crossing the porch and climbing down the steps, Wendy plucked a twig off the sidewalk bordering the newly sodded front lawn. "Maybe Gunter wrote that letter because he thinks I'm the one who put money in his prison account."

"Even if he suspects you're the one, he'll never know for sure." They crossed the new concrete parking pad on the side yard between the inn and the ranch house. "What have you decided about showing Gunter's letter to Chris?"

"The jury's still out."

"You're seeing him tonight, so I suggest you decide one way or the other beforehand."

Wendy huffed. "Amanda already reminded me." She stepped up her pace and rushed through the carport then straight to the kitchen door.

Regretting the comment about Wendy's date with Chris, Erica released a sigh. Her young partner didn't need more unsolicited advice. She waited a full minute before entering the kitchen and making her way across the den. Grateful Wendy's bedroom door was closed, she continued down the hall to Abby's room.

Her daughter curled up on her beanbag chair tapping her phone. Dusty, Abby's golden retriever sprawled on the floor beside her. "What's on your mind, sweetheart?"

"Since I'm a few weeks from graduating, I've been thinking a lot more about my future."

Erica sat on the single bed closest to her daughter. "Have you made some decisions?"

"Back in Asheville I wanted to go away to college because that's what all my friends planned to do."

Erica's brow pinched. "What about now?"

"You know how much I love tutoring kids at the crisis center—" Abby hesitated. "The thing is, I don't want to leave Blue Ridge."

Erica probed her daughter's expression. "Does this have something to do with Tommy?"

She nodded. "After graduation, he plans to work for his dad's construction company and eventually take over the business."

Erica stroked Dusty's back. "I always regretted not having the chance to attend college."

"I know, Mom. But I have a plan all figured out." Abby handed over her phone. "That's what's available at the University of Georgia, Blue Ridge Campus."

Erica read the list of social service classes. "The local campus only offers pathways, not degrees."

"I don't need a degree to keep doing what I'm doing."

"True." Erica returned the phone. "Except tutoring is volunteer work, not a career."

"Did Amanda and Wendy agree to let me work as the inn's housekeeper?"

"Of course."

"Well, okay then. That'll be my paid job."

Erica reached for the only toy her five-year-old child had taken with her when they sought refuge in a Baltimore women's shelter all those years ago. She fingered the pink ribbon tied around the bear's neck. "You've obviously given this a lot of thought, and I understand how your experience has shaped your desire to help those children—"

"You're about to say but, aren't you?"

How could she express her opinion without questioning her daughter's rationale? "Helping children who are forced to flee troubled domestic situations is noble, and I'm proud of you. It's just...keeping your options open is wise."

"I've already considered my options, and this is what I want to do with my life, Mom."

"You know I'll always support you, sweetheart. Now, here comes the but..." Erica set the bear back on the bed. "If you ever have the tiniest doubt about your choice, promise you'll talk to me."

Abby traced an X on her chest. "I promise."

"Good." Erica stood. "By the way, your first chore as the Hilltop Inn housekeeper begins the day after tomorrow when Millie checks out of the Rainbow room."

"I hope she's not messy."

Chapter 4

Wendy's pulse quickened as she grabbed her pinging phone off the dresser and read the text from Chris. "Bringing dinner. Dine in gazebo?

On their last two dates, he had fixed dinner at his house and now the gazebo? Despite his claim about not caring what people thought, he obviously didn't want to be seen dating a woman who could no longer hide her bulging belly. She couldn't blame him, especially since half the town's residents had expected him to marry his high school girlfriend. Well maybe not half, but a lot. Wendy breathed deeply to slow her pounding heart as she tapped her response. "Meet you in gazebo at six."

He responded with a thumbs-up.

Wendy tossed her phone on the bed beside the white teddy bear Gunter had given her when she knew him as Kurt Peterson. Amanda was right about the man she thought was her husband. Given his lies, he had no claim on her or the child he had fathered. Wendy grabbed the bear then hastened to Abby's room. She stopped by the closed door before knocking. Was she making a decision based on emotion? Whatever the reason, she couldn't back down. She rapped her knuckles on the door.

"Come on in."

Wendy stepped into Abby's private space. "Hey."

Dusty's tail slapped the floor beside the teenager who had turned eighteen two weeks earlier. Abby looked up from her book. "Back at you."

"Are you studying?"

"Biology final. Ugh. What's up?"

Wendy sat on the edge of the single bed closest to Abby. "I've been thinking about the kids you tutor at the crisis center, and well—" She held out the bear. "Maybe this will bring comfort to one of them."

"Isn't that for your baby?"

"Not anymore."

"Okay then. I'll give it to the sweet little girl who came in with her mother yesterday."

"Perfect." Pleased with her decision, Wendy set the bear on the bed then returned to her room. Her muscles tensed as she changed into an outfit more suited for a picnic than a dinner at a fancy restaurant. She grabbed Gunter's letter and slid it into her back pocket.

"Giving away that bear was a smart move."

Wendy whirled and eyed Amanda standing at her door. "You heard from across the hall, didn't you?"

"Clear as a bell. Is Chris treating you to dinner at his house tonight?"

Wendy shook her head. "We're picnicking in the gazebo."

"How fun." Amanda stepped in. "Perfect for a private conversation."

Could she be any more obvious? "Just because the letter's in my pocket doesn't mean I'm gonna show it to Chris."

"When the time's right, you'll make the best decision."

"Whatever that is," murmured Wendy as she brushed past Amanda and made her way out the front door. The sun warmed her skin as she traipsed across the driveway and onto the path leading to the gazebo. Water cascading down the five-foot-tall bronze fountain's three tiers splashed into the circular pool. Wendy sat on the concrete barrier and swirled her fingers in the cool water. Her mind drifted to the first time Chris kissed her. Passion had surged through her limbs. She was falling deeply in love with a man she'd only known for a few months.

"Perfect weather for a picnic."

Wendy yanked her hand from the pool and spun toward Chris.

"I didn't mean to startle you."

No point trying to deny it, given his lawyerly ability to read body language. She eyed the Bob's Eatery sack in his left hand. "What's on tonight's menu?"

"Sandwiches and milkshakes."

"Perfect choice for a warm April night."

Chris helped her to her feet and wiped her wet hand dry with his shirttail. His touch sent a wave of desire cascading through her as he pressed his hand to her back and escorted her to the gazebo. Had he chosen to bring take-out here so they could spend time alone, away from crowds and prying eyes? Chris pulled out a chair for her then placed the drinks and Styrofoam containers on the white wrought-iron, glass-top table.

"Oh my gosh, you brought my favorite." Wendy slid a straw into the thick Oreo milkshake and tasted. "Yum."

"I'm glad you approve." Following a two-sentence blessing, Chris opened his container. "I brought us BLTs with avocado spread." He bit into the sandwich.

Following his lead, Wendy took a bite. "Another good choice."

Chris swallowed. "How are the grand-opening plans coming along?"

"We finalized everything during today's board meeting." Wendy shared the details. "We'll send invitations to everyone on your mother's list."

"The response would quadruple if you include her name on the invitation."

"Should I ask her if it's okay?"

"I'll do it for you." Chris removed his phone from his belt clip and tapped the screen, then set it on the table.

Wendy focused on the mountain of whipped cream topping her milkshake. A question wrestled its way to the surface

"What's going on in your head?"

She blinked. "What makes you think—oh yeah, lawyers know how to read people."

"Effective lawyers. So, what gives?"

Wendy tilted her head. "The first time I visited your home you told me your family was close."

"Your comment isn't about the invitation, is it?"

Did she dare ask the question begging for an answer? Better to learn the truth now. "Do your parents know we're seeing each other?"

Chris stared at her for a long moment. "They know."

Wendy blinked. She'd gone this far. Why stop now? "Do they approve?"

"They don't interfere with my personal life."

"You didn't answer my question."

"Dad's my law partner. He knows about Gunter."

"So, he doesn't approve?"

"That's not what I said."

"Then what do you mean?"

Chris set down his sandwich. "Blue Ridge is a small town."

Wendy caught her bottom lip between her teeth and mentally teetered between two options. If she shredded Gunter's letter without showing it to Chris, she'd protect him from the drama. On the other hand, not showing it to him could destroy his trust as her lawyer.

He reached across the table and touched her arm. "I can handle whatever's troubling you."

His expression spoke volumes. He deserved to know. "Gunter sent me a letter."

Chris pulled his hand away. "I'm not surprised."

"Do you want to read it?"

"As your attorney, I need to know what he's up to."

Wendy hesitated. *As my attorney? What about as my boyfriend?* She swallowed against the dryness in her throat, then pulled the letter from her back pocket and pushed it across the table.

Chris silently read Gunter's words. When finished, he turned the paper face down and locked eyes with Wendy. "Please tell me you didn't respond?"

"I didn't."

"Good."

"I'm curious." Wendy's head tilted. "How much was that necklace he gave me worth?"

"A little more than a grand." Chris's jaw tensed. "In case you're wondering, his comment about you funding his account is nothing more than a fishing expedition."

"Did I make a mistake giving him that money?"

"It's never a mistake to do what you believe is right in your heart."

Even if it hurts? "Before I learned that Kurt wasn't Gunter's real name, he gave me a white teddy bear." She broke eye contact. "Today, I gave it away."

"I'm surprised you've kept it this long."

A bundle of knots took up residence in Wendy's belly. Why had she told him? "It wasn't the bear's fault—"

"You don't need to explain. About the letter—it's best if you let me determine how to respond. As your lawyer."

Again, as her lawyer...and not the man I'm dating. "I assume you'll let me know what you decide. As your client."

"Of course." Chris pocketed the letter then bit into his sandwich, making it clear he considered the subject closed—at least for tonight.

Following an hour of idle conversation about random topics, Wendy could no longer ignore her full bladder. She pushed away from the table. "Sorry, nature calls. I'll be right back." She dashed past the fountain and onto the patio. Grateful for the unlocked French doors, she scurried to the powder room in the nick of time. Relieved, Wendy traipsed through the den and stepped outside. Chris stood on the patio with the Bob's Eatery sack in his hand. Her brows furrowed then released. "Are you leaving?"

"I need to prepare for a client meeting early tomorrow morning." He gripped her elbow as they headed toward the driveway. When they arrived at his car, he pulled his hand away and kissed her cheek with a peck as if he was a pal thanking his buddy for sharing a sandwich. "I'll call you tomorrow."

Wendy choked back tears as Chris climbed into his car, then backed onto the parking pad and eased down the driveway. Had Gunter's letter driven a deadly stake in their relationship? She trudged to the fountain, dropped onto the barrier, and released her tears to the cool water.

Chapter 5

Amanda sealed the last envelope and placed it atop the second stack on the dining room table. "Eighty open-house invitations stamped and ready to mail."

Erica massaged her right hand. "If we had used Evite, as Wendy suggested, we would have saved a lot of money."

"Except a formal hand-addressed invitation is more sophisticated."

"I suppose you're right. I'll drop them off at the post office after I take Dusty to the crisis center."

"For another tag-team effort?"

"Abby wants to convince me she's making the right choice about her future." Dusty plodded over and sprawled beside Erica's chair. "I can't help but wonder how much Tommy's choice to skip college has influenced her decision."

"I'm curious." Amanda leaned back. "Before you moved here, did Abby have her heart set on a specific career path?"

Erica shook her head. "Only that she wanted to go away to college."

"So, volunteering as a tutor is her first honest-to-goodness passion?"

"A noble cause best pursued in addition to—" Erica flinched. "Not instead of a profitable career."

"If you want my opinion—even if you don't—I suggest you lighten up and trust your daughter to do what's best for her."

A smirk replaced Erica's benign expression. "Easy for you to say, since Morgan's graduating with an engineering degree and skills to land a great job."

Amanda shrugged. "I would have supported my daughter no matter what she decided to do with her life. Besides, if Abby and Tommy have fallen deeply in love—"

"How's that possible? They're still teenagers."

"When I met Preston—"

"I know." Erica's tone mocked. "You had barely turned nineteen, and he was the love of your life."

Amanda probed Erica's expression. "You're still allowing Jack to influence your attitude about young love, aren't you?"

She studied her nails. "It's difficult not to. He was a police officer who showed up the day my brother was shot and killed. Naturally, I trusted him."

Amanda scooted her chair close to Erica. "You were heartbroken and vulnerable. I remember you telling Wendy and me that Jack was your rescuer. But not one time have I heard you say you loved him."

Erica hesitated. "What do you expect? I was his punching bag."

"Not until you'd been married for nearly a year. The fact is your relationship with Jack Nelson was based on emotional and financial desperation. Abby's relationship with Tommy Bennett comes from mutual respect and heartfelt love. Pay close attention the next time you see them together."

Erica's brows knitted together. Given her failures, how could she possibly distinguish between love and infatuation? "I married two losers. There's something seriously wrong with me."

Amanda slid an arm around her shoulder. "Nonsense. You're an incredible woman—"

"Who's thirty-seven-years-old and has never once fallen in love."

"Only because you've yet to meet the right man. If you want to know what I think—"

"I don't." Erica folded her arms across her chest.

"Well, I'm going to tell you anyway. You're a beautiful, intelligent woman who's poured your heart into raising an amazing daughter. Maybe it's time to put yourself out there and meet new people."

"By people I assume you mean eligible men. If your advice is so wonderful, why don't *you* put yourself out there?"

Images of waking up beside Preston in their beloved shotgun house the morning before his fatal accident broke through. "There's no need to. I already found my soulmate."

"It's time we face the fact that we married Gunter to provide for our daughters. Now, because of his deception, we're both terrified of making another huge mistake." Erica pushed away from the table and traipsed to the sliding-glass door.

Amanda's attempt to shrug off the sting of truth pricked her conscience. "When reality smacks a person across the face, they either deny it or deal with it head-on."

"Which are you doing?"

"A little of both, I suppose." She eased beside Erica and looped her arm around her friend's elbow. "I addressed two envelopes to single men. What about you?"

"I know what you're suggesting, but it'll be a long time before I trust another man enough to let him into my life—if ever. Besides, I have two new careers to keep me busy."

"What if at least one of the single men we invited is a good prospect?"

"Forget it." Erica wrestled her arm away from Amanda's grip. After clipping a leash to Dusty's collar, she scooped the invitations off the table then headed straight to the kitchen. The clang of keys and the slam of the back door attested to Erica's opinion on dating again.

Amanda dismissed her tinge of disappointment as irrational. Especially since the only reason she'd suggested meeting men was to help her friend move on with her life. Unless Erica changed her mind, the subject would remain off the table.

After her daughter's faithful companion bounded onto the truck's back seat, Erica slid behind the steering wheel and set the invitations on the seat beside her. She lowered the back window for Dusty then eased down the driveway. Her jaw clenched as she backed onto the two-lane road. She didn't have a clue how to tell the good guys from the jerks, so there was no way she'd open herself up to more disappointment. Besides, Amanda had only suggested the ridiculous idea because she felt sorry for her. At least by rejecting Amanda's outlandish proposal, she wouldn't make a fool out of herself.

Erica braked at the intersection and turned left. What if Amanda had commented about the single men on their list because she was interested? Ridiculous. Despite the fact that Preston had been the love of her life, she had married again, even if it was for all the wrong reasons. Conflicting thoughts collided in Erica's head. Somehow, she had to sort through the confusion muddling her brain.

The moment she parked at the crisis center, Dusty's tail set her backside in motion. Erica opened the back door and grabbed the leash. "You know where we're going, don't you, girl?" The golden retriever led the way into the building and on to a cozy classroom. A dark-haired little girl hugging Wendy's white teddy bear sat on a sofa between Abby and Tommy. The child's face lit with a smile the moment Dusty padded over, sat on her haunches, and plopped her head on the child's lap.

Tommy stood. "Hey, Ms. Nelson. Thanks for bringing Dusty."

"You're welcome. Are you volunteering here now?"

He nodded. "Abby hooked me into helping these kids."

Erica's eyes shifted to her daughter. "She's definitely persuasive."

"She's also the smartest and kindest person I've ever met." Tommy dropped back onto the sofa.

Abby's dreamy-eyed expression spoke volumes. "Tommy and I are a great team."

"So, I see." Erica leaned down and smiled at the child. "What's your name, sweetheart?"

The child's chin lowered. "Nyla."

"That's a pretty name. Do you like your new bear?"

Her eyes lit. "Uh-huh."

Abby patted the little girl's knee. "Nyla came here two days ago with her mom and baby brother."

The child held up four fingers. "I'm this many."

"And she already knows all her letters," added Abby.

"Wow, you're a smart little girl."

Nyla clutched her bear tight against her chest. "Daddy made Mommy's face bleed."

Erica cringed as memories of the night she and Abby fled to a shelter came streaming back.

"Know what we need to do now?" Tommy tapped the bear. "Give your new friend a cool name." He rattled off a list of suggestions that made Nyla giggle.

Abby shot Erica what appeared to be an I-told-you-he's-a-great-guy expression. "Thanks, Mom."

Erica blinked. Was her daughter thanking her for bringing Dusty or for grasping the truth about her relationship with Tommy? "You're welcome, sweetheart." She straightened. " I have errands to run, so I'll leave Dusty with you." When Erica returned to the truck, curiosity nudged her. She settled behind the steering wheel and eyed the invitations. She'd addressed one envelope to a single man, which combined with Amanda's two invitations, meant three bachelors might attend their open house. If they bothered to show up. Were the single men they'd invited young or old? Were they divorced or never married? The idea of dating again churned her stomach. Erica dismissed the mental questions as irrational, then cranked the engine, pulled onto the street, and drove straight to the post office.

Chapter 6

Dusk settled over Blue Ridge as Amanda stood at the Rainbow Suite's French doors leading to the rear patio. Her eyes drifted to the brass plaque dedicating the backyard garden to Eleanor. How many of the guests they'd invited to the open house had known the Harringtons or visited their home? Her eyes drifted to the free-standing building. Would their guests accept the invitations to satisfy their curiosity about the three out-of-towners who'd transformed the house to an inn and the garage to a spa?

"Impressive."

Amanda whirled away from the glass. "This room, or that you always seem to sneak in without making a sound?"

"This is what I'm talking about." Millie strode in waving the guest list she'd found on the kitchen island. "Business owners, public figures, even my son and daughter-in-law. Every person you invited is a VIP in town."

"That's the point. Since you seem to know everyone, how many do you suppose will accept our invitation?"

"I'd say at least eighty percent, including your competition." Millie handed the list to Amanda then ambled to the bed and palmed the colorful comforter Erica had purchased. "I've lost count of the number of times I've read what Eleanor wrote in her journal about the daughter she gave up for adoption. I still tear up when I read how she wrote a love letter to her child every year on her birthday, then threw it away so her husband wouldn't discover her despair."

Amanda eyed the painting of a rainbow Wendy had found at a local gallery. "I can't imagine living my entire life without ever meeting my only child."

Millie heaved a sigh. "And I can't help but wonder if her daughter ever attempted to find her birth mother."

"Which couldn't happen unless Eleanor's name is in one of those ancestry databases."

Millie straightened the lampshade on her friend's nightstand lamp. "She is now."

"How do you know?"

"I sent one in."

Amanda shot Millie a questioning look. "Don't those require DNA samples?"

She nodded. "Which is why I sent the toothbrush I found in the bathroom—"

"Hold on." Amanda aimed an open palm toward Millie. "When we gave you her journals, we'd already cleaned everything out of all the bathrooms—"

"Except the one for the turret bedroom."

"Why would Eleanor have a toothbrush up there?"

Millie strode across the room and lifted a photo of Eleanor and Warren off the dresser. "I'm glad you're leaving this for guests to see."

"Only because you insisted. Back to my question." Amanda propped a fist on her waist.

"During the last summer the Harringtons spent in this house, Warren came down with the flu. Eleanor slept in that room for a week."

"And left her toothbrush?"

"That's what I call fate." Millie lifted a shoulder.

"Or some odd coincidence. Have any results popped up?"

"I didn't check." Millie set down the photo. "It's best if I don't know."

"Because you don't want to be tempted to contact your friend's daughter?"

"I opened the door. It's her place to walk through. Now, if you don't mind, I'm ready to begin my guest experience."

"Well then, Ms. Cunningham." Amanda pasted on her best smile. "Welcome to Hilltop Inn and Spa. We'll serve breakfast in the dining room at eight tomorrow morning. Before you turn in tonight, take time to visit the beautiful garden out back."

"Good speech. But you also need to tell guests that Eleanor's best friend, who's also the inn's chef, designed every inch of it."

"Or we could let them discover your many talents on their own."

Millie propped her hands on her hips. "The garden is one of the inn's best features, so don't you believe I deserve the credit?"

Amanda resisted rolling her eyes. "Of course, you do. For now, I'll run along and leave you to enjoy your time as our first official guest." She strode through the den to the kitchen and placed the list back on the island before heading out the front door and across the parking pad. Inside the ranch house, Amanda plopped onto the den sofa beside Erica. "You won't believe the conversation I just had with our chef."

Erica aimed the remote toward the television pausing a program. "Try me."

"First, she contacted one of those ancestry companies." Amanda explained. "What happens if Eleanor's daughter stumbles across her mother's name and finds out about these two properties?"

"After all these years, that's about as likely to happen as a full-blown hurricane making it all the way to Blue Ridge."

Amanda tilted her head. "Why'd you choose that particular analogy?"

"Because you're from one of the most hurricane-prone areas in the country. Anyway, we have too much going on to fret about some remote possibility."

"You're right. So, I'll put that aside to address a more immediate issue. Millie wants us to tell our guests that she designed the backyard instead of letting them find out on their own."

Erica peered up. "Why is that a problem?"

"If our guests ask her questions about the garden or Eleanor while she's serving breakfast, she'll talk a blue streak."

"She's likely to anyway, so why not give her the recognition? Especially since she paid for the project. Besides, we have a photo album with pictures of the entire transformation on display in the inn's living room."

Amanda plucked a dog hair off the cushion beside her. "I suppose if you're okay with mentioning our chef's contributions in our welcome speech—"

Erica's eyes widened. "I didn't know we had to give a speech."

"We don't. But we need one."

Erica stared at Amanda for a long moment. "Don't you think a prepared spiel would come across as boring and trite? Especially since we're innkeepers welcoming guests into their home away from home? Doesn't it make more sense to treat our guests as if they're friends while we show them around and casually share the amenities that make our inn special?"

Amanda failed to suppress a groan. "You want us to wing it?"

"Not exactly."

"Then what exactly are you suggesting?"

"The thing is—" Erica drew in a deep breath. "You put me in charge of staff...and well, in my opinion, guests who choose to stay at a luxury inn expect a relaxed atmosphere."

Amanda blinked as her mind drifted to the streets of New Orleans. "Back when I worked as a tour guide, I mastered the art of balancing a prepared spiel with spontaneous responses to tourists' off-the-wall questions. Maybe prepared spontaneity is our best approach."

Erica nodded slowly. "Hmm. In a weird sort of way, that makes the most sense."

"Well played, partner. You skillfully brought me around to your way of thinking."

"As Awesam's CEO, I am in charge of strategic direction." Erica pinched her chin between her thumb and finger. "I've been thinking about the people we invited to our open house. Maybe we should find out more about them."

Amanda studied Erica's expression. Did she mean all the guests, or had she changed her mind about meeting the single men? "Millie seemed to know everyone on the list. We could ask her tomorrow during breakfast."

Erica snapped her fingers. "Great idea."

An hour and a half after sunrise, Erica nudged Amanda as they strode into the Hilltop Inn's den. "It's obvious our first official guest is an early riser."

Millie rose from the sofa cradling a mug. "I made us a pot of coffee. Is Wendy joining us?"

"She's sleeping in." Erica led the way to the kitchen. "Amanda and I are going to treat your tastebuds to Awesam's Saturday morning special a day early—chocolate chip pancakes and crisp bacon."

Millie climbed onto a stool. "That's an interesting combination."

"We're smart enough not to compete with your culinary expertise." Amanda removed a package of bacon, a carton of eggs, and a gallon of milk from the fridge. "Which is why we're playing it safe."

Erica measured pancake mix into a bowl. "We're eager to hear about your overnight experience."

"The subtle landscape lights and gazebo's chandelier make Eleanor's garden a magical place after dark. I imagine your open house and future inn guests will spend a lot of time walking those paths."

Erica stirred eggs and milk into the pancake mix. "I wish we knew more about the folks on our list."

"I know a good many of them." Millie pulled the list close. "For example, Mrs. Bishop owns one of the downtown boutiques, and her husband is my dentist. Their daughter—she's also a dentist—and her husband are also on your list."

Amanda lined bacon strips on a microwave platter. "We've obviously invited important guests."

"Especially the second couple." Millie tapped the list. "He's our mayor, and his wife is one of our high school teachers."

Erica poured batter onto the griddle while listening to their neighbor share tidbits about each couple she knew and speculated about those she didn't. By the time she plated the pancakes, Erica's brain reeled with names. Would she remember anything about anyone Millie described?

Millie poured syrup on her pancakes then tasted. "I have to admit these are much better than I expected." She pulled the list close. "Judge Livingston's wife died a few years back. The three of us were high school classmates. If I wasn't too set in my ways... Anyway, he'd be a good catch for some old lady."

Erica stifled a chuckle as she swirled a forkful of pancakes in a puddle of syrup.

In between bites, Millie prattled on about who was who. She described the second single male as an old codger who'd never married. Halfway down the second page, she grinned. "If I was thirty years younger, I'd definitely have my eye on this guy."

Amanda swallowed a bite. "What's special about him?"

"To start, Brad's movie-star handsome. His parents were two of the Harringtons' regular dinner guests. They were such a nice couple. Brad's sweet wife died a few years ago. His sons both found jobs in other states. It's a shame he's all alone, especially since he's one of the good guys." Millie hesitated as if an idea suddenly struck home. "He's in his early forties, and you're both unattached—"

Erica held up her hand. "Forget it."

Millie scoffed. "Relax, I was just thinking out loud. Anyway, this next couple..."

Erica tuned out Millie's prattle. Had she been too quick to dismiss Millie's comment? She stole a quick glance at Amanda's faraway stare. Was it possible their chef piqued her friend's curiosity? Erica dismissed the notion. More likely Awesam's president was on mental overload.

Chapter 7

Wendy's stomach churned as she gripped the steering wheel and braked at a red light. A young woman pushed a stroller in front of the truck and onto the sidewalk. Was she alone with her child late Saturday afternoon because she was a single mother, or because her husband was playing golf? How did locals treat unmarried mothers—especially those who were new in town?

A horn beeped from behind. Wendy blinked. Green light. She waved over her shoulder, then pulled forward and drove past the bright blue train engine parked on the track. Four months had passed, and she still hadn't experienced one of the town's most popular tourist attractions.

At the next intersection, Wendy turned right and drove past Blue Ridge Inn's parking lot. Would she have met Chris if Gunter had revealed his true identity to a different lawyer? She drove two more blocks then turned onto Armstrong Law Firm's parking space, and eased beside Chris's late-model sedan. Where would he take her for dinner after their meeting? To a restaurant or to his house where no one would see them? Wendy plucked her purse off the passenger seat and plodded into the single-story building's empty reception area. Should she text Chris to let him know she'd arrived? Better to wait a few minutes.

Wendy ambled to the window and stared with unseeing eyes at the parking lot. Today was the second time she'd meet Chris at his office.

She closed her eyes. Memories of meeting Private Investigator Vincent in the law firm's conference room for the first time bubbled up. Weeks later she and Amanda sat in Cynthia Thomason's living room—the woman who had abandoned her five years after bringing her into this world. The same woman whose husband and three other children had no idea their mother's first-born child existed. Wendy pressed her hand to her swollen belly. No matter what happened, she would never abandon her child.

"You're right on time."

Startled, Wendy's eyes popped open. She spun toward Chris. His jeans, running shoes, and polo shirt that accentuated his muscular arms made him look more akin to a professional athlete than a lawyer. "Is today Casual Saturday?"

"In a sense. We'll talk in my office." He escorted her down the hall past the conference room where they'd met with Vincent. Inside his office, Chris motioned toward a couch. "Please."

Wendy settled on the smooth tan leather and laid her purse on the cushion beside her thigh. Her eyes darted around the room painted a subtle shade of blue. "Nice colors."

"They're intended to put our clients at ease."

"Does it work?"

Chris sat on an easy chair catercorner to her. "You tell me."

Wendy shrugged. "Jury's still out."

His eyes met hers. "I've thoroughly reviewed Gunter's letter."

Wendy blinked. Had Chris found a way to erase Gunter from her and her son's life? "What's the verdict?"

"He was smart enough to avoid threatening or harassing language."

Wendy's brow pinched. "What are you telling me?"

"From a legal perspective, the letter doesn't meet the standard for a cease-and-desist order—"

"Are you saying there's nothing we can do?"

"Unless he changes tactics, we're limited. But we're not completely without options."

"Meaning what?"

"I prepared a letter to clarify our intentions." Chris lifted a folder off the end table and removed a single sheet of paper. "Do you want to take a look, or would you rather I read it to you?"

Wendy caught her bottom lip between her teeth. She stared at the paper. Maybe it was best not to know. Except she had to face reality. "Read it to me."

"It's short and to the point. *Dear Mr. Benson. I am writing on behalf of Wendy Thomason regarding the letter you addressed to her as Wendy Peterson. Ms. Thomason wishes to cease all communication with you. We believe it is in the best interest of both parties for you to adhere to her request. Should you attempt further communication, I've advised Ms. Thomason to forward any and all unopened letters to my office for review and response. In addition, please use her legal name in all future communications.*

Sincerely, Christopher Armstrong, Attorney at Law.

Wendy cringed at the vision of Gunter reading the letter inches from the photos of her he'd taped to his cell walls. "Based on your experience, will that letter force him to leave me alone?"

Chris hesitated for a long moment. "No, but at least knowing anything he writes will end up in my hands should prevent him from crossing any legal lines."

What did he mean by *should*? Wendy looped her arms around her belly as reality struck home. The father of her child wasn't capable of loving anyone except himself. "In your opinion, what's the real reason he wrote to me?"

"Given his history and narcissistic nature, the source of the letter is either misplaced pride or greed or both. No matter what he does, you have the law on your side."

"You expect him to pull some kind of shenanigans, don't you?"

"He's an imprisoned con man with nothing but time on his hands. What do you think?"

Chris's harsh tone sent a chill skittering up Wendy's spine.

"I'm sorry." He leaned forward and touched her knee. "I don't want to upset or frighten you. However, it's important for you to understand who you're dealing with."

Why had he said '*you're* dealing with' instead of *we're* dealing with? "What's the next step?"

Chris withdrew his hand from her knee. "Wait for Gunter to make a move, then decide."

Wendy slumped back. How long would she have to wait? A week? A month?

"About tonight—" Chris placed the letter folder back on the end table. "Since it's Casual Saturday, do you mind if I have dinner delivered here?"

And there it was. The truth. She'd become a burden. Maybe even an embarrassment. Chris deserved a woman who wasn't weeks away from giving birth to another man's son. A woman who didn't have to wait for the next letter from a criminal. No matter how much it hurt, she had to do what was best for him. Wendy tucked her purse under her arm and pushed off the couch. "I'm not hungry and, well...I'm really tired."

Chris stood. His eyes met hers as he clasped her shoulders. "What's really going on, Wendy?"

I love you far too much to hold on to you? She lifted her chin. "I appreciate everything you're doing to help me, and I expect to pay you for your legal services." Wendy choked back tears as reality hit home. Gunter Benson had sealed her fate. "With everything going on in my life…it's…um…best if we stop dating at least for a while."

Emotion-laced silence enfolded the moment as Chris gazed deep into her eyes. "Are you sure that's what you want?"

What I want is to melt into your arms and tell you how much I love you. But that's not what you need. Wendy averted her eyes. "I'm positive."

Chris released her shoulders and gently brushed a strand of hair away from her cheek. "I'll give you all the time you need."

Fearing his touch would erase her resolve, Wendy whispered thank you then forced her legs to carry her away from the man she loved and out to the reception area. Her hand froze on the front door knob. Had she just made a huge mistake? If Chris followed her, she'd rush to him and tell him how much she loved him. If he didn't, she'd walk out of his life. A quick glance over her shoulder told her everything she needed to know.

Wendy trudged to the truck and climbed behind the wheel. A half block from the Armstrong Law Office the tears she had kept at bay erupted and tracked down her cheeks. She pulled to the curb, covered her face with her hands, and wept.

A tap on the passenger window startled her. Wendy swiped her fingers across her cheeks and cut a glance to her left. An elderly woman stood staring at her.

"Are you okay, honey?"

Get a grip. Wendy forced a smile and lowered the window. "It's um…"

The woman smiled. "Pregnancy hormones?"

Wendy patted her belly. "Big time." Would she ever see the woman again? "I'm fine now. Really." Did she at least sound convincing? "Thank you for checking on me."

"You're welcome. You take care of yourself now." The woman straightened and walked away.

Wendy pulled down the visor mirror and stared at her reddened eyes. No way she could deny she'd been crying. She wet her fingers and dabbed the mascara smudges from beneath her eyes. Amanda and Erica knew she'd planned to have dinner with Chris. Maybe she should stay downtown for a couple of hours. And do what? Postpone the inevitable? Better to come up with some version of the truth—which called for serious reinforcements. She pulled away from the curb, drove to North Main Street, and found a parking spot less than a block from her destination.

Chapter 8

Erica opened her laptop and pulled up Hilltop Inn's email. "Only three couples have RSVP'd."

"Folks have barely had time to receive the invitations, much less respond." Amanda ambled from the kitchen and set two plated BLT sandwiches on the dining room table.

"Our open house is two weeks from tonight."

Amanda pulled out a chair. "We've done all we can do, so we might as well relax."

"That's a lot easier said than done. Especially since Millie is planning to prepare appetizers for more than a hundred people." Erica opened Hilltop Inn's website. "Good news. We have our first reservation—four nights in the Azalea Suite beginning grand-opening day. Does our promo to book one night and get the second night free mean we should only bill them for two nights?"

"Although we didn't specify, that's the right thing to do."

Erica sighed as she pushed her laptop aside. "There's still a lot we need to learn about innkeeping."

"We'll figure it out along the way." Amanda cut her sandwich in half. "How's massage school coming along?"

"I'm adding extra classroom days, so I can earn my credentials in time for our grand opening."

"Now that your massage room is all set up, how about giving me and Wendy the massages you promised?

She'd dragged her feet long enough. Besides, she'd practiced a number of times on other students. "How about tomorrow afternoon?"

"That works for me. I wonder how Chris decided to respond to Gunter's letter?" Amanda took a bite of sandwich.

"Maybe he'll accuse the con man of stalking Wendy."

Amanda shot her an incredulous look. "Gunter's locked in a prison on the other side of the country. How could he possibly stalk anyone?"

"You're right. Still, Chris needs to find some way to stop him from hounding Wendy." Erica bit into her sandwich while eyeing the mysterious pink envelope lying on the table. Was Amanda right about who had sent it? Dusty sprang to all fours at the sound of a vehicle pulling into the carport. "Seems we have company."

The kitchen door swung open. Wendy tossed keys into the bowl then strode into the den and set a Sweet Shoppe box on the table. "I brought us cupcakes."

Erica studied Wendy's face. Had she been crying, or had pollen reddened her eyes? "How'd everything go with Chris?"

Awesam's CFO plopped onto a chair. "He's sending Gunter a letter telling him not to write to me. If he ignores the request, Chris wants me to turn the unopened envelopes over to him."

"That makes sense." Amanda pushed her sandwich aside. "But it doesn't explain why you're here instead of with Chris."

Struggling to control her emotions, Wendy lifted a cupcake topped with a swirl of vanilla icing and a drizzle of caramel from the box. "I saw the cutest little outfit for a baby boy after I left his office." She dipped her finger into the icing. "This is my favorite."

"Enough chitchat about outfits and cupcakes." Amanda drummed her fingers on the table. "Are you going to tell us what's going on, or keep us guessing?"

Afraid to make eye contact, Wendy licked the icing off her finger. "There's nothing my lawyer can do to make Gunter go away, unless he breaks some law."

Amanda stopped drumming. "You broke up with Chris, didn't you?"

"It's for the best."

"Best for you or best for Chris?"

Wendy's shoulders tensed. She shot Amanda a stern look. "Trust me. I know what I'm doing."

"Do you?"

There was only one way to convince her partners that she'd made the right decision. "When I first met Chris, I was in shock and mistook his kindness as infatuation. After my first ultrasound...I was afraid of raising a boy by myself. That's when I set out to trap Chris into becoming my baby's daddy."

"Except—"

Wendy aimed her palm at Amanda. "Let me finish." She shared details about Chris's letter to Gunter. "Trust me, breaking up is best for both Chris and me, so please...no lectures. Besides, I'm perfectly capable of raising my son on my own." Struggling to control her emotions, Wendy pushed the box to Awesam's president. "The one with strawberry icing is for you."

Amanda hesitated as if deciding how to respond. "Since you brought our favorite cupcakes, I'll share my BLT with you." She scooted to the kitchen then returned and placed half her sandwich on a plate. "Especially for you." She pushed the half sandwich to Wendy.

Had Amanda accepted her explanation? What about Erica? They'd believe her if she kept from falling apart. Summoning steely resolve, Wendy peeled the wrapper off her cupcake. "Any news about Hilltop's grand opening?"

Amanda glanced at Erica, then eyed Wendy. "Our first reservation came in today for a four-day stay."

"Cool. We'll charge them for two nights." Wendy bit into her cupcake. "Anything else exciting happen while I was gone?"

"Actually—" Erica lifted a pink envelope off the table. "This came in the mail for you."

Wendy choked.

Erica handed her a glass of water. "It's not from Vegas."

Wendy gulped a mouthful. Relieved, she lifted the sandwich off her plate. "Who's it from?"

"There's no return address." Erica set the envelope beside Wendy's plate. "But it's postmarked Nashville."

Wendy's hands froze halfway to her mouth. The sandwich dropped onto the plate as she gawked at the handwritten name and address. She only knew one person who lived in Nashville.

Erica reached across the table and touched Wendy's hand. "Do you want me to open it?"

Wendy caught her bottom lip between her teeth. Did she have any courage left to discover what was inside? Not knowing would be far worse. She released her lip. "Please."

"All right." Erica slid her finger under the flap and removed a folded sheet of pink stationery. A photo dropped onto the table.

Wendy stared at a family gathered around a white baby grand piano. What kind of cruel joke was this?

"There's a letter. Do you want me to read it to you?"

Wendy leaned back and wrapped her arms around her belly. "No, but go ahead anyway."

Erica unfolded the letter. "It says, *"Dear Wendy. Seeing you for the first time in eighteen years came as quite a shock."*" She looked up.

"Is that all she wrote?"

"No."

Wendy's brow pinched. "Then why'd you stop?"

"Because..." Erica hesitated. "What she wrote next is hard to read."

"It's too late to back out now."

"All right, here goes. *"Especially since I had all but erased you from my memory."*"

Amanda slammed her fist on the table. "That woman's heart is as cold as the snowman in our freezer."

The mental image of the souvenir Wendy had rescued from the miniature snow family on Blue Ridge Inn's front porch eased the tension gripping her shoulders. "Way colder. What else did the ice queen write?"

"*Since I've had time to reflect on your visit, I realize that in my heart I have always cared about you.*"

"Not enough to rescue me from any one of seven different foster homes." Wendy tapped her finger on the photograph. "Why did she send that to me?"

Erica's focus returned to the letter. "*"I'm sending you a picture of my family so you will understand why you must remain a secret part of my past."*"

Amanda sneered. "To ease her guilty conscience, that's why."

Erica plucked the photo off the table. "Even though she looks normal—except for that bright pink streak in her hair—she's mentally off-balance."

"Another reason other than appearance, why our CFO is nothing like her mother."

Wendy blinked. Her eyes shifted from Amanda to Erica. "Is there more?"

She nodded. "'*It's good to know you've grown into a successful young woman with a bright future. If one day you find your father, I hope he is free to accept you into his life. In closing, I wish you all the best. Cynthia.*'"

Wendy slapped the photo face down on the table. "She couldn't even bring herself to sign as my mother."

Amanda faced Wendy. "You know why, don't you?"

Her brow pinched then released. "So, if any of her kids or her husband happened to see the letter, she could claim I was a long-lost acquaintance?"

"Exactly."

Erica placed the letter back into the envelope and handed it to Wendy. "What do you want to do with this?"

Wendy hesitated, then slid the photo in with the letter. "Keep it as a reminder of what kind of mother I never want to become."

Amanda reached across the table and squeezed Wendy's hand. "You have more love in one tiny little corner of your heart than Cynthia has in her entire body, honey."

With a response stuck in her throat, Wendy pushed away from the table then headed straight to her room and closed the door. The tears she had held at bay erupted as her eyes drifted to Chris's photo beneath her baby's sonogram. Would her broken heart ever mend after walking away from the man she loved?

Chapter 9

Amanda opened the blinds letting the early morning sunshine in. She spun around and eyed the living room which they'd eventually convert to a room for Wendy's son. Unless Chris and Wendy reconciled. At some point they'd need to find a spot to set up a proper office with a real desk. Until then, this space would have to do.

She moved a folding chair close to the card table then set her coffee mug and phone beside her laptop and pulled up the inn's website. Three more guests had taken advantage of their grand-opening special and reserved the Daffodil, Bluebell, and Rainbow Suites. She blinked as a new two-night reservation for six rooms in July popped up. The comment section made it clear their tech guy's sister had chosen Hilltop Inn for her annual sorority reunion. Hopefully their open house would lead to more successful referrals.

Morgan's ringtone startled Amanda and triggered alarm bells. Her daughter never called this early. She swiped her finger across her phone. "Hey, honey, is everything okay?"

"I have a final exam in two hours..." Sniffles.

"What's wrong?"

"Kevin and I had a terrible fight last night. I called him a few minutes ago. It went straight to voicemail. I didn't know what to say, so I hung up without leaving a message."

Time for a little loving guidance. "Did I ever tell you about the blowout your dad and I had two weeks before our wedding?"

More sniffles. "Over what?"

"Whether I should move into his apartment or he move into mine. A couple of days later, we kissed and made up."

"Where did you end up living?"

"In his apartment, but that's not the point. Unlike you and Kevin, Preston and I weren't dealing with final exams and looming career decisions. We let pre-wedding jitters get the best of us."

A long moment of silence. "I said some terrible things to Kevin."

"Strong relationships survive all sorts of challenges, including harsh words spoken in the heat of the moment."

"I never heard you and Dad argue, much less fight."

"Because we kept those moments private."

"Should I try to call Kevin again or wait for him to reach out to me?"

Amanda carried her phone to the den and settled on one of the two club chairs angled toward the sofa. "Give him a little time to cool off while you decide how to best apologize for your part in the argument."

"What if he doesn't accept my apology?"

"Trust me. He will. In fact, there's a good chance he'll apologize first."

A sigh resonated through the phone. "Thanks for the pep talk, Mom."

"You're welcome, honey. Now go ace that exam." After pocketing her phone and opening the sliding glass doors to let Dusty in from the backyard, Amanda ambled to the kitchen and refilled her mug. Her anger at Gunter intensified as her eyes drifted to Wendy's purse lying beside the key bowl.

Awesam's CFO hadn't joined her and Erica for a meal since Saturday. Their attempts to cheer Wendy up when she ventured out of her room to fix a sandwich or walk across the hall to the bathroom had done little to improve her mood. Even Dusty's tail wags failed to bring even the hint of a smile.

Amanda set her mug down then pulled her pinging phone from her pocket and eyed the text from Chris. "Need to talk. Meet me for coffee?" Her brow pinched. Did he have news about Gunter or questions about Wendy? Amanda tapped the screen. "When? Where?"

She waited.

"Ten. Mountain Mama's."

Amanda responded with a thumbs-up. Assuming Chris didn't want Wendy to know about the meeting, Amanda tiptoed to her room. After tucking her purse under her arm, she returned to the hall and hurried past Wendy's door. Back in the kitchen, she poured her coffee down the drain then grabbed the truck keys and headed next door. A loud clang drifted from the kitchen as Amanda stepped into the den. "Is that you making all that noise, Millie?"

"Burglars are stealing Eleanor's silverware and fancy dishes." Millie's tone mocked. "Of course, it's me. Who else would be in here?"

Typical Millie. Amanda joined Hilltop Inn's chef. "What are you do-ing?"

Millie stooped to pick a silver platter off the floor. "What do you think I'm doing?"

"Rearranging the cabinets?"

"I tackled that task yesterday. Today I'm getting ready for our open house." She set the tray atop the island beside an assortment of glass and silver platters. "How many RSVP's so far?"

"Forty-eight as of last night. I haven't checked today."

"You can count on that at least doubling." Millie removed a silver punch bowl from a bottom cabinet and set it on the counter. "I haven't seen Wendy in a couple of days. Is she okay?"

No way she'd reveal their CFO's latest drama. Amanda slid onto a stool. "She's resting up for the big day."

Millie eyed her with a raised brow. "That's not all that's going on, is it?"

"I'm curious." Amanda lifted a ladle off the island. "How old is your son?"

"Fifty-four. What does he have to do with my question about Wendy?"

Amanda set down the ladle and eyed Millie. "I just wanted to know how many years it's been since you were pregnant."

"You obviously don't want me to know anything that's going on around here."

"Are you going to be suspicious of every guest who checks into the inn?"

Millie waggled her finger at Amanda. "It's good to keep a watchful eye on strangers without them suspecting they're being watched."

Amanda rolled her eyes. Managing Millie would put the entire team's patience to the test. "We didn't bring you onboard to function as a secret service agent or amateur private investigator, so lighten up."

She rolled her eyes. "Hmph."

"Unless you need help doing whatever you're doing, I'm off to run errands." Amanda headed toward the den, then spun back toward their chef. "By the way, Wendy needs all the rest she can get before her baby arrives, so promise you won't bother her."

"You don't need to worry about me. I know my place."

That's debatable. "Okay, then." Amanda made her way out back and across the inn's driveway to the carport. She climbed into the truck for the short drive downtown. With a half hour to kill, she parked across the street from the coffee lounge then wandered in and out of Main Street's shops. Were any of the customers or staff members on their guest list? Five minutes before ten, she crossed back over the railroad track and headed up the driveway. Memories of the week she'd first met Wendy and Erica bubbled up. Chris was Awesam's attorney, so maybe this meeting with him had nothing to do with Wendy. Whatever the reason, she had to get a grip.

Amanda breathed deeply, as Mountain Mama's location came into view. She entered the coffee lounge and glanced around. No sign of Chris. Should she order or wait? Her eyes drifted to a table where her partners and their lawyer had celebrated Erica's birthday. The same table where Chris had first revealed Gunter's inheritance. Did he have news about the con man he didn't want to share with Wendy or Erica?

"Which coffee would you like?"

Amanda spun toward Chris. At least he wasn't carrying a manilla envelope. "Mountain Mama latte."

"One of my favorites." Chris stepped up to the counter.

The barista smiled. "Good morning, Mr. Armstrong."

"How's it going, Gloria?"

Amanda studied Chris's profile. Was the woman a client, or did Chris know everyone in town? What was this meeting all about?

The barista grinned. "Did you hear about my son's acceptance to your alma mater?"

"I did. Tell him congratulations."

"He's over the moon. Especially about attending all those Georgia football games. Anyway, what would you like?"

"Two mountain mama lattes."

"Coming right up."

Chris escorted Amanda to a small high-top table tucked in a corner. "Thank you for agreeing to meet me."

"I must say you've piqued my curiosity." As Amanda climbed onto a stool, her focus shifted to the door leading to the Blue Ridge Inn. "Is this a favorite hangout with friends or a convenient location for important meetings?"

"My office is a few blocks from here. Seems Mountain Mama's has outgrown this spot. They're moving to a new location in a few weeks."

"Today are we here for a friendly chat or an official meeting?"

"A little of both."

"Armstrong, two mountain mama lattes." The barista's voice rang out, drawing Chris back to the counter.

Amanda swallowed against the dryness in her throat. What did he mean by both?

Chris returned and placed their coffees on the table. "Mountain Mama's coffee is among the best in town."

Amanda wrapped her fingers around her cup. Was he stalling because he had disturbing news about Gunter? "You didn't invite me here to discuss the coffee."

"No." His eyes trained on hers. "What did Wendy tell you about our meeting?"

How much should she reveal? Enough but not too much. "She mentioned the letter you wrote to Gunter."

"The criminal knows enough about the law to keep our hands tied." Chris hesitated as if debating his next comment. He pushed his cup aside and crossed his arms on the table. "Wendy wants us to stop seeing each other."

So that's what this was about. Amanda sipped her coffee while struggling with the dilemma. As much as she believed Wendy had made a mistake, she respected her too much to intervene in her personal life. Besides, if Chris loved her, he'd find a way back into her heart. "All the trauma during the past five months along with raging hormones have taken a toll on Wendy. She needs time to sort through her emotions."

"I understand."

Did he?

"I respect her decision." Chris paused for a long moment. "I just wanted to make sure she's okay."

"Wendy's strong. She'll survive." If she changed subjects, would Chris take the hint? "The day after the three of us first checked into the Blue Ridge Inn, we met here before heading out to shop. If I'd had the slightest inkling of what lay ahead, I would have bought a proper winter coat."

Chris uncrossed his arms and clutched his coffee cup. "How are the grand-opening plans coming along?"

Relieved he'd read her ploy loud and clear, Amanda smiled. "We have our first reservations."

Following a half hour devoid of any mention of Wendy, Chris swallowed the last of his coffee. "If you don't mind, I'd prefer you keep our conversation between the two of us."

So, this had been about Wendy after all. "I understand."

Wendy leaned against her headboard with her laptop balanced on her legs and stared at the online sudoku she'd started hours ago. Three days of playing games and surfing the net had failed to fill the empty space in her heart. Yet somehow she had to accept reality—Chris could never be more than her attorney and friend.

Stomach grumbles forced Wendy to set her laptop aside. She climbed out of bed and slipped her phone in her pocket. The succulent scent of spaghetti sauce greeted her as she opened the door and ambled toward the kitchen. Her stomach grumbled again as she eyed the Caesar salad wend four place settings on the dining room table.

"Perfect timing, Ms. CFO." Amanda smiled. "Our favorite Italian dinner is ready." She lifted the pasta pot off the stove and set it in the sink.

Erica opened the oven releasing the mouthwatering aroma of butter and garlic. "Complete with fresh baked bread." She set the baking sheet on a hot pad, then cut the bread and transferred the slices to a platter. "We're celebrating our sixtieth open-house RSVP."

Hoping she'd masked her surprise, Wendy plucked a slice of bread off the platter and took a bite. She didn't want to admit that she hadn't checked the email or logged onto the Inn's website since Saturday morning.

"Millie's confident we'll double that number." Amanda poured the sauce over the spaghetti and carried the bowl to the table.

Erica followed with the bread while Abby bounced in and plopped onto her chair. "I'm starving."

Grateful no one asked questions or mentioned Chris, Wendy settled across from Abby. Following Erica's blessing, the Awesam team indulged on Amanda's signature dish while chatting about upcoming graduations and Hilltop Inn's open house. When they finished, Amanda pushed away from the table. "Everyone sit tight for dessert and a surprise for our CFO." She scooted to the kitchen then returned and placed a Sweet Shoppe box and gift bag on the table in front of Wendy. "Do you want to start with the cupcakes or the present?"

"What are we celebrating now?"

"Open it and find out."

Wendy removed the blue tissue paper and peeked into the bag. "Oh my gosh." She lifted the first item for her baby's wardrobe. "This is the most adorable little outfit I've ever seen."

"Perfect for our family's first boy. There's more."

Wendy reached into the bag and pulled out a card. Tears welled as she read the signatures. "Erica, Abby, and Nana." She reached across and squeezed Amanda's hand. "That's the perfect name for my son's grand-mother."

Amanda smiled. "I'm glad you approve of my choice."

After helping with kitchen cleanup, Wendy settled in the den with her family to watch a chick flick. By the time the credits rolled across the screen, she could barely keep her eyes open. She lifted off the sofa. "I'll see y'all in the morning." Wendy ambled to her room and changed into pajamas then curled up in bed and fell asleep.

Other than two trips across the hall, thanks to her little guy pressing on her bladder, Wendy managed to sleep through the night until a ping nudged her awake. Sunlight shone around the edges of her blinds as she lifted her phone off the nightstand. She stared at the screen. A text from Chris. Did he have news about Gunter, or had he sent her a personal message? Her heart pounded against her ribs as her finger inched toward the screen. What if... She swallowed the question and pressed the icon. "Want to make sure you're okay. I'm here if you need me."

Wendy squeezed her eyes shut and imagined Chris pulling her into his arms, kissing her, and telling her how much he loved her. *What I want is not what you need.* How should she respond? As a friend thanking a friend, that's how. She opened her eyes and tapped the screen. "Thanks for checking on me. All's good here." Wendy hesitated for a moment then pressed send.

She waited.

A thumbs-up emoji.

Heartbroken, Wendy plodded to the dresser and pulled Chris's photo off the dresser. Tears pooled and tracked down her cheeks as she dropped his picture into the top drawer.

Chapter 10

Amanda drew in a deep satisfying breath as she flicked a leaf off the inn's Hilltop Inn and Spa sign and glanced up at the grand three-story Victorian house. What the Awesam partners had achieved in fewer than five months was nothing short of miraculous. Her focus shifted to the mail truck as it stopped beside Millie's box then headed in her direction.

"Afternoon, Ms. Smith. The place has never looked better." The driver handed over mail for both properties.

"Thanks." As he drove off, Amanda flipped through the items. Relieved there were no envelopes from Nevada, she headed up the driveway to the inn's front sidewalk where guests would be greeted by the row of newly planted azaleas in full bloom. Morgan's ringtone sounded as she climbed onto the front porch. Amanda set the mail on the railing then pulled her phone from her pocket and pressed Facetime. "Based on your smile, I'm guessing you've landed a great job."

"I received an offer from a big company in Texas."

Even further away than Louisiana. Amanda masked her disappointment with a weak smile of her own . "That's good news."

"Except, Kevin has an even better offer in Atlanta, so I turned mine down. His job starts the first week in June." Morgan paused. "Which is why I'm calling."

"Let me guess." Warmth spread through Amanda's chest. "You're sending resumes to Atlanta companies, which means you'll only live a couple hours away."

"Yes, but first...Kevin and I are moving our wedding up to the day after graduation. "

Amanda blinked. Had she heard correctly? "That's fewer than two weeks from now. How can you plan a wedding in such a short amount of time?"

"We've decided on an intimate ceremony at his parents' home with family and a few close friends. So, there's not much to plan."

Amanda dropped onto a rocking chair. "Are you sure that's what you want?"

"Positive. Besides, big expensive weddings are way overrated. After we honeymoon in Atlanta and find a place to live, I'll send out resumes. Oh, and Kevin's mother invited you to stay with them the entire time you're here. You'll love his parents. They remind me of you and Dad."

Tears formed and spilled down Amanda's cheeks.

"You're thinking about Dad, aren't you?"

"He would have been so proud to walk you down the aisle and place your hand in Kevin's."

Morgan's eyes appeared to redden. "Daddy will be with us in spirit, Mom."

"I know." Amanda swiped her fingers across her cheeks. "Now, what can I do to help you prepare for your big day?"

"Can you change your plans and come two days before graduation, so we can go shopping together?"

"Absolutely, I'll make that happen."

"Thanks, Mom. I love you."

"I love you too, honey." As Amanda pocketed her phone and lifted off the rocking chair, Millie trekked across the front lawn carrying a foil-covered plate. "You're twenty minutes early."

Their neighbor climbed onto the porch. "This is the first time you invited me to one of your board meetings. I don't want to miss anything, so I brought fresh-baked cookies."

"We might as well go on in." Amanda led the way into the dining room.

Millie glanced around. "Does it matter where I sit?"

Amanda pointed to a chair facing the pocket doors opening to the living room. "How about there?"

"Okay." Millie skirted the table and set the platter on the table beside four bottles of water. "What's on today's agenda?"

"Final plans for our open house." After laying the mail on the sideboard, Amanda took her place at the end of the table and opened her laptop. "By the way, we currently have a hundred and fifty RSVP's."

Millie snapped her fingers. "I told you we'd have a great turnout. From now on, you need to invite me to all your board meetings."

If Erica hadn't insisted, she wouldn't be attending this one. Amanda leaned forward. "You're still not an officer or a voting member of our company."

"You do know that without me you wouldn't have that fabulous backyard or a first-class chef." Millie peeled off the foil releasing mouthwatering chocolate and brown-sugar scents. "We should put fresh cookies out for guests every afternoon."

"We'll consider your suggestion." Amanda tapped her keyboard. "Now, if you don't mind, I need to prepare before the rest of the team arrives."

"I'll leave you alone." Millie grabbed a water bottle then pushed away from the table and ambled into the living room.

Amanda's fingers rested on the keyboard. Should she lighten up on Millie, especially since she had become an important member of their team? A lot depended on her behavior during today's meeting. She turned her attention to her screen until footsteps struck the foyer floor.

Wendy's voice came from the living room. "Something smells yummy."

Erica accompanied her. "I think it's chocolate."

Millie's chest puffed. "Compliments of Hilltop Inn's professional chef."

"This is the first time we've had fresh-baked cookies at a staff meeting." Wendy ambled into the dining room, dropped onto a chair, and set her laptop on the table.

Awesam's CEO settled beside Wendy while Millie returned to her seat. Erica smiled at their chef. "Thanks for bringing them."

"Next staff meeting I'll bring snickerdoodle cookies."

Amanda failed to resist an eye roll. "Before we begin, I...um—" She stole a glance at Awesam's CFO reaching for a cookie. How would Wendy react to Morgan's news? Maybe she should hold off until the end of the meeting to find out.

Wendy took a bite of cookie. "Oh my gosh, this is delicious. Another signature recipe?"

Millie nodded with more than a little enthusiasm. "One of many, including my own twist on the snickerdoodles."

Definitely best to wait to break the news about Morgan and Kevin. "Now that we have snacks settled, we need to discuss our roles during the open house."

"Actually—" Erica uncapped a water bottle. "I thought about that all the way back from school, and in my opinion, we need prepared spontaneity."

Wendy's brows shot up. "What in the heck are you talking about?"

"We want everyone to feel welcome while learning everything about the inn. . Tours seem too formal, right?"

Amanda eyed Erica. "What's your point?"

"First a question." Erica faced Millie. "How many different appetizers have you planned?"

"Eight."

"What if we spread the appetizers around the main floor to encourage guests to browse on their own. We could each host a room and promote the inn's amenities."

Amanda nodded. "That makes sense."

"Hold on." Millie raised an open palm. "How can I answer questions about my hors d'oeuvres if they're spread all over the place?"

"We can put little signs out for each appetizer." Wendy reached for another cookie. "Such and such by Chef Millie."

"Good idea, Wendy." Erica turned back toward Millie. "Besides, you'll be busy telling everyone about Eleanor and your English-garden master-piece—"

Millie waggled her finger at Erica. "Are you suggesting I stay outside the whole time?"

"Goodness no. However, you are the perfect team member to encourage guests to step out back and walk along the paths."

"All right, I'll go along." Millie shrugged. "But only if I'm the one who decides what appetizers go where. And if I'm busy talking to guests, someone will need to replenish the food."

Erica nodded. "We'll make that happen."

Amanda stifled a grin. *Way to go, Erica.* "Now as for the three of us—" After nailing down responsibilities, Amanda closed her laptop. She couldn't postpone the inevitable any longer. "I have some news about Morgan. It seems Kevin landed a job in Atlanta." She stole a quick glance at Wendy. "Which is why they've decided to move their wedding up to a week from Saturday so they can find a place to live as a married couple."

Erica eyed Amanda. "Are you disappointed about missing the opportunity to help plan the wedding?"

Amanda shrugged. "A little, I suppose. Although Morgan would have taken care of most details on her own, no matter what the date. Anyway, I'll be back home before our grand opening."

Wendy stared at Amanda. "You didn't tell us earlier because you were afraid I'd be upset, weren't you?"

"I thought it was best to wait."

"Wendy's jaw tensed. "Do you have anything else to tell us?"

Amanda shook her head.

"Then I'm gonna head home and take a nap." Wendy lifted her laptop off the table then padded across the living room and out the front door.

Millie's eyes darted from Amanda to Erica then back to Amanda. "Wendy and Chris broke up, didn't they?"

Amanda shot their neighbor an incredulous look.

"Don't look so surprised. I'm not blind. Besides, Wendy didn't mention Chris once during the entire meeting, and the way she responded to Morgan's news was a dead giveaway."

No point denying. "It's best if you don't say anything to Wendy."

Millie huffed. "You don't have to worry about me. When's our next staff meeting?"

Amanda broke eye contact and closed her laptop. "We'll let you know."

Chapter 11

Grateful to have the house all to herself, Wendy grabbed the remote off the coffee table and aimed it at the television. Dusty padded over and sprawled on the floor between the coffee table and the sofa. "What should we watch, girl?" She scrolled through the recorded programs and chose a *Cheers* rerun. Funny how a comedy that was filmed before she was born could make her laugh. At least most days.

While Wendy's eyes remained focused on the screen, her mind drifted from the Boston bar to Amanda's news about Morgan and Kevin. They belonged together. If she wasn't pregnant, so might she and Chris. Wendy pressed her hand to her belly. "It's not your fault, little guy. It's mine for allowing myself to fall in love. After Morgan and Kevin's big day, chances are Abby will end up the next family member to walk down the aisle. Right, Dusty?"

The dog's tail thumped the floor in a lazy motion.

"I knew you'd agree." Wendy propped her feet on the coffee table. At least single motherhood had certain advantages, especially with Amanda and Erica to help out, although they'd be busy innkeeping. She shifted her focus back to the program. Chris was way more handsome than Sam Malone and smarter than Frasier. Wendy rolled her eyes at the absurdity of comparing Chris to television characters. How long before she could go an hour without thinking about him?

She flicked off the television, then ambled to her room and dropped onto the edge of the bed. Dusty followed her and sat on her haunches. Wendy's bottom lip caught between her teeth as she rocked the cradle her baby's nana and aunt had brought home yesterday. Last time she'd checked, Chris hadn't RSVP'd for their open house. He hadn't called her other than that one time he texted. Chris had obviously moved on.

Dusty's ears perked at the sound of the doorbell.

Wendy followed Abby's canine companion and opened the front door as the UPS driver dashed down the driveway. Her eyes drifted to the box addressed to her from a local store. "Who do you suppose it's from?"

Dusty released a muted bark.

"You're right. There's only one way to find out." Wendy carried the box to the kitchen and set it on the counter. After slicing through the packing tape, she opened the flaps, peeled back tissue paper, and removed the brown teddy bear. She stroked the silky blue ribbon tied around the bear's neck, her eyes drifting to the envelope lying on the bottom of the box. Wendy's heart pounded against her ribs. She recognized the handwriting. Swallowing the lump in her throat, she set the bear on the counter. After hesitating for a long moment, she removed the card from the envelope. *A gift for your little guy to replace the bear you gave away. Chris.*

Tears erupted and tracked down her cheeks. She lifted the bear and hugged it to her chest. Why did he make it so difficult to fall out of love with him? Wendy carried the gift to her room and placed it in the bassinet. She swiped her fingers across her cheeks, grabbed her phone, and tapped the screen. "Thank you for the bear." She hesitated. What else should she say? Wendy added a smiley face then pressed send.

Five minutes passed before her phone pinged a response. "You're welcome."

Wendy stared at her phone. Maybe one day... No. She had to accept the fact that Chris would never be more than her lawyer and her friend. Grateful for the sound of the mail truck, she hastened to the front door. The sun warmed her cheeks as she headed down the driveway. Wendy removed the inn's mail then emptied the ranch house box and carried the stack back up the driveway and into the kitchen. She rifled through the stack to the last envelope. A gasp escaped as she glared at the familiar handwriting. Did she dare open it, or should she follow her lawyer's instructions?

Fearing she couldn't face Chris without falling apart, Wendy carried the dreaded envelope to the den and dropped onto the sofa. She stared at the postmark for a long moment. It had been mailed a week ago. Cold sweat broke out on the back of her neck as she slid her finger under the flap. Maybe she should rip it to shreds and toss it in the trash. Wendy's heart pounded against her ribs. Better to find out what Gunter wrote. In one swift move, she removed then unfolded the single sheet of lined paper. She drew in a deep breath to slow her pulse then released the air. *I can do this.* She forced her eyes to focus on the handwritten words.

Dearest Wendy,

After I wrote expressing my love for you and for our baby, I was disappointed to learn that you had shared my letter with Chris Armstrong. I believed you would understand that my intentions were honorable. Should you pass this on to your attorney without first reading it, I will assume your misplaced loyalty.

Given that I'm an innocent man, I'm confident the appeal process will reverse the travesty done to me. Once I am free, I will reclaim what rightfully belongs to me. In the meantime, know that you are in my thoughts every waking moment. I hope I am also in yours.

Yours forever,

Kurt

Did he sign with that name to intimidate her? Wendy's pulse pounded. Or was prison driving him mad? She squeezed her eyes shut and envisioned the assistant DA's closing argument against Gunter—the indisputable evidence proving his guilt as a murderer. No way he'd ever win an appeal.

Wendy opened her eyes then folded the letter and slid it back into the envelope. Now what? If she shared it with Chris, would he be angry at her for ignoring his instructions? Maybe it was best to keep it a secret. Except, how could her attorney protect her if she failed to tell him the truth? The truck engine whirred in the carport. Erica had returned from school.

Wendy escaped to her room and closed the door. Her heart pounded as she opened her top dresser drawer and stared at Chris's photo. *Will I ever stop loving you?* She slid the letter under her clothes and pushed the drawer closed. If Chris showed up at the open house, she'd share the letter. If he didn't, she'd rip it to shreds and find a way to move on without him.

Chapter 12

Amanda waited in front of the window while the open-house team gathered in the downstairs turret room for a last-minute pep talk. Given Wendy's sour mood during the past few days, the role as Awesam's cheerleader had landed squarely on Amanda's shoulders. Especially since every attempt to cheer their CFO had fallen on deaf ears. She pasted on her best smile. "What our team has accomplished during the past few months is nothing short of miraculous. Tonight, our VIP guests will experience the hospitality and luxury of a first-class inn."

"—featuring the best chef in Blue Ridge." Millie pulled her apron over her head and smoothed her red tunic. "The professional appetizer stations are all set up."

Abby gazed dreamy-eyed at her boyfriend. "Tommy and I are ready to keep those stations stocked." Her eyes shifted to Millie. "Oh, and your snickerdoodle cookies are scrumlicious."

Their chef's brows raised. "Did you invent that word, or is it some sort of young-person slang?"

"Scrumptious and delicious." Abby stared at Millie as if she didn't have a clue. "You know, scrumlicious."

"Definitely made up, but clever. Anyway, we all need to remember that in addition to promoting the inn, tonight is about honoring Eleanor Harrington. After all, if she and Warren hadn't built this house, we wouldn't be here."

Amanda's gaze shifted to the turret room's elaborate ceiling molding. "I imagine your friend is smiling down on us at this very moment, Millie. And when you show guests your backyard masterpiece, they'll know how much you loved her. For now, are there any last-minute questions about our responsibilities tonight?"

Erica shook her head.

Wendy shrugged. "I'm good."

"Me too," added Millie.

"All right then. Let's wow our guests with amazing southern hospitality."

As the team headed to the French doors, Amanda clutched Wendy's arm. "Hold on a second." She waited for the others to walk out. "I want to make sure you're okay."

"Why wouldn't I be?"

"The past few days you haven't been the enthusiastic charmer we all know and love."

Wendy's bottom lip caught between her teeth. "I...um..."

"You can talk to me, honey." Amanda patted Wendy's belly. "After all, I'm your baby's nana."

Wendy blinked then pointed to the window. "Our first guest is here."

Amanda glanced over her shoulder at a car pulling up in the driveway.

Wendy pulled her hand away. "You don't need to worry about me. I'll charm the socks off our guests with mountains of Mississippi charm." She whirled away, ambled to the foyer, and turned toward the den.

Amanda breathed deeply as she stepped into the foyer and headed to the console table close to the front door. She opened the guestbook and stared at the blank page. Had interest in the new inn or curiosity about the newcomers enticed nearly all of the invitees to respond favorably to their invitation? Did their reasons for accepting even matter? She grabbed a stack of brochures and tapped her foot. The doorbell rang. Amanda stilled her foot, then painted on her most engaging smile and pulled the door open. An elderly couple stood on the porch. "Welcome to Hillside Inn and Spa. I'm Amanda."

The gentleman gripped the woman's elbow as he introduced himself and his wife. "This is the first time we've been in this house since the last summer Warren and Eleanor stayed here."

The woman leaned on her cane. "They hosted such fun dinner parties."

Amanda handed the gentleman a brochure showcasing the inn. "Are you two aware that Mildred Cunningham is Hillside's chef?"

"I talked to her yesterday." The woman patted Amanda's arm. "You ladies have made her happier than she's been in years. You know she and Eleanor were close friends."

"Yes. In fact, Millie will show you the garden we've dedicated to Eleanor. You'll find her delicious appetizers throughout the downstairs and in the upstairs hall." Amanda nodded toward the console. "After you sign our guestbook, Erica will share details about restoring the Harrington home."

"Thank you, dear. We're looking forward to seeing what you and your friends have accomplished."

While Millie's dinner-party friends signed the book, Amanda turned and greeted the middle-aged couple walking in. The gentleman introduced himself as the mayor. "You've done wonders with this place."

His wife handed Amanda a gift bag from Owl's Nest. "A little present to welcome you as our town's newest business."

"Thank you for the gift and for helping us celebrate."

"Folks are curious, so I imagine you'll have a big turnout."

Curious about the inn or its innkeepers? "It's a pleasure to meet you both." While the mayor and his wife signed the guestbook, Amanda greeted the next couple. "Welcome to Hillside Inn and Spa..."

Erica stared out the front window and mentally ticked off the list of tasks she and the team had tackled. Had they forgotten any important details? Her eyes drifted to the elderly couple approaching the front porch. Erica spun away from the window and glanced around the living room. Everything was in place. Candles on the mantel. Pillows on the sofa.

The doorbell rang. Erica moved close to the bookstand and tuned into the voices drifting from the foyer. While waiting, she mentally rehearsed her spiel. The moment the couple walked into the living room Erica greeted them with a smile. "It's an honor to meet two of the Harringtons' friends. Millie has told us how much she enjoyed the dinner parties they hosted."

The woman glanced around. "We always looked forward to Eleanor and Warren coming back to Blue Ridge. It's a shame she never returned after he passed away. We heard she'd married again."

To a scoundrel. Best not to touch that subject. "Before you taste the first of Millie's amazing appetizers—" Erica pointed to the bookstand. "We've documented our entire renovation project."

The gentleman swept his arm in a wide arc. "I can already tell you've done an amazing job."

"Thanks to my Awesam partners. That's the name of our company." Erica explained how Wendy had come up with the name.

"You're such clever ladies." The woman gripped her cane. "This was always my favorite room. Sometimes after dinner while the men watched a baseball game, we ladies sat in here and chatted about our families. It's sad Eleanor and Warren never had children, although they were happy with each other. They were quite wealthy, you know."

"Warren was a real car enthusiast," added the gentleman. "Do you know what happened to that vintage Cadillac he kept in the garage?"

Erica hesitated. How much should she share? Did it matter? After all, they'd probably find out anyway. "Actually, that car funded a good bit of our restoration."

"I call that a good trade."

The mayor and his wife ambled in and greeted the older couple. "You two look as spry as ever." The two women embraced. "Don't you just love what they've done to the place?"

Erica stepped away as the foursome continued to chat. Her focus drifted to the two women entering from the foyer. The brunette looked familiar. She blinked. The salesclerk from the store where she, Amanda, and Wendy had shopped the day after they arrived at the Blue Ridge Inn. Would she remember Wendy's denied credit card? Surely, she wasn't the only customer whose card had been turned down. Erica smiled as the ladies wandered in. "Welcome to Hilltop Inn. I'm Erica."

The women introduced themselves. "We're co-owners of a Main Street boutique." The brunette handed Erica a business card. "Come in and see us sometime."

"Thanks, I will." Either she didn't remember them, or she was too polite to say anything. After sharing tidbits about the restoration, Erica pointed toward the dining room. "Please make yourselves at home and enjoy the appetizers."

"We heard Ms. Cunningham had taken the job as the inn's chef."

Did everyone in town know about Millie? "Lucky for us. She also designed our English country garden. Be sure to check it out."

"We will."

The women joined the mayor and his wife while another couple meandered in from the foyer. Although Erica had never met them, there was no mistaking the man as Chris's father. "Welcome, Mr. and Mrs. Armstrong. I'm Erica."

He slid his arm around the pretty, middle-aged woman with stylish, highlighted hair. "Tonight's a social gathering, so please call my wife and me Linda and Keith."

Chris's mother glanced around. "Our son told us about the wonderful job you ladies have done with this place."

Did either of them know that Wendy had broken up with their son? "It was a labor of love."

"And a wonderful addition to our thriving tourist business."

As Chris's partner, his dad had to know the whole Gunter story, but did his mother? "We're all delighted to be part of this community. Especially my daughter, Abby. She and her friend Tommy are around here somewhere."

"Tommy Bennett?"

Was he the only Tommy in town, and why hadn't she called him Abby's boyfriend? "Yes."

Linda smiled. "The Bennetts are a wonderful family, and Tommy's a terrific young man."

Another couple strolled in.

"You have more guests to greet." Linda touched her arm. "It's a pleasure finally to meet the rest of the Awesam team."

Wendy chewed on her fingernail as unfamiliar voices drifted from the foyer. Last she'd checked, Chris hadn't RSVPed, but his parents and sister had. Did his family have any idea she and Chris were no longer dating? Since they'd waited until the second hour to show up, maybe it was intentional, so she'd be too busy with other guests to spend time with them. How many people who planned to show up knew she was a single mother? What should she say if they didn't know and asked about her husband?

Millie touched her arm. "Are you okay?"

"Why is everyone asking me that question?" Wendy plucked a stuffed mushroom off the snack table and popped it into her mouth.

"You seem a bit anxious."

"Yeah, well—" She swallowed. "I'm about to greet hundreds of people I've never met—maybe not hundreds, but a lot. So, what if I'm a little distracted?"

"All you need to do is relax and turn on your Wendy charm."

Easy for her to say. She wasn't a pregnant woman who couldn't go an hour without rushing to the bathroom.

"Oh my goodness." Millie rushed toward an elderly man and a woman walking with a cane. "Wendy, meet Midge and Stan, two of Eleanor's favorite dinner-party guests. Wendy is our chief financial officer."

Time to turn on some Wendy charm. She smiled ear to ear and extended her hand. "Welcome to Hillside Inn."

Stan sandwiched her hand between his. "You're beautiful and charming."

Wendy tilted her head. "Thank you for the compliment, but I don't hold a candle to your lovely wife and my dear friend Millie."

"You're also smart." He grinned and released her hand.

"You two won't believe what Millie has created out back."

When their chef linked arms with her friends and escorted them out the French doors, Wendy's mind drifted to Eleanor Harrington's journals. Having read every word she'd written, she sensed an intimate connection with Millie's closest friend. A kick drew her hand to her belly and triggered a smile. One of these days she had to give her little guy a name.

"You and your partners have created a beautiful inn."

Wendy's pulse accelerated as she spun toward Linda and Keith. "It was a labor of love." Why had she used that term? Her eyes drifted to a young man sporting a neatly trimmed beard heading in their direction. The elderly woman clinging to his arm looked vaguely familiar. Wendy blinked. Was she the same woman who had tapped on the truck window the day she'd broken up with Chris?

Chris's father turned toward the couple. "Wendy, meet our son-in-law Mark, and my mother, Susan."

"One of Allison's patients is in labor; otherwise she'd be here." Susan touched Wendy's arm. "How are you holding up, my dear?"

That voice. She was the same woman. Did Chris's grandmother recognize her? How much did she know about her grandson's personal life? "A bit tired, but I'm fine."

Susan's eyes remained locked on Wendy's. She nudged Mark's arm. "Go fetch one of those dining room chairs for this lovely young lady. At eight months, she doesn't need to spend hours on her feet."

Wendys swallowed against the dryness in her throat. *How'd she know how far along I am?*

Keith slid his arm around his mother's shoulders. "Mom's a retired obstetric nurse, so don't be surprised if she checks your pulse."

Oh. That's how she knows.

Mark returned.

Wendy stared at the chair he placed beside the appetizer table. "I'm fine, really."

Susan touched Wendy's arm. "Of course you are. Which is why you need to take care of yourself and that precious child you're carrying, sweetie."

Wendy hesitated.

"Mom is one persuasive lady." Linda smiled. "Believe me, she won't give up until you follow her instructions."

Although she didn't want to admit it, her feet and legs screamed for a rest. "All right, then." Relieved no one had mentioned Chris, Wendy lowered onto the chair.

His sweet grandmother patted Wendy's cheek. "Now, you rest while we tour this lovely inn."

"Yes, ma'am." No matter what had happened between her and Chris, Wendy couldn't help but love his family.

Chapter 13

An hour after the first guest had arrived, the inn buzzed with activity and lively chatter. Amanda read the guestbook signatures. For whatever reasons folks had responded to their invitation, they all seemed to accept the newcomers with open arms.

A good-looking young man ambled in from the front porch and introduced himself.

The moment Amanda greeted him and handed him a brochure, his name rang a bell. "You're Blue Ridge Inn's owner, aren't you?"

"I am." His face lit with a warm smile. "Congratulations on everything you've accomplished. This open house is a smart way to launch your new business."

"Your beautiful inn and the way your staff treated us during the blizzard has been such an inspiration. We hope you don't mind the competition."

He glanced at the brochure. "Each inn has its own unique qualities and advantages. If you ever need advice or suggestions, feel free to give me a call."

It felt right that her competitor bore her no ill will. "Thank you, we will. By the way, your assistant innkeeper and her husband arrived a few minutes ago."

His eyebrows lifted. "Ah, Faith. She's a treasure."

"Yes she is." Amanda pointed toward the console. "Please sign our guest-book, then make yourself at home."

"Thanks."

After he added his name to the signatures and disappeared into the living room, Amanda turned toward the dark-haired young woman entering from the porch. "Welcome to Hilltop Inn."

"Thank you." The woman glanced around. "It appears your open house is quite a success."

"We're delighted with the turnout. My name's Amanda, and you are?"

"Actually, I'm not one of your invited guests." She handed over a business card.

Amanda's muscles tightened. "Gail Weston. Freelance Journalist." She pocketed the card. "How did you hear about our event, Ms. Weston?"

"Keeping tuned in to everything that happens in North Georgia is how I make a living. Are you one of the three women who were stranded at the downtown inn during December's blizzard?"

Amanda hesitated. "I am."

"I want to write a story about your experience and how you ended up owning this property."

Alarm bells jangled in Amanda's head. How much did this stranger already know about them? "I appreciate your interest. However, I can't commit to anything without consulting my partners." She swept her arm in a wide arc. "As you can see, it's not a good time to discuss your request tonight."

"I understand. Why don't I look around and call you tomorrow after-noon."

"All right. First, come meet our chief executive officer." After introduc-ing the journalist to Erica and relaying their conversation, Amanda made a beeline to the den to warn Wendy and Millie.

Grateful for the heads-up, Erica escorted the journalist to the dining room. "As long as you're a guest, you should try the appetizers prepared by our chef. You can start here, then visit the other rooms." She handed the woman a plate then glanced over her shoulder. "If you'll excuse me, I need to greet another guest." Erica hastened back to the living room and extended her hand to the gentleman with curly brown hair strolling in from the foyer. "Welcome to Hilltop Inn and Spa. I'm Erica Nelson, one of the owners."

His deep blue eyes twinkled before he gently took her hand. "It's a pleasure to meet you, Erica. I'm Brad."

Erica's pulse accelerated as her eyes remained focused on the widower Millie had called movie-star handsome. She'd definitely nailed that description. "We're delighted you're joining us."

His eyes lingered on hers. "So am I."

Erica's daughter dashed toward them. "He's here—" She halted mid-sentence. "Hey, Mr. Barkley."

"Hi, Abby."

Erica pulled her hand away from Brad's. Millie should have mentioned his last name, so she wasn't caught off guard. "You're the high school principal."

"For the past twelve years. We'll catch up later."

Erica's eyes followed Brad as he strode toward the dining room and clapped his hand on a man's shoulder. "What were you about to say when you walked in?"

"The judge who sentenced me for running the stop sign and texting while driving is in the den."

Erica turned toward her daughter. "I'd hardly call a couple hundred dollars and a few hours of community service a sentence—which, by the way, turned out to be a blessing."

"True. But what if he recognizes me?"

"That was nearly five months and hundreds of cases ago." She patted her daughter's cheek. "Besides, if he does happen to remember you, it's because you're memorable in a good way."

"I suppose you're right. Did you know Mr. Barkley's wife died a few years ago?"

"I'd heard."

Abby leaned close. "For an older guy he's pretty hot."

She resisted the urge to nod. "How did he know I was your mother?"

Abby lifted a shoulder. "Why wouldn't he? I bet he comes back to talk to you as soon as I walk away."

"Why? To spill the beans about mischief you and your friends pulled?"

"No, Mom." Abby rolled her eyes. "Because you're a good catch."

"Yeah, well, Miss Matchmaker, it's time for you to go back to work."

"I'm on my way." As if on cue, Brad returned to the room.

Abby whirled around in the foyer and signaled a thumbs-up.

Sensing her cheeks were seconds from flushing, Erica shuffled from one foot to the other.

A grin lit Brad's face. "If I didn't know otherwise, I would have sworn you and Abby were sisters."

Was he flirting with her? "We've been through a lot together." *What a dumb comment.*

"I understand."

What did he understand? That she was a thirty-seven-year old woman who'd married an abusive cop followed by a con man who was in jail for murder? Erica blinked. "Millie mentioned that your parents and the Harringtons were friends."

"They were. Dad and Warren were golf buddies."

"Do you play?"

"Every Saturday. What about you?"

Why do I suddenly feel as if I'm Abby's age? "I've never had the chance."

"Our local pro is an excellent coach. Who knows, you might be a natural."

A man who appeared to be the same age as Brad strode in and clasped a hand on his shoulder. "Sorry I had to miss last Saturday's game—" Taking advantage of the opportunity, Erica stepped away. Halfway across the room, she glanced over her shoulder. Her eyes met Brad's. He smiled, then turned toward his friend.

Would he have talked to her if she wasn't one of his students' parents? A warm sensation flowed through Erica. Whatever the reason, at least she had enjoyed the moment.

Grateful the journalist had breezed in and out of the den without approaching her, Wendy peered out the French doors. The landscape lighting and gazebo chandelier cast a warm glow on the backyard.

"By all accounts, the open house is a success."

Wendy's heart jumped to her throat at the voice. She spun around and breathed in the scent of Chris's cologne. "So, it seems."

"I hear you met my grandmother tonight."

Wendy nodded. "Thank you again for the bear."

"You're welcome again."

Chris showing up made it clear she could no longer keep her attorney in the dark. "There's something I need to show you, next door."

"All right."

She fell silent while leading the way across the side yard and into the ranch house den. Wendy pointed to the sofa. "Wait there." She headed to her room and pulled the envelope from her dresser drawer. Would Chris be angry at her for ignoring his instructions? Maybe showing him the letter was a mistake. Ridiculous. He was her attorney; he needed to know. She plodded back to the den and handed Chris the envelope. "I'm sorry I couldn't resist opening it."

"Understandable." Chris settled on the sofa, then removed the letter. His jaw clenched as he silently read Gunter's words.

"Did he cross any legal lines, and why do you think he signed the name Kurt?"

"To answer your first question, not exactly."

"What does 'not exactly' mean?"

"He's sending a clear message, but he hasn't directly threatened you. As far as his signature goes, he wants you to think of him as the man you married instead of a criminal behind bars."

"Fat chance of that happening." Wendy collapsed against the back of the sofa. "If he sends more letters, should I return them unopened?"

"No. To protect you, I need to know what's on his mind. I'll send him another letter in response to this one. Do you want to read it before I mail it?"

"I trust you, so no."

"All right then." Chris pocketed the letter.

Drawing on every ounce of strength in her body, Wendy resisted the overwhelming desire to tell Chris how much she loved him. "I should return to our open house."

Chris stood and helped Wendy to her feet. "I'll walk you over."

"You don't have to."

"I'm heading back to indulge on Millie's appetizers, so I might as well." They walked out the kitchen door. "What did you think of my grandmother?"

"She made me get off my feet."

He chuckled. "That definitely sounds like her."

He shared stories about his grandmother while they strolled back to the inn. Moments after they stepped inside, an attractive young woman waved him over. Chris leaned close to Wendy. "We'll talk later."

Wendy's expression pinched as Chris approached and embraced the woman. By the time he left the party, she had come to one undeniable conclusion. The man she loved with all her heart had moved on.

Chapter 14

Sunday afternoon, Amanda gathered the Awesam board, plus Millie, around the inn's dining room table. "By all measures last night was a huge success for our new business."

"Think about it." Erica scooted her chair closer to the table. "Two days ago we were the town's mysterious strangers. Today we're welcomed members of the Blue Ridge community."

"Which brings us to the purpose of this meeting." Amanda leaned forward and placed her phone on the table. "We need to decide how to respond to that journalist's request to write a story about us."

"Let's make a list of all the pros and cons." Wendy uncapped a water bottle. "Starting with the pros."

Millie peeled the wrapper off the plate of cookies. "First of all, a positive story about a business beats the heck out of paid advertising."

"Good point." Wendy grabbed a cookie. "Are those snickerdoodles from last night?"

Millie nodded. "The last eight."

"You're right about the impact of positive publicity." Amanda leaned forward and crossed her arms on the table. "Except for one glaring fact. Gail Weston wants to write about how we ended up owning this property."

Wendy swallowed a bite of cookie. "We could tell her that we met during the blizzard, became friends, and decided to buy it."

"Out of the blue, we packed up and left our homes? That's illogical at best." Amanda eyed their CFO. "Besides, I suspect journalists are similar to detectives—"

Erica tapped her fingers on the table. "Meaning they probe until they arrive at the truth."

"Exactly."

Wendy huffed. "Sounds like you two have already made up your minds."

"We could tell her she can only write about the garden I designed and dedicated to Eleanor, especially since my friend was the inn's original owner. That's an inspirational story."

Amanda shook her head. "This morning I researched Gail's bylines. Believe me, she doesn't write fluff pieces."

Erica's brow pinched. "She might already know a lot more about us than we realize."

Millie scoffed. "I still believe my idea will work."

"Maybe for some gardening magazine." Amanda tapped her fingers on her arms. "Definitely not for a hard-hitting journalistic piece."

Amanda's phone buzzed. "It's Gail. What are we going to tell her?"

Wendy shrugged. "Guess we'd better tell her no."

Erica nodded. "I agree."

Millie raised her hand. "Does my vote count?"

"Sorry, Millie, you don't have voting privileges." Amanda slid her finger across the screen and tapped the speaker. "Good afternoon."

"Have you and your partners discussed my proposal?"

"We have. Although we appreciate your interest, we respectfully decline."

A long moment of silence. "We need to meet in person. Today."

Amanda's chest tightened. "Why?"

"I have information that will change your mind."

Erica gasped.

Wendy pressed her hand to her belly.

Millie folded her arms across her chest.

Amanda glared at the phone. "What information?"

"Not over the phone."

Amanda muted the sound. "We need to find out what she knows. What do you think, Erica?"

"I agree."

"Wendy?"

"Yeah."

Amanda eyed their chef. "What about you?"

"Now you're letting me vote?"

Amanda scoffed. "I'm asking for your opinion, not your vote."

"Invite her over."

"All right." Amanda unmuted her phone. "Meet us at the inn."

"I'll be there in an hour." Gail ended the call.

Amanda grabbed her phone and pressed the screen.

Erica's brow pinched. "Who are you calling?"

"Our attorney."

Twenty minutes after Amanda spoke to Chris, the doorbell rang. She eyed Wendy. "Do you want to let him in?"

Wendy shook her head. "You go."

"All right." Amanda hastened to the foyer then escorted Chris to the dining room and motioned toward Abby's seat.

He pulled the chair out then placed his phone on the table. "Tell me what you know."

"Not much." Amanda relayed Gail's comments. "Maybe calling you was an overreaction—"

"You can never be too careful when it comes to reporters."

Wendy picked at a cuticle and appeared to avoid eye contact with Chris. "What do you suggest we do?"

"Inform her that I'm your attorney, then listen to what she has to say."

Erica drummed her fingers. "What if she won't talk with you here?"

"If she wants the story, she'll talk."

Millie pushed the cookies to Chris. "We have two snickerdoodles left. One for you and one for the journalist."

"Why don't we leave both for Gail?"

Millie raised a brow. "As a bribe or a treat?"

Chris grinned. "A little of both."

"You know what would hit the spot? A pitcher of ice-cold lemonade." Amanda nudged their CFO. "I could use your help."

"Okay." Wendy followed Amanda to the kitchen. "What do you want me to do?"

She brushed a stray hair away from Wendy's cheek. "I want to make sure you're okay."

"Why does everyone keep asking me that question? I'm perfectly fine." Her tone belied her response.

Amanda patted her arm. "It's best not to keep your emotions bottled up."

Wendy's shoulders slumped. "Stop worrying about me. I'm okay. Really. What do you want me to do?"

Amanda hesitated. Best not to probe. "Help me carry the glasses."

Back in the dining room, Wendy remained silent while the group chatted about the open house. The second the doorbell chimed, a palpable tension infused the space. Amanda stood. "I'll tell her you're here, Chris." She hastened to the foyer and pulled the door open.

Gail stepped inside clutching a manila envelope. "Thank you for agreeing to meet with me."

"We invited our attorney to join us."

"Chris Armstrong?"

How'd she know? "Yes." Amanda led the journalist to the dining room and motioned to the chair opposite Chris.

Gail set the envelope on the table. "Are any of you familiar with Nancy Campbell?"

Erica shook her head. "I've never heard of her."

"Neither have I," added Millie.

Wendy remained silent.

"She has a podcast called Nancy's Nuggets—"

Millie's brow pinched. "What's a podcast?"

Gail explained. "Anyway, her podcast is about people living in North Georgia and Eastern Tennessee. Nancy's also a friend who knows I'm interested in your story. We met this morning for breakfast." She tapped the envelope. "I'm here because she received this in the mail yesterday."

Chris propped his arms on the table. "Where's it from?"

"Las Vegas." Gail slid the envelope to Chris.

He pulled out a photograph of Gunter posing arm in arm with a dark-haired young woman dressed in what appeared to be a cocktail-waitress uniform.

Amanda pointed to the photo. "Is that from him?"

Chris scanned the single sheet of paper he'd also pulled from the envelope. "Based on the letter, it's from the woman in the photograph." He faced Gail. "I assume you've read what she wrote."

"I have, so go ahead and share it with everyone."

Chris glanced at Millie.

"It's all right." Amanda leaned forward. "Millie knows all about Gunter."

"All right. It begins, "*Dear Nancy Nugget. I'm giving you first crack at breaking a story about Gunter Benson, a man who's been wrongly accused of a crime and cheated out of his inheritance by his three clueless wives. Even though he made a mistake by marrying them all at the same time, he loved each of them with all his heart. Just as he now loves me.*"

Amanda's eyes narrowed. "That woman is the one who's clueless."

Erica flicked a cookie crumb across the table. "She's his latest pawn in some sort of cruel chess game."

Amanda faced Chris. "What else did she write?"

"*They conned a crooked lawyer into helping them steal the two houses in Blue Ridge, Georgia, that Gunter inherited from his wife Eleanor Benson. When Gunter needed them to help prove his innocence, they turned on him so they could keep what they'd taken from him.*"

Amanda slapped her palm on the table. "No one stole anything from that man, and he's guilty of murder."

Gail nodded. "Nancy and I both figured as much. Read the rest."

"*If you refuse to tell his story, he will find a reporter who isn't afraid to reveal the truth. I'm starting a gofundme page to help pay his legal expenses.*"

"Gunter's latest con." Chris faced the journalist. His jaw clenched. "Is your friend planning to run with this story?"

"No, but you can bet someone will."

Millie swallowed a sip of lemonade. "How could anyone believe that malarkey?"

Gail crossed her arms on the table. "For some reporters, truth isn't a prerequisite for covering a story. Sensationalism sells."

Amanda's nostrils flared. "Can we sue that woman or Gunter for libel?"

"She didn't sign her name, and there's no return address." Chris slid the letter and the photo back in the envelope. "Even if we found her, she'd claim she believed he was telling the truth. Conning her into writing the letter was another smart move."

Erica stared at Chris. "Are you telling us there's nothing we can do?"

"In these cases, it's best to take a proactive approach."

"Meaning what?"

"If I may offer the best solution." Gail laced her fingers on the table. "Let me tell your story the way you want it told."

Wendy's face paled. "All of it?"

Chris cleared his throat as his eyes shifted from Wendy to the journalist. "I appreciate you bringing this to our attention, Ms. Weston. Let me confer with my clients before they respond to your offer."

"I understand. Call me when you've come to a decision." Gail stood. "I'll let myself out."

The moment the front door closed, Amanda eyed Chris. "You want us to beat Gunter at his own game, don't you?"

"Exactly. Which is why controlling the narrative is a good move."

Erica's brow peaked. "How could we control what Gail writes?"

"We'd require her to sign an agreement allowing you to approve the story before she attempts to sell it."

"What if she changes the story after we approve it?"

Chris tapped the envelope. "She wouldn't have brought this to your attention if she wasn't an honest journalist. Look, this is a lot for you ladies to digest." He lifted off his chair. "I suggest you discuss her proposal among yourselves and call me after you make a decision."

After an hour of discussion, Wendy remained the one holdout. Even Millie agreed with Erica and Amanda. Why couldn't anyone other than her understand the humiliation they'd suffer if people discovered they'd been married to the same man at the same time? "What if I write Gunter a letter—"

Amanda stared at her. "And tell him what?"

Wendy shrugged. "Maybe sweet-talk him into leaving us alone?"

"No amount of southern charm will stop that man."

"Amanda's right." Millie refilled her glass. "Based on everything you've told me about Gunter Benson, he doesn't give a flip about anyone except himself. In my opinion, he wants to create enough doubt through the letter he wrote to con a greedy lawyer into helping him reclaim his inheritance."

"How could he?" Wendy glared at Millie. "We have all the proof on our side."

"Do you want your attorney to be tied up in a long, expensive legal battle with a slick con artist?"

Wendy's shoulders slumped. "No."

Amanda released a heavy sigh. "I don't know about you three, but my stomach's growling and my head's spinning. So, I suggest we table the discussion for today and find something to eat."

"We have enough leftover appetizers in the fridge for a meal." Millie scooted her chair away from the table.

"Perfect. I'll open a bottle of wine." Erica followed Millie to the kitchen.

Amanda moved to the chair beside Wendy. "Gunter's maneuver is harder on you than it is on the rest of us."

Wendy's eyes drifted to the envelope sent by Gunter's latest patsy. "All those years I spent in foster homes, I believed no one could love a child whose own mother abandoned her." Tears pooled and spilled down her cheeks. "I want my son to grow up knowing he's loved *and* respected. If people around here find out Gunter's his father—"

"Last night our guests welcomed us into the Blue Ridge family. They'll welcome your child as well."

Wendy dabbed her cheeks. "Telling our story will be risky."

Amanda rested an arm around Wendy's shoulders. "Imagine how impressed our new friends will be when they learn how three strong women refused to become victims and risked everything to turn their lives around."

"Not everyone."

"Everyone who matters."

Her baby's kick drew Wendy's hand to her belly. "We don't have a choice, do we?"

"Your son will grow up knowing his mother is an amazing woman who refused to let the past define her."

Wendy turned toward her son's chosen grandmother. "You're gonna be an awesome nana."

Chapter 15

Erica tossed her purse on the passenger seat then clipped her phone into the mount attached to the windshield. A fellow student strode past the truck and waved. Next week she'd drive away from the Cleveland Massage Institute one last time with a massage therapist license in hand. She'd miss the friends she'd made. At least they could stay in touch and compare notes about their new careers.

Erica pulled out of the parking lot and drove the familiar route toward home. She'd also miss the hour-long drive through the foothills. Her alone time. A familiar routine. So many unknowns lay ahead. Would the Awesam team be able to effectively manage a luxury inn? What about Abby's relationship with Tommy? Erica's phone rang. Amanda's ringtone. She swiped her finger across the screen. "Hey, what's up?"

"Gail's meeting us at Chris's office today at four."

"She didn't waste any time." A siren sounded behind her. Erica glanced in her rearview mirror at the ambulance speeding toward her. She pulled onto the shoulder.

"Gail wants to pitch the story to the local paper for next week's edition."

Erica waited for the ambulance to pass, then pulled back onto the road. "I suppose it's best if that happens before our grand opening."

"Unless..." Amanda's voice broke up. *Unless what*? Erica glimpsed her phone. She'd driven into a dead zone. Although she loved Amanda and

Wendy as her new family, their expectation of her to function as Awesam's peacemaker was exhausting. Especially with Millie added to the mix. Fortunately, her massage-therapist career promised a calm working environment, and there was that private office off the massage room where she could find peace and quiet.

Erica switched on a music station and hummed along to the music until she drove into the ranch house carport. Inside, she plopped onto the den sofa, kicked off her shoes, and propped her feet on the coffee table.

Her phone pinged a text from Abby. "Shopping with Hannah." Erica responded with a thumbs-up. The earlier phone call came to mind. Someone had left a message. She listened. Stunned, she played the message a second time.

Amanda ambled in from the hall. "How was class?"

Erica stared at her phone. "You won't believe who left me a voicemail."

Awesam's president settled on the sofa. "A national television station wants to do a story about Gunter's private wives club?"

"You're hilarious. It was Brad—"

"Movie-star handsome Brad Barkley?"

"Who's also Abby's high school principal." Erica blinked. "I think he invited me on a date."

"What do you mean, you think?"

"He wants to take me to dinner. Maybe he wants to talk about Abby."

"If that were the case, he would have asked you to meet him at his office. He definitely invited you on a date."

Erica blew out a breath. "I don't know what to do. He seems nice enough, but so did Jack and Gunter aka Brian."

Amanda stretched her arm across the back of the sofa. "You were a vulnerable girl when you married Jack. And you accepted Gunter's proposal because Abby wanted a daddy—"

"But why would Brad invite me to dinner?"

"Are you kidding me? You're beautiful. You're smart. You're successful. Besides, it's just dinner, not a lifetime commitment."

Wendy padded in from her room. "What's not a lifetime commitment?"

"Brad Barkley invited Erica to dinner."

"The high school principal? Cool." Wendy settled on the other side of Erica. "Where's he taking you?"

"I haven't even decided if I'll accept his invitation."

"I'll give you three excellent reasons why you should." Wendy held up a finger. "He's handsome as all get out." Second finger. "Millie says he comes from a good family." Third finger. "He's a widower, which means there aren't any ex-wives hanging around."

Erica trilled her lips. "I'll think about it. In the meantime, we need to make sure we're still on the same page about our meeting with Gail."

"Okay." Amanda crossed her leg over her knee. "Never fear, we'll continue the Brad conversation tonight."

An hour later, Chris escorted the Awesam partners into the Armstrong law firm conference room and motioned them to sit. He took his place at the head of the table and tapped the document in front of him. "Gail will need to sign this binding agreement before I'll allow her to interview you. It stipulates that the three of you approve the article before she publishes, and it prohibits her from making any changes afterwards."

Amanda lifted a bottle of water off the table. "What if she refuses to sign?"

"I did my due diligence. Trust me, Gail's a reputable journalist." Chris leaned back. "She won't refuse."

Erica eyed the painting of downtown Blue Ridge on the wall behind Chris. Would Brad have called her if their story had already been published?

"No matter what Gail asks, you three are free to share your story the way you want it told."

Amanda uncapped her water bottle. "We've elected Erica as our spokesperson. Except those posed to us individually, she'll respond to all of Gail's questions."

"Good decision. I'll stay here to prevent you from responding to any inappropriate questions."

Erica released a sigh. "I'd hoped you'd stay."

The law firm receptionist eased the door open. "Ms. Weston is here."

Chris stood. "Show her in."

The receptionist stepped aside. Gail breezed in.

"We appreciate you agreeing to meet us here." Chris aimed his palm toward the seat across from Awesam's partners.

Gail sat and set her purse on the table. "I assume you want me to sign some sort of agreement."

"Yes." Chris lowered to his chair and pushed the document and a pen across the table.

Gail read the agreement then signed and removed a small recorder from her purse. "With your permission, I'll record our conversation to ensure accuracy." She pressed a button. "Why don't you begin by telling me how long you three have known each other."

Erica drew in a deep breath then slowly released the air. "Last December we met at the Blue Ridge Inn..." The tension in Erica's shoulders eased as she continued to tell their story the way they'd planned. Her partners responded to personal questions with confidence, and Chris only intervened one time.

At the end of ninety minutes, Gail stopped recording then dropped her recorder in her purse. "Thank you for trusting me to tell your story." She stood and extended her hand to each partner. "I'll email the draft in two days."

Chris stood. "Copy me on the email."

"I will."

Chris escorted her to the door.

The moment Gail walked out, Amanda nudged Erica. "Thanks to you, that interview turned out a lot better than I expected."

"Hopefully, she'll write a story that will stop Gunter from whatever monkey-muck business he's trying to pull."

Wendy pushed away from the table. "Why don't we grab a bite to eat on the way home."

Erica tucked her purse under her arm. "Can you take time to join us, Chris?"

"Thanks, but my grandmother is preparing dinner for the family tonight." He escorted them through the empty reception area.

Outside, Amanda slid behind the truck's steering wheel. "Instead of going to a restaurant, let's order a pizza, then go home and convince our chief executive officer to accept Brad's dinner invitation."

Erica buckled her seatbelt. "I'll go along with your pizza suggestion."

Wendy tapped Erica's shoulder. "And let us talk you into going out with Brad."

Would her partners hound her until she gave in and accepted his invitation?

Chapter 16

After stashing her carry-on in the overhead bin, Amanda slid to the window seat and placed her book on her lap. Five months ago when she and Wendy had driven to Asheville to convince Erica to move to Blue Ridge, Morgan had only known Kevin for a month. Now they were two days away from making a lifelong commitment. Did his parents have any qualms about their son's rushed wedding?

A woman and a young girl sat in the seats beside her. Hoping for a conversation-free flight, Amanda greeted them before buckling her seatbelt then closed her eyes. Returning to New Orleans summoned an array of emotions. She'd experienced immense joy in her hometown—marrying her soulmate and bringing her child into this world. Amanda cringed as heart-wrenching memories surfaced. Losing her mother to cancer and her soulmate to a fatal accident. Discovering Gunter had taken everything from her. At least she had landed on her feet. An involuntary smile formed. A young woman she'd met six months earlier had chosen her to be her child's honorary grandmother. Now Wendy, Erica, and Abby were part of her growing family.

Amanda opened her eyes and peered out the window while the pilot eased away from the gate. After the plane sped down the active runway and lifted into the clear blue sky, the child beside her played a game on her phone while her mother read. Perfect. Amanda opened the book she'd begun reading months earlier at the Blue Ridge Inn, before her world turned upside down. By the time the plane dropped onto the runway at the Louis Armstrong International Airport, she had read a third of her book uninterrupted.

Eager to see her daughter, Amanda hurried into the terminal, pulling her bag behind her.

Morgan, looking radiant, waved her over. "I'm thrilled you're here."

"So am I, honey." Amanda drew Morgan into her arms. "You look amazing."

"So do you, Mom. I can't wait for you to meet Kevin's parents. But first, we're going on a serious shopping spree."

"For your trousseau?"

"That's too old fashioned and a huge waste of money. We're on a mission to find the perfect mother-of-the-bride dress for you and wedding gown for me."

Amanda stared wide-eyed at her daughter. "Aren't you cutting it kind of close?"

"I didn't want to make such important decisions without you." Morgan linked arms with her mother as they headed toward the exit. "Besides, I found the perfect off-the-rack discount bridal shop."

Amanda smiled. "My practical daughter."

"What can I say? My amazing mother taught me well."

They made their way through the terminal and into the parking garage. Amanda hesitated for a moment before climbing into Morgan's passenger seat. "How's your car holding up?"

Her daughter cranked the engine. "Good, considering the scumbag who gave it to me."

Amanda buckled her seatbelt. Her daughter had first viewed Gunter's gift wrapped in a giant pink ribbon the day she turned sixteen and stepped off the school bus. Despite his gesture, Morgan had never warmed up to the man they'd known as Paul Sullivan. Turned out she'd been right.

Morgan backed out of the parking space. "During our drive, I want to hear everything that's happening with our Awesam family." By the time they entered the bridal shop, Morgan was up-to-date on all the news. She led Amanda straight to the bargain rack. "Yay. The four dresses I picked out yesterday are still here. All marked down fifty-percent."

"You really are a bargain hunter. What about attendants' dresses?"

Morgan lifted her selections off the rack. "Kevin and I decided against the whole bridesmaid and groomsmen scene."

"So did your dad and I—mostly because Mom, Preston, and I barely scraped together enough money to pay the preacher and photographer."

"I still miss Dad."

"So do I, honey." Amanda followed her daughter to the dressing room.

After modeling the first two options, Morgan stepped out wearing a fitted white gown flaring mid-thigh to the floor. She twirled "What do you think?"

"Wow." Amanda pressed her hand to her heart. "That's definitely the one."

"I agree." After changing back into her street clothes, Morgan led Amanda to a rack and pulled out a teal floor-length gown with an off-center floral applique at the waist. "This is what I picked out for you, Mom. It's the perfect color for a redhead."

"It's beautiful. You have exquisite taste." Amanda fingered the smooth satin. "Did you ask Kevin's father to walk you down the aisle?"

"No." Morgan stroked her mother's cheek. "Since Dad isn't here, I want to take that walk with you. In his place."

Tears pooled as Amanda pulled her daughter into her arms. "I'm honored beyond words, sunshine."

Morgan sniffled. "That was Daddy's pet name for me."

"Because you brought so much joy into our lives." Amanda released her daughter. "After I try on this gorgeous dress, what do you say we drive by the house where our little family of three first lived?"

"A trip down memory lane, so to speak?"

"Something like that."

"Sounds fun."

Amanda stepped into the dressing room. As she changed into the gown, her heart swelled with pride. How many daughters would even think to ask their mother to walk them down the aisle? She glanced up and imagined Preston smiling down at her. "You and I created a beautiful soul, sweetheart," she whispered. Amanda blinked, then caught her image in the three-way mirror. Not bad for a forty-three-year old. She walked out and turned in a slow circle. "What do you think?"

"Oh, Mom." Morgan pressed her palms together. "It's perfect, and you're gorgeous."

"All right then, it seems we've made two important decisions."

They paid for the gowns and returned to Morgan's car. Amanda slid onto the passenger seat. "How much do you remember about the shotgun house?"

"Even though it was small, it seemed big to me." Morgan pulled into traffic. "My room was all the way in the back. Most nights Daddy read me a bedtime story. After he was gone, you took his place." Morgan braked at a red light. "Kevin will be a great dad."

Amanda stared at her daughter's profile. "Are you—"

"Goodness no. We both plan to establish our careers before we start a family, so you'll have lots of time to practice being a nana. Has Wendy named her baby?"

"Not yet." Amanda faced the side window as they drove past Café du Monde. "Some Sundays after church, you, your dad, and I joined the tourists and indulged on beignets."

"A New Orleans tradition." Morgan turned onto a side street and drove past tiny houses without front yards. She braked at a stop sign, her mouth agape. "This can't be right."

Amanda gawked at the full block cleared of every single building. She peered at the street sign, hoping they'd made a wrong turn. No such luck. A construction-company sign was posted at the corner.

Morgan drove through the intersection. Halfway up the street, she pulled over to the curb. "It's gone."

Amanda swallowed the lump in her throat as she stepped onto the sidewalk. She approached a woman sitting on the front porch and pointed to the cleared land. "What's going on over there?"

"A developer tore down all those charming little houses to build a bunch of bodacious condos. They call it progress." The woman scoffed. "I call it a crying shame. Do you know someone who lived in one of those houses?"

Amanda nodded. "My husband and I owned the house across the street years ago."

"Oh dear. It must be quite a shock to see it gone."

"I almost wish I didn't know." Amanda plodded back to Morgan's car. "The little fixer-upper your dad and I sacrificed so much to transform into a beautiful home survived dozens of hurricanes and floods, but it couldn't survive so-called progress."

Morgan reached across the console and touched Amanda's arm. "Progress can't steal our memories from us."

"I know." Amanda released a sigh. "It's just...this is one more unexpected discovery in a year full of changes."

"Which you've survived like a champ."

Amanda placed her hand over her daughter's. "Are you taking on Wendy's role as Awesam's cheerleader?"

"Yeah. How am I doing?"

"Well, I haven't succumbed to a torrent of tears."

Morgan smiled. "I call that emotional progress."

"Or I've become shockproof. Anyway, what do you say we continue our shopping spree, so I can buy you the perfect wedding gift from your Blue Ridge family."

"You're on."

Amanda stole one more glance at the vacant lot as they pulled away from the curb.

An hour and a half later, they carried a digital photo frame and a cutglass crystal vase to Morgan's car. "I forgot to mention tonight's plans." Morgan drove out of the parking garage. "Kevin and I are going out to dinner with his best friend while you and his parents spend the evening together."

"Okay." Amanda turned toward the passenger window and focused on the passing scenery.

"What are you thinking?"

Amanda blinked. "Today, for the first time in my life, I feel as if I'm a stranger in my hometown."

"Because you've moved on to a new life with exciting opportunities."

"More cheerleading?"

"I'm simply stating the facts."

Twenty minutes after leaving downtown, Morgan turned onto a circular driveway fronting a stately, two-story brick house. Manicured shrubbery added an air of sophistication to the front lawn

"Impressive."

They climbed out and walked up the three steps to the front portico.

Kevin swung the door open. "Welcome to my parents' home, Ms. Smith."

Amanda smiled. "I believe it's time for you to begin calling me by my first name."

"Good idea." Kevin kissed Morgan's cheek, then escorted them to an elegant living room. "Amanda, meet my mother, Monica Hartman."

The attractive, slender woman with shoulder-length brown hair smiled. "Welcome to our home, Amanda."

"It's a pleasure to meet you."

"My husband will be home from work in an hour, which gives us time to enjoy a glass of wine while we become acquainted." Monica linked arms with Amanda and escorted her to the kitchen.

"Your home is beautiful."

"Thank you." Monica motioned to a banquette anchoring a corner. "We raised Kevin and his older brother here. He married a local girl several years ago." Monica poured white wine into two glasses. "I understand you recently moved to Georgia."

How much did Kevin's parents know about the reason she'd left New Orleans? "My partners and I had an opportunity to start a new business."

"Morgan told us about Awesam's project. I'd love to hear more about the inn."

Careful not to indulge any information about the real reason for the move, Amanda shared tidbits about the renovation and the open house.

"Now I understand where Morgan's ambition comes from." Monica paused to take a sip of wine. "What's your opinion about this wedding happening so fast?"

Caught off guard by the sudden subject change, Amanda broke eye contact and fingered her wineglass stem. How had Monica responded to her son's announcement? "I was surprised but pleased by the way your son asked for my daughter's hand. I assume you asked me for a reason."

"Morgan is an incredible young woman, and Kevin loves her dearly." Monica paused. "It's just...six months is such a short amount of time, and they're moving so far away."

Amanda studied Monica's pinched expression. "In addition to being an extraordinary person, Kevin is the perfect man for my daughter." She placed her hand on his mother's arm. "I'm proud to call him my son-in-law."

Monica's features relaxed. "I understand why your daughter speaks so highly of you." She tilted her glass toward Amanda. "We're family now."

"Indeed, we are." Amanda clicked her glass to Monica's. "Here's to the beginning of a life-long friendship."

"And one day to two grandmothers loving on a couple of grandbabies."

Chapter 17

Wendy plopped onto the den sofa and propped her feet on the coffee table, balancing her laptop on her knees. She tapped her keyboard and pulled up a website that shared tips for single mothers raising sons—the second one she'd discovered since leaving Chris's office yesterday.

Dusty padded over and laid her head beside Wendy's thigh. She stroked the canine's muzzle. "Someday I'll buy my baby a dog as sweet as you." A giggle escaped as a kick drew Wendy's hand to her belly. "See? He's already excited about having a pet." The back door opened, sending Dusty scampering to the kitchen.

Erica wandered in and settled beside Wendy. "How are you feeling?"

"Very pregnant and eager to introduce my baby to his aunt, nana, and cousin."

"We're all looking forward to loving on your little guy." Erica kicked off her shoes and propped her feet beside Wendy's. "One of these days you need to give him a name."

Why couldn't she decide? "I will."

"Hopefully, before his first birthday."

Wendy's baby kicked again. "He kind of likes being called *little guy*. Anyway, how was school?"

"I'm three days from becoming a licensed massage therapist. Your idea to transform the garage into a spa was brilliant."

"Yeah, I know. Not that I'm bragging."

Erica thumped Wendy's arm. "You earned bragging rights." She pulled her ringing phone from her purse. "Chris is calling. Should I answer?"

Wendy shrugged. "Why wouldn't you?"

"No reason." Erica swiped her finger across the screen and pressed the speaker. "Hey, what's up?"

"If you haven't already done so, open your email. Gail sent the article."

"Oh my gosh." Wendy tapped her keyboard. "There it is."

"Read it, then call me back." Chris ended the call.

Wendy handed her laptop to Erica.

"I assume you want me to read it."

"Good assumption."

"All right. The headline reads, '*Triumph over Tragedy.*'"

"Catchy. What's next?"

"*The Hilltop Inn and Spa in Blue Ridge, Georgia, is far more than a new business. The luxury property stands as a testimony to the determination of three women. Their story began three days after Amanda Smith, Erica Nelson, and Wendy Thomason first met at the Blue Ridge Inn. Having endured last December's once-in-a-century blizzard, they discovered a man they all had trusted deceived them.*"

Wendy wrapped her arms around her belly. "At least Gail used our legal names. Lucky for us she didn't call Gunter by name or write that we were all married to him."

"Because she considers us the story, not Gunter."

"And she knows he's a scumbag."

"As any woman would after hearing our story. '*Days away from fleeing the country, that same man deeded two Blue Ridge homes he'd inherited*" *from Eleanor Harrington to the three women. What appeared to be a generous gift was shackled with thousands of dollars in unpaid property taxes. Unable to come up with the cash, the women opted to sell the properties. Upon returning to their respective towns, they faced more devastating news. Their homes had been foreclosed, their cars repossessed, and their bank accounts emptied. In a culture where people are too often encouraged to embrace the role of victims, Amanda, Erica, and Wendy rejected victim-hood and its limitations to take charge of their lives and embrace new possibilities."*

"Oh my gosh." Wendy pressed her hand to her chest. "We really are incredibly strong southern gals. What'd Gail write next?"

"After selling most of their possessions and all their jewelry, the women stepped out in faith, moved to Blue Ridge, and paid the back taxes. Thus began their five-month-long journey to transform the larger of the two homes into a luxury inn. With limited cash reserves, the women tackled the daunting task with resolve and sweat equity. Then days away from halting the project to find jobs, they discovered a goldmine—a 1960 Eldorado in pristine condition in the home's garage. Left behind by the original owner, the Cadillac was sold to a collector and provided the cash the women needed to turn their vision into reality."

"So far, it seems Gail wrote the story exactly as you told her."

"Chris assured us she's a reputable journalist."

"He was right. Continue reading."

"Partnering with Mildred Cunningham, their neighbor and close friend of Eleanor's, the four women created a seven-room luxury inn featuring a spa and an exquisite English country garden. Amanda, Erica, and Wendy are an inspiration to all women who face unsurmountable challenges, and I am proud to call them my friends."

"One fact is certain. Gail is one heck of a writer." Erica set the laptop on the coffee table. "Do you want to call Chris?"

Wendy shook her head. "He called you, not me."

"Which makes sense, given you and Amanda insisted I answer most of Gail's questions." Erica tapped her phone.

Chris answered. "Impressive article, huh?"

"It's beyond anything we hoped for."

Wendy leaned close to the phone. "The most important question—is it enough to stop Gunter?"

"When he reads the article along with the letter I intend to write, maybe he'll accept the fact that he's no match for three gutsy ladies."

Wendy ran her finger along the sofa's cushion. "What if he doesn't?"

"We won't give up until he does. By the way, according to Gail, the blogger who gave her the letter and photo from Gunter's patsy wants to interview the three of you for her podcast."

"A live interview seems risky." Erica's brow pinched. "You're our attorney. How should we respond?"

"The four of us should listen to a few of the woman's podcasts before making a decision. In the meantime, are you ready to give Gail permission to submit her article?"

Erica glanced at Wendy.

She nodded.

"As long as Amanda's onboard." Erica ended the call. "Morgan's graduation was earlier, so hopefully Amanda is free to talk."

Two hours after leaving Baton Rouge with Kevin's parents, Amanda's euphoric mood dampened. The route to Commander's Palace to celebrate Morgan and their son's graduation would take them past Gunter's house.

Monica nodded toward the iconic streetcar easing along the track separating the lanes. "I always love driving down St. Charles Avenue. You must have enjoyed watching that lovely old streetcar pass your house."

"Most of the time." Were Monica and Adam unaware of her history with Gunter, or were they too polite to say anything? Amanda pulled her phone from her purse. "My business partner is calling." She pressed the phone to her ear. "Hey, Erica."

"How was the graduation?"

"Long but exciting." Especially since Morgan was the first person in her family to graduate from college. "What's up?"

"Are you free to read Gail's article?"

"I am."

"Good. Text me when you finish."

Monica glanced over her shoulder. "Is everything okay?"

Amanda nodded. "I have a bit of business to take care of." Her heart pounded as she pulled up Gail's email. An involuntary smile formed as she read the journalist's words. When finished, she texted Erica, Wendy, and Chris. "It's perfect. Give Gail the go-ahead." Erica responded with a thumbs-up. Amanda dropped her phone into her purse and peered out the window. They were a block away from Gunter's house. At least for the moment, her Awesam family had outsmarted the con man.

Chapter 18

A ringtone perked Erica's ears. Was it her phone or the one on TV? She aimed the remote and paused the mindless sitcom. The ringing continued. Definitely hers. She plucked the phone off the coffee table. No name. Her brow pinched. Did the number look familiar? Should she answer? If someone important called, they'd leave a voicemail. Erica set her phone on the cushion beside her and resumed the program. A minute passed. A ping. Whoever left her a message could wait. Unless...was it possible?

Erica turned off the television then tapped the screen and pressed her phone to her ear.

"Hi, it's Brad Barkley."

That's why the number looked familiar. Shrugging off the sting of guilt for failing to respond to his first call, Erica pressed play.

"I don't answer calls from numbers I don't recognize either. Hopefully, curiosity about a second message will pique your interest. I enjoyed meeting you at the open house, and if you're willing, I want to become better acquainted over dinner. Give me a call."

Conflicting thoughts collided in Erica's head. Millie had called Brad one of the good guys, and he was a high school principal for goodness sakes. Except her last date had been seven years ago—with Brian Parker, aka Gunter Benson. She needed to talk to someone before making a decision.

Wendy had turned in early and Amanda was in New Orleans. Millie was out of the question. Which left her with one option. Erica pocketed her phone then headed down the hall. She hesitated. Was it appropriate for a mother to ask her teenaged daughter for dating advice? They were living in the twenty-first century, so why not?. She tapped on the door.

"Come on in."

Erica entered and closed the door behind her.

Abby looked up from her beanbag chair. "Hey, what's up?"

"Are you reading something fun?" She sat on the twin bed closest to her daughter.

"More like interesting." Abby stroked Dusty's back. "Are you still super-excited about Gail's article?"

"Excited as well as a little apprehensive." Maybe asking her daughter's opinion wasn't such a good idea, although she and Abby had always been close.

Abby's head tilted slightly. "What's going on, Mom?"

"The thing is...I've been invited to dinner...and it's been a long time since I've been on a date."

"So?" Abby shrugged. "What's the big deal?"

Erica hesitated. "It's mostly about who invited me."

Abby's brows shot up. "Oh my gosh. Mr. Barkley wants to go out with you, doesn't he?"

"So it seems."

"That is way cool." Abby closed her book. "You told him yes, didn't you?"

"I haven't decided."

"Because you're gun-shy, right?"

"For good reason."

"Well, if you want my opinion, I think you should definitely go. All the kids are crazy about Mr. Barkley, and half the girls have a crush on him."

Erica relived the moment Brad walked toward her in Hilltop Inn's living room. "As you said, for an old guy he's pretty hot."

"Even better, Mr. Barkley cares about all of his students, and he's only six years older than you."

"How do you know?"

"The internet, Mom." Abby rolled her eyes. "Everyone knows everything about him."

Erica trilled her lips. "I imagine most of the people in Blue Ridge know Mr. Barkley."

"Especially because he was our school's winningest football coach." Abby offered a pert smile. "You asking for my opinion is sweet."

"Mother seeking daughter's dating advice is an interesting role reversal."

Abby set her book on the floor. "Do you remember making me promise to talk to you if I ever had the tiniest doubt about my choices?"

Was Abby having a change of heart? "I do."

"Half my friends who are going away to college are talking more about what sororities they want to pledge than what they want to study. Except for Hannah. She's planning to major in business administration and one day start her own company."

"That's an impressive goal."

"The point is, she's my best friend, and she knows what she wants." Abby lifted off her beanbag and sat beside her mother. "The past few weeks, I've thought a lot about my future. After I finish courses at the local campus, I plan to earn an online child psychology degree."

Erica studied Abby's profile for a long moment. "Is your decision based on your feelings for Tommy?"

"In part, but also because staying in Blue Ridge will allow me to continue volunteering at the crisis center and graduate without a mountain of debt."

Erica wrapped her arm around her daughter's shoulders. "You're a bright young woman."

"Then you're okay with my decision?"

"I'm a little disappointed about you missing an on-campus experience—"

"Because you missed that chance?"

An involuntary smile curled Erica's lips. "You'll be a terrific psychologist."

Abby elbowed her. "I'll take that comment as your approval."

"I'm proud of you, sweetheart."

"We're a good team."

"Indeed, we are." Erica paused. "Now it's my turn to offer an opinion."

"I'm listening."

"It's best if you and Tommy allow your relationship to mature before making any long-term commitments."

"Trust me, Mom."

Erica squeezed her daughter's shoulder. "I'll take your comment as a commitment. Now, about Mr. Barkley—Is it too late to call him tonight?"

"It's only nine o'clock."

"All right then." Erica stood and headed to the door. She paused with her hand on the doorknob and glimpsed over her shoulder. "I love you, sweetheart."

"I love you too, Mom."

Erica strode to her room and closed the door. She pressed Brad's number before her courage had a chance to evaporate.

He answered after the second ring. "Hi, Erica."

"Hi." Impressive. He'd already added her number to his contacts. "I'm sorry I didn't respond to your first call."

"No need to apologize. I was in my twenties the last time I invited a woman to dinner, so I hope I didn't come across as awkward."

"A little, but not too much."

"In that case, are you willing to go out with a guy who's totally out of practice?"

No wonder the kids are crazy about him. "Sounds fun, especially since we'll compete for which of us is the most out of practice."

He chuckled. "Will this Saturday work for you?"

"Yes."

"I'll pick you up at six."

"Perfect." A warm sensation washed over Erica as she and her daughter's principal wished each other a good night.

Following a knock, her door eased open. Abby stepped inside. "Did you call him?"

"I did."

"And?"

"We're going to dinner Saturday night. Please don't tell all your friends—"

"Give me a little more credit. Besides, the news will spread once people see you two out for dinner."

"Maybe everyone will think he invited me for a principal-parent conference."

"Yeah, right." Abby rolled her eyes.

Erica laughed. "Good night, sweetheart."

"Good night, Mom."

After changing into pajamas and climbing into bed, memories of Erica's first conversation with Brad surfaced. Whatever happened, at least she'd enjoy a nice dinner and conversation with a good man.

Chapter 19

Amanda eased to the guest-room window and stared at the white tent covering the entire backyard. Although Morgan and Kevin had opted for a small wedding, thanks to Monica, the ceremony and reception promised to be an elegant affair. Responding to a knock, she moved away from the window and pulled the door open. Her heart warmed at the sight of her daughter's smile. "You look happy."

"Deliriously. I want to enjoy my last breakfast as Morgan Smith alone with my mom."

"Perfect."

Morgan strode in and set a tray on a small round table between two plush chairs. "Hot coffee, beignets, and fruit."

Amanda sat and lifted a mug off the tray. "The perfect New Orleans morning treat."

Morgan settled beside her. "Do you remember the first boy who came to our house to pick me up for a date?"

Amanda nodded. "The neighbor from down the street whose parents drove you to a middle-school dance."

Morgan giggled. "He was so awkward I ended up spending most of the time talking to my girlfriends."

"The first boy I dated—long before I met your dad—took me to the second *Jurassic Park* movie. It was more of an adventure than an actual date."

"My first date with Kevin was at an LSU football game. Afterwards we ate burgers and talked for hours—as if we'd known each other for years instead of a few weeks. By the end of the evening, we both knew we were meant to be together."

"Your dad and I came to the same conclusion during our first date."

Morgan bit into a beignet. "When we told Kevin's mother we wanted a simple backyard wedding, we didn't know she'd go all out with a big tent and a catered dinner."

"She created a beautiful setting for you. Which was smart considering how often it rains in New Orleans." Amanda lifted a strawberry off the tray. "I've been wondering, how much do Kevin's parents know about Gunter?"

Morgan licked powdered sugar off her lips. "Since your second husband is no longer part of our lives, nothing. Kevin and I both agreed you should tell them when you feel the time is right. And don't worry about them judging either one of us. They're good-hearted people."

"Monica's taking me to breakfast before my flight tomorrow. Depending on how our conversation goes, I'll consider telling her then. For now, I want to hear all about your honeymoon and Kevin's new job."

"We're spending two nights in a luxury suite at the Roosevelt before driving to Atlanta."

"You know that your dad and I splurged and celebrated our first anniversary in the hotel's Italian restaurant?"

Morgan nodded. "That's the main reason we chose the Roosevelt. The other is to enjoy our hometown one last time before moving away."

Hours after reminiscing with Morgan and helping with last-minute wedding details, Amanda donned her gown then padded across the hall and tapped on the door.

Monica, wearing a royal blue gown, pulled the door open. "Your dress is beautiful."

"So is yours." Amanda stepped into the Hartmans' bedroom suite complete with a sitting area and a fireplace. Morgan's gown lay across the king-size bed. "What a lovely room."

"This is Adam's and my compromise of masculine and feminine decor."

Amanda smiled. "The bedroom Preston and I shared was a fraction of this size, but also a blend of our styles."

"The day Morgan told us she wanted you to walk her down the aisle in place of her father—" Monica patted her hand on her chest. "She reached in and touched my heart."

"Mine too." Amanda blinked. "If I'm not careful, tears will unleash a river of mascara."

"We can't let that happen."

Amanda laughed as Monica recounted a shenanigan Kevin pulled as a young boy. "Don't tell my son I shared that story with you."

"Not a word."

Following a tap, the door swung open. Morgan breezed in. "What has you two tickled?"

"A little fun between two proud mothers-in-law while Kevin's brother and his sweet wife greet our guests."

Morgan strode across the room and fingered her gown. "How's your oldest son holding up?"

"Amazingly well." Monica lifted the gown off the bed. "After all, he's about to become one with the love of his life."

Morgan slipped out of her robe and stepped into her wedding gown.

After zipping up the back, Amanda secured her daughter's hair behind one ear with an elegant pearl-and-rhinestone floral clasp, revealing the diamond earring she'd borrowed from Monica. "I'm glad you left your hair down."

"Especially for my groom." Morgan stood in front of the freestanding full-length mirror while fingering the silver bracelet adorning her left arm—Preston's fifth anniversary gift to Amanda. "Daddy would have loved Kevin."

"The same way Adam and I love you." Monica's phone pinged. "The caterers are all set up in the kitchen, and our guests are ready for the big moment. I'll scoot out back and take my place."

"Mom and I will be down in a minute." Morgan fingered her hair flowing across the right side of her chest to inches above her strapless gown. "Daddy's here with us in spirit."

Fearing words would summon tears, Amanda nodded while stroking her daughter's cheek.

Morgan lifted the white and pale blue rose bridal bouquet off the dresser. "I'm ready."

"So am I, honey." After descending the stairs, they walked out back and stepped under the open tent where fifty guests sat in rows facing an elegant white arbor. Strings of miniature white lights twinkled overhead. Behind the guests, chairs draped with shimmering gold covers encircled round tables covered with white cloths. Candles set in ornate glass jars served as centerpieces.

The piano player leaned close. "Are you ready?"

Morgan nodded.

The woman transitioned to the wedding march, signaling the guests to rise. They turned toward mother and daughter as they moved past the tables and began their stroll. When they arrived at the end of the aisle, Amanda placed her daughter's hand in her groom's hand. "Morgan's father and I are proud our daughter has chosen you as her life partner, Kevin."

"I'll treasure Morgan with all my heart forever." Her son-in-law's eyes focused on his bride as Amanda carried her daughter's bouquet to the chair across the aisle from Monica.

Kevin's brother assumed the role of photographer while the Hartmans' pastor and long-time friend opened a small book. "We are gathered here in the sight of God…"

The ceremony summoned memories of the morning Amanda became one with her soulmate. She had walked alone down the chapel aisle. The few friends they'd invited sat in the first rows with her mother and Preston's parents. As she gazed into her groom's eyes, she had imagined spending the rest of her life by his side.

A warm sensation flowed over Amanda as memories of their life together played in her mind. Even though they would never grow old together, she had been blessed to have loved one man with every fiber of her being. A man she would meet again in eternity.

"You may kiss your bride."

Amanda blinked.

Kevin gathered Morgan into his arms. Guests stood and applauded while the pianist began to play "Here and Now." Amanda returned the bouquet for Morgan's stroll down the aisle with her husband. While the newlyweds stepped into the reception area and prepared to greet their guests, Monica eased across the aisle and embraced Amanda. "Our two families are now one."

"Yes, they are." The tears Amanda had kept at bay pooled in the corner of her eyes.

Monica leaned close and handed her a tissue.

"You came prepared."

"A newlywed's mother always needs tissues when her baby marries the love of his life."

Amanda smiled as she dabbed the tears before they spilled down her cheeks. "Thank you for creating this beautiful setting."

"It was a labor of love." Monica linked arms with her. "Now you and I are ready to host our children's reception."

As if on cue, two tuxedo-clad young men stepped out carrying trays of Champagne-filled flutes while Kevin's brother continued his role of photographer.

A half hour into the reception, Adam announced dinner. While the guests were taking their seats, Amanda settled beside Adam's eighty-year-old mother everyone called Miss Gertie. As soon as the pastor returned thanks, the waiters began serving the meal. The muted overhead lights and soft piano music created an intimate atmosphere while guests dined and engaged in lively conversation.

Halfway through the main course, Miss Gertie nudged Amanda's arm. "You're too pretty a young lady to have me as your dinner partner."

Amanda smiled at the woman whose appearance belied her age. "I'm having a lot more fun sitting next to you. Besides the love of my life is smiling down from heaven."

"So is mine. Do you mind taking advice from an octogenarian?"

"Is it good advice?"

"That's the only kind I give."

"Well, okay then."

"You should find yourself a good-looking man to fill the gap until it's time to reconnect with your soulmate."

"Thanks, Miss Gertie, but I'm busy starting a new career."

"That's good, except—" Adam's mother leaned closer. "A career won't warm your bed, sweetie."

Amanda laughed. "Your son and daughter-in-law need to bring you to spend a few nights at our luxurious inn. You'd be a breath of fresh air for our chef. Millie's in her mid-seventies and a terrific cook, but a bit too cranky."

"How long has she been alone?"

"For years, but she claims her husband was an old curmudgeon."

"See what I mean?" Miss Gertie tapped Amanda's arm. "Don't you wait too long."

Adam grinned as he caught Amanda's eye. "Is my mother enlightening you with some of her homespun advice?"

"The most interesting advice I've received in a long time." By the time the bride and groom cut their cake, Amanda had secured a promise from Adam to bring Miss Gertie and Monica for a visit to Blue Ridge before the end of the year.

An hour after the night sky blanketed New Orleans, everyone followed the newlyweds to the front lawn. Kevin swept his bride—still wearing her wedding gown—off her feet and carried her to the white stretch limo parked at the curb amid a flurry of rose petals.

Sandwiched between the bride and groom's mothers, Miss Gertie pressed her palms together. "Isn't young love grand?"

Monica wrapped her arm around her mother-in-law's shoulders. "The grandest."

As the limo drove away, Amanda laced her fingers, then closed her eyes and sent up a silent prayer for Wendy and Chris to find their way back into each other's arms.

Miss Gertie nudged Amanda. "Who'd you pray for?"

"A young couple who need a lot of divine guidance."

Chapter 20

The morning after their children's wedding, a chill skittered up Amanda's spine as she and Monica stepped under the awning hovering over the entrance to Brennan's Restaurant. In years past she'd guided tourists past the iconic pink building, but she'd only ventured inside one time. Moments after they entered, the hostess seated them at a table beside the wall of glass showcasing the courtyard. "It's amazing how many such gems there are in New Orleans."

"Little havens hidden from the crowds."

Their waiter arrived with menus. "Good morning, ladies. May I start you out with coffee, orange juice, or perhaps a glass of Champagne?"

Monica's eyes met Amanda's. "How about celebrating our new role as in-laws with mimosas?"

Maybe a little Champagne would give her enough courage to reveal her past. "Perfect."

"Two mimosas coming up." The waiter stepped away.

Amanda scanned the room brimming with old-world elegance. "Brennan's is well-known for breakfast." *Now she sounded like a tour guide.* "Do you and Adam come here often?"

"About once a month after church. Is this one of your favorite morning indulgences?"

"Actually, I've only eaten here one time." Eager to change the subject, Amanda lifted her menu off the table. "I imagine the newlyweds ordered room service this morning."

"Their first morning together as a married couple, they won't want to leave their suite." Monica lowered her menu. "How close is Blue Ridge to Atlanta?"

"A couple of hours away."

The waiter returned with their beverage. After he took their orders and walked away, Monica tapped her flute to Amanda's. "To our new family."

"And to our friendship." Amanda took a sip, then set her flute down.

"When Kevin chose an engineering major, I knew one day he'd move away from Louisiana." Monica sighed. "At least Atlanta is a direct flight from New Orleans. Enough about our children moving away. Where did you and Morgan's father spend your honeymoon?"

"A historic bed and breakfast in Lafayette was all we could afford. What about you and Adam?"

"We jetted off to Napa Valley. We've returned twice to celebrate an anniversary." Monica wrapped her fingers around her flute. "I admire your courage. Especially since I don't know any women who would be brave enough to pull up stakes, move hundreds of miles away, and become president of their own company."

Amanda shrugged. "My partners and I simply took advantage of an opportunity."

Monica broke eye contact while wrapping her fingers around her glass. "Years ago, I graduated from Tulane with a business degree."

"Impressive. Did you meet Adam at school?"

"During my junior year. He was a senior. When we married a month after I graduated, Adam was already established in a high-paying career, and his family is well off. Miss Gertie is a character, but she's also an important presence in New Orleans' high society. She introduced me to all the right people." Monica's eyes seemed to glaze over." I've never told anyone, not even Adam...but I regret choosing that path rather than taking advantage of my degree."

She lived in a beautiful home with the man she loved. How could she possibly have regrets? "A successful marriage and a happy family are more important than a career."

Monica blinked. "I love being a wife and mother, and my social life has plenty of perks. But if I had put my education to use, I'd have the best of both worlds."

How should she respond? With encouragement, that's how. "It's not too late to pursue a career, especially since you have a marketable degree."

"From twenty-five years ago, and other than volunteer work, I don't have any professional experience."

Monica had made herself vulnerable. The time had come to do the same. Amanda pushed her glass aside and crossed her arms on the table. "What did Morgan tell you about my background?"

"Not a lot. Except that you dropped out of high school to take care of your mother when she was diagnosed with cancer. When she passed away, you sold her home to pay the medical bills and returned to school to earn your degree. Soon after, you married Preston, and the two of you tackled a fixer-upper."

"Other than a little volunteer work, guiding tourists around New Orleans was the only job I ever had before I moved to Georgia."

"You obviously learned a lot from that experience."

Amanda hesitated. How would a socially-connected woman whose biggest regret was not earning a paycheck react to a soap opera-worthy scandal? Morgan had seemed confident her mother-in-law wouldn't judge her. Besides, she'd opened the door. "I need to show you something."

Amanda removed her phone from her purse, tapped the screen, then pushed it across the table. "That article will appear in next week's Blue Ridge newspaper."

Monica pressed her hand to her chest as she read. When she finished, her eyes met Amanda's. "I admire you even more for your courage."

"It hasn't been easy. I've always preferred to work alone, so the idea of moving into a house with three women—"

"Three?"

"Erica's teenaged daughter came with us. Anyway, starting a business with strangers terrified me. Until Morgan helped Wendy and me accept our situation as an opportunity to turn our lives around."

Monica's brow pinched. "Who was the man you trusted, and why did he give that property to the three of you?"

Time to share the rest of the story and find out if Morgan had been right about her mother-in-law. "His name is Gunter Benson, but we knew him as Paul, Brian, and Kurt. Although we didn't know when we met him, we found out he's a con man addicted to gambling." Amanda pulled in a deep breath then slowly released the air. "Erica, Wendy, and I were all illegally married to him...at the same time."

Monica's mouth fell open. "Oh my gosh, what a terrible man."

"At least now he's behind bars in Nevada."

"For bigamy?"

Amanda shook her head. "He's a convicted murderer, and Wendy is weeks from delivering his child. The one other time I breakfasted here was the first day of my honeymoon with Paul Sullivan aka Gunter."

Monica's shoulders curled. "I feel foolish for complaining about not having a career, and I'm so sorry for choosing this place."

"Please, don't apologize. We all have regrets. Yours isn't any less important." Amanda forced a smile. "Besides, you confiding in me gave me the courage to share my story."

Monica straightened her shoulders. "You're the bravest woman I've ever met."

"Thanks to my daughter and our Blue Ridge family."

"Everything you've overcome—the heartache, the deception—maybe I'll find the courage to step out in faith and pursue a career."

Amanda reached across the table and touched Monica's arm. "Our children falling in love is as much a blessing for us as it is for them."

"In so many ways."

Amanda spread her napkin across her lap as their waiter arrived with their food. "While we enjoy our meal, I want to hear all about your social activities."

"And I want to hear about your inn."

"Deal." During breakfast and their ride away from the city, the two women chatted as if they'd been friends for years. When they arrived at the airport, Monica escorted Amanda to her gate. "I look forward to meeting your Blue Ridge family. In the meantime, I want to hear all about your grand opening."

"And I look forward to updates on your mission to launch a career." When Amanda's zone was called for boarding, she stood. "These past few days have meant the world to me."

Monica embraced her. "You and I will celebrate many milestones in the years to come."

"Yes, we will. Beginning with our new journeys."

Chapter 21

Erica splayed her hands on the table while Abby applied a coat of polish. "I still say you're going to a lot of unnecessary effort for one date."

"You wouldn't let me schedule an appointment at a nail salon—"

"A manicure is a luxury I can't afford until I begin earning a salary."

"Which is why today I'm your manicurist. Where's Mr. Barkley taking you?"

"I don't have a clue."

Abby dipped the brush into the bottle. "I bet he kisses you when he brings you home."

"Are you suddenly a dating expert? Besides, we're two adults going out for dinner, not a couple of love-struck teenagers."

"Don't be so dramatic, Mom."

Wendy wandered in. "Are you also gonna treat your mother to a pedicure?"

"I already did."

Erica rolled her eyes. "This was all Abby's idea."

"So was you treating yourself to a massage the day after you first checked into the Blue Ridge Inn. And now you're a massage therapist."

"Are you suggesting one manicure will change my life?"

"No, but one date might." Wendy's expression clouded over. "If he's the right guy for you."

Erica shared a knowing glance with her daughter. Despite Wendy's insistence that any discussion of Chris was off the table, her Awesam family recognized how much she missed him. Morgan and Kevin's wedding had added to Wendy's gloom. Best to change the subject. "As of an hour ago, we have two new Hilltop Inn reservations."

Abby applied polish to Erica's pinkie. "I'll be plenty busy as Hilltop Inn's adorable housekeeper."

Erica laughed. "It's obvious my daughter doesn't suffer from a lack of self-confidence."

"Hey, you guys gave me the title of vice president." Abby dipped the brush into the bottle. "At least the housekeeper job comes with a paycheck."

"Before long, we'll all have paychecks." Wendy patted her belly. "Which won't go far considering the huge hospital bill I'll have to pay after delivering this little guy."

Abby looked up. "Are you gonna wait 'til he's born to give him a name?"

Wendy scoffed. "Maybe." She spun away from the table and headed toward her room.

"Sorry, Wendy. I didn't mean to come across as insensitive."

Wendy flicked her hand over her shoulder. "Not a problem." She stormed into her bedroom and swung the door closed.

Erica eyed her daughter. "Wendy doesn't need us pressuring her."

"I didn't mean to." Abby brushed the second coat on Erica's right hand. "Do you suppose she and Chris will ever get back together?"

"Not unless he makes the first move, which seems less likely every day. At least the three of us are here to support her."

A tap on the back door perked Dusty's ears and lit Abby's face with a smile. "He's here." She rushed to the kitchen then returned with her boyfriend.

"Hey, Ms. Nelson."

"How's it going, Tommy?"

"Really good." He pulled up a chair. "I start working for my dad next week. In a few months, I'll have enough money to move into my own apartment."

"Do you think you'll miss going away to college?"

"Nah. I'm good at construction, and Dad's training me to take over the business. Besides, studying isn't my thing, so college would be a waste of my parents' money."

Erica couldn't help but admire the young man. "Where are you two going tonight?"

Abby finished the manicure with quick-drying spray. "A cookout in Hannah's backyard with a bunch of grads."

"Sounds fun."

"So does your date."

"Mr. Barkley's a cool guy. Don't worry, Ms. Nelson, Abby didn't tell anyone except me and Hannah."

"I'll see you later, Mom." The teenagers linked arms as they headed to the back door.

At least Tommy was a practical young man. Erica glanced at her watch. In thirty minutes the cool high school principal would knock on her front door. She waited ten minutes, then scurried to her room and flung open her closet door. Blue Ridge was a casual sort of town, so overdressing wouldn't do. She pulled out a bright pink casual dress and held it up in front of her dresser mirror. The color matched her nail polish and worked well with her complexion and dark hair. Erica slipped into the dress then pulled on three-inch-heeled sandals.

"You look gorgeous." Amanda stepped in. "Especially for a gal who adamantly rejected the idea of putting herself out there."

"I have no idea what attracted Brad to me, or if we'll even have a second date. Although he does seem to have a good sense of humor."

"Handsome, smart, and easygoing combine for a winning combination." The doorbell chimed. "Your date has arrived."

Erica's pulse accelerated. "I hope I'm not too casual."

Amanda thumped her arm. "Stop obsessing and go meet your date."

"I'm going." Erica stole one last glance in the mirror before grabbing her clutch purse and scooting out to the hall. She paused in the foyer to take a deep breath then pulled the door open and eyed Brad's dark slacks and long-sleeved, button-down shirt matching his blue eyes. "Hey."

His face lit with a smile. "Hi."

Erica stepped out and closed the door behind her. A sleek red sportscar with a tan convertible top sat at the end of the sidewalk. "You drive a fancy car. Is it new?" *What a dumb comment and a dumber question.*

"If you call eighteen-years-old new. I bought it five years ago."

At least she recognized the logo on the hood, and thankfully it wasn't the same make as Gunter's sports car. "I've never ridden in a Corvette."

"I promise not to drive over the speed limit." Brad opened the passenger door.

Erica lowered onto the tan leather then swung her legs to the floor and buckled her seat belt.

Her date hastened to the driver's side and backed onto the street. "My every-day car is a fifteen-year-old SUV."

"My partners and I share a pickup. Abby has her own car." Erica stifled a giggle. They were definitely competing for the most awkward title. "How fast have you driven this car?"

"Not too much over the speed limit." He grinned. "It wouldn't do for the principal to be presented with a fast-driving award."

After chatting about the weather for the remainder of the drive, Brad pulled into a parking space across from the Black Sheep, the same restaurant where Chris first dined with Wendy. He dashed to the passenger side and held out his hand. "Climbing out of a car this low to the pavement is a trick."

Especially with any shred of grace. Grateful for his help, Erica swung her legs to the pavement and stood.

Brad released her hand as they crossed the street and headed up the sidewalk to the white single-story building with black trim and large windows flanking the entrance. Inside, the hostess smiled. "Good evening, Mr. Barkley." Brad greeted the young woman by name. He spoke to three people as the young woman led them to their table. Erica recognized one couple from their open house.

After they were seated, Erica glanced around. Was it her imagination, or were other diners catching glimpses of them? How many of them would read Tuesday's article? Her focus returned to Brad. "Do people recognize you wherever you go?"

"More from my years as the high school football coach than as the principal. We southerners are football fanatics."

Their waiter arrived. "Welcome back, Coach."

"Thanks, Eddie."

After ordering beverages, Brad's eyes met Erica's. "See what I mean?"

"Abby called you the school's winningest coach."

"I had a great team. Four of my players, including my youngest son, were granted college scholarships. Two of those young men are playing professional ball."

"That's quite an accomplishment."

"I loved coaching those kids."

"Why'd you give it up to take on the role of principal?"

"When the job became available, the assistant principal tossed her hat in the ring. Unfortunately, she didn't have a clue how to relate to the students. So, I stepped up."

"And gave up the job you loved?"

"For the greater good, I suppose. Although I still miss coaching."

Their waiter returned and placed two glasses of wine on the table. "Are you ready to order?"

"Give us a few more minutes, Eddie."

"Yes, sir." The young man stepped away.

Brad's eyes remained trained on Erica. "You're the first woman I've invited to dinner since my wife passed three years ago."

Did he invite her because she reminded him of his wife? "Was she also a brunette?"

"No, but she was also beautiful."

Sensing her cheeks were seconds from turning multiple shades of pink, Erica focused on her menu. "What do you recommend?"

Brad chuckled. "Up to this point, it's obvious I'm winning the who's-most-out-of- practice competition."

Erica lowered her menu. Her date's bemused expression warmed her heart. Everything about Brad seemed the polar opposite of Jack and Gunter. "Considering I had no idea how to respond to your compliment, I'd say we're even."

"I imagine by the end of the evening we'll both end up winners."

Two hours after Wendy turned in for the night, an engine's purr drew Amanda's attention and perked Dusty's ears. She glanced at her watch. Eleven p.m. "Which Nelson do you suppose has arrived home first? Mother or daughter?" Amanda chuckled at the canine's cocked head. "If the kitchen door opens, it's Abby."

A minute passed. Two more. Footsteps clicked the foyer floor. Erica meandered into the den. "Did you stay up to grill me about tonight?"

"It's only eleven." Amanda tossed her book on the coffee table. "So, where did Brad take you?"

"The Black Sheep." Erica settled on the sofa beside Amanda.

"And?"

"And what?"

Amanda propped her elbow on the back of the sofa and rested her chin on her knuckles. "Unless you ordered a nine-course meal or moved to the bar, you didn't spend five hours at the restaurant."

Erica slipped out of her sandals and propped her feet on the coffee table. "After dinner we walked through the park and downtown."

"You two obviously hit it off."

"Brad's easygoing and a good listener. He only mentioned his wife one time, and I didn't say anything about my past relationships."

"Ideal first dates should be get-acquainted events, not true-confession affairs."

"Yeah, well—" Erica leaned back. "Tonight was more akin to two pals catching up, and I know a lot more about Blue Ridge than I did this afternoon."

"Romantic relationships often begin as friendships."

"You're getting way ahead of yourself."

"Are you seeing him again?"

"Next Saturday—"

"Well, there you go—"

"Unless Gail's article scares him off."

"It's more likely to impress him."

Another engine whir sent Dusty racing to the kitchen.

Amanda lowered her forearm and glanced at her watch. "You beat your daughter home by five minutes."

"Have you appointed yourself as our curfew monitor?"

"I don't know. Do you need one?"

"Hardly."

Abby breezed in and plopped beside her mother. "How long have you been home?"

"A few minutes."

"Did Mr. Barkley kiss you in the car or at the front door?"

Amanda laughed. "Talk about a role reversal. Daughter interrogates mother after first date."

Abby rolled her eyes. "Don't be so dramatic."

Erica patted her daughter's knee. "There was no kissing or hugging, just a widower and a divorcee enjoying dinner and conversation."

"Hmm. When's your next date?"

"What makes you think Mr. Barkley asked me out again?"

Abby's brows raised. "Well, did he?"

"He did."

"I've read that date number two is the magic number for older guys."

"At least my inquisitive daughter didn't call her principal ancient." Erica lifted off the sofa. "I'll see y'all in the morning."

"I'm also ready to call it a night." Amanda ambled to her room and pulled the door closed. After changing into pajamas and climbing into bed, she closed her eyes and prayed for God's will for her Awesam family's lives.

Chapter 22

Desperate to ignore the internal turmoil playing havoc with her emotions, Wendy inserted her earbuds and pressed the playlist Abby had uploaded for her. She pulled her hair into a ponytail, then pocketed her phone. After stretching, she headed out the front door and down the driveway for her daily walk—a routine she'd adopted to relieve the melancholy after breaking up with Chris.

At the end of the driveway, she turned left and strolled past the Hilltop Inn sign. Hopefully when the first guests arrived in six days, she'd stay busy enough with innkeeping duties to keep Chris from invading her thoughts and weakening her resolve.

The music in Wendy's ears drowned out the roar of the guy mowing Millie's front lawn—the same man they'd hired to take care of the inn's front yard. Another expense adding to their tight budget. At least they had enough prepaid reservations to stock the kitchen and keep the lights on. Sometime in the next few weeks, she'd have to buy a baby car seat and diapers. Those items would have to come out of her first paycheck.

Uh-oh. Was Millie motioning her to come up to her front porch? She could pretend she hadn't seen her. Except there was no ignoring her vigorous arm waves as if she were one of those airport guys signaling to a pilot. Hoping Millie would control her meddling antenna and resist asking about Chris, Wendy drew in a steely breath then trudged up the driveway and removed her earbuds. "Hey, what's up?"

"I need an expert taste tester." Hilltop Inn's chef motioned Wendy to follow her inside to the kitchen. Sharp cheese and herb scents wafted across the space. Millie plated a slice of quiche and set it on the table then pulled out a chair. "Take a bite, then give me your honest opinion."

Wendy hesitated. If she sat, she'd be a captive audience—especially since lifting off a chair took more effort every day.

Millie propped her hands on her hips. "Well? What are you waiting for?"

Wendy heaved a sigh and lowered onto the chair. Millie's calico curled around her leg before emerging from under the table and pouncing onto the kitchen counter.

Millie shooed the cat to the floor. "My naughty kitty knows better. She's showing off for company."

Hoping a stray cat hair hadn't found its way into the quiche, Wendy tasted.

Millie's brows raised. "What do you think?"

Should she tell the truth? Their chef asked for honesty, so yeah. "It's not my favorite."

"Mine either, but I needed a second opinion." Millie poured two glasses of orange juice then sat catercorner to Wendy. "How are you feeling?"

"Very pregnant."

"It won't be long now before you cuddle your baby in your arms."

Presuming where the conversation was headed, Wendy lifted the calico off the floor. "I've always wondered why some people prefer cats and others prefer dogs. What's your opinion?"

"Cats don't bark."

"And dogs don't jump onto kitchen counters. Both pets are curious but in different ways."

Millie's eyes probed Wendy's. "A couple of weeks ago, you couldn't go twenty minutes without talking about Chris, and now you never mention his name."

And there it was, the real reason Millie had invited her in. Their nosy neighbor obviously didn't intend to stop prying, and she had become part of the Awesam family. Maybe the time had come to bring her up-to-date. "Chris and I are no longer seeing each other. Except for legal stuff."

"That's too bad."

"Actually—" This situation called for a little fib. "Our decision was mutual."

Millie reached across the corner of the table and patted Wendy's arm. "Sometimes women in your condition make decisions based on emotion rather than reason."

Wendy stared at Millie's thin fingers. "What are you really saying?"

"Parting ways wasn't mutual, and Chris didn't break up with you, did he?"

Wendy shot Millie an incredulous look. Was she fishing or had someone told her? But who and why? She pulled her arm away and stroked the calico's back. "It's complicated."

"Raising a child alone isn't ideal. That's why Rupert and I stayed together when he discovered I was in love with another man."

Wendy's mind drifted back to Eleanor's journal entry about Millie's illicit love affair. "With Amanda, Erica, Abby, and even you to help out, I'm not alone. Besides Chris and I are still friends."

"Honey, I might be old and a little out of touch, but I know a young woman doesn't ask for help preparing a special meal for a young man who's simply a pal."

Wendy shrugged. "Circumstances change."

"You can't let Gunter influence your decisions."

Why had the Awesam partners agreed to tell Millie the whole truth about the con artist? Wendy swallowed a mouthful of orange juice. "You know what? You're absolutely right. Which is why I've taken charge and am doing what's best for everyone, including my son." She lifted the cat off her lap and pushed her chair away from the table.

"I didn't mean to meddle in your business."

"Of course, you did."

Millie shrugged. "You're right, I'm a meddling buttinsky." She held up her index finger. "However, you're family, and I'm a wise old woman who doesn't want you making decisions you'll live to regret."

Wendy's breath caught. How should she respond—especially since Millie had offered what she considered good advice? "Before I met Chris, I thought I was in love with the man I'd known as Kurt Peterson. When I discovered the truth about him, and that my baby is a boy..." Wendy hesitated. "For the first time since I met Chris, I'm doing what's best for him."

"The question is, what's best for you—"

"Look." Wendy aimed her open palm at Millie. "I appreciate you caring about me, but nothing you say will change my mind."

"I've said my piece. The rest is up to you."

"All right then. You don't need to show me out." Wendy gripped the table's edge and pushed off her chair. "About that quiche—"

"No need to worry, I'm not adding it to Hilltop's menu."

"Good, because everything else you're planning is delish."

"I know. Before you go—" Millie scooted to the counter, removed a cookie from an apple-shaped cookie jar, and handed it over. "A thank you for taste testing."

Wendy bit into the snickerdoodle. "I want you to bake the cake for my little guy's one-year birthday celebration."

Millie's face lit with a smile. "With lots of icing."

"Definitely." Wendy inserted her earbuds then made her way to the front door and out to the porch. Given how much time had passed since she began her walk as well as the full glass of orange juice she'd downed, she gobbled down the cookie and cut across Millie's side yard.

While trekking across the inn's front lawn, images of the first moment she'd laid eyes on Eleanor's vacation home played in her mind. She and her Awesam partners had transformed the rundown mansion into a beautiful inn. Wendy stopped dead in her tracks. Had she made a huge mistake and done the opposite with Chris? A squirrel skittered across the sidewalk fronting the inn before scampering up the steps to the front porch.

Wendy squared her shoulders and resumed walking. No, love and respect for Chris had influenced her decision to let him go. As she crossed the driveway and parking pad, Erica turned from the street and eased into the carport. Wendy cringed. Gunter's truck was a subtle reminder that she would never be free from the man who had fathered her child.

Chapter 23

Eager to discover if Gail's article had been published as written, Amanda settled at the dining room table then booted her laptop and pulled up the online weekly newspaper. Her pulse raced as she scanned each page. "There it is." She pointed to the photo of Hilltop Inn on page three.

Erica peered over Amanda's shoulder. "*Triumph Over Tragedy*. At least the headline is the same." She continued reading aloud, pausing for a brief moment before reading the last line. "'*Amanda, Erica, and Wendy are an inspiration to all women who face what appear to be unsurmountable challenges, and I am proud to call them my friends.*' The editor didn't change a single word."

Amanda breathed a sigh of relief. "While we wait for the readers' reactions, we need to make a decision about that blogger's request to interview the three of us."

"Doing a live interview is way too risky. Especially since we have no idea what questions she'd ask,"

Amanda cut a glance over her shoulder. "I've listened to a couple of Nancy's Nuggets podcasts, and she seems fair. Besides, more publicity for the inn is worth the risk."

"Not if she mentions Gunter by name or grills us about our relationships with him." Erica returned to her chair and sipped her coffee.

Amanda pushed her laptop aside and leaned back. "We could ask Millie to conduct a mock interview and throw tough questions at us, the same way Chris prepared us for Gunter's trial."

Erica shook her head. "There's one huge difference. Chris is an experienced attorney who knows what to anticipate. Millie has never even heard of a podcast."

"Doesn't matter. She'd come up with some real zingers."

A furrow appeared between Erica's eyebrows. "There's another important reason to reject the offer. Wendy's too fragile—"

"We could do the interview without her."

"And make her think we don't trust her?"

Amanda blew out a breath. "You're right, that's not a good idea. Besides, there's no way we'll consider doing the interview unless the three of us agree."

"By that time, the blogger will have given up on us and taken the decision out of our hands." Erica grabbed her ringing phone. She stared at the screen, her brows pinched. "It's Brad. Why do you suppose he's calling?"

Amanda rolled her eyes. "You're seriously out of practice. He obviously wants to talk to you."

"At least I'm not totally clueless." Erica swiped her finger across the screen. "Hi." She listened. "I understand." More listening. "You too." She tapped her screen.

"Well? What's up?"

Erica set her phone on the table. "He canceled tomorrow night."

Amanda's brows raised. "Did he say why?"

"One of his sons is coming to town for the Memorial Day weekend."

"Spending time with his kid is a legitimate reason."

Erica shrugged. "Unless he read that article and used the visit as a way out."

"Did he say he'd call you again?"

Erica nodded. "Next week."

Amanda thumped Erica's arm. "Well, there you go."

Erica wrapped her fingers around her coffee mug. "The last thing I need in my life is more relationship drama."

Someone knocked on the back door.

"I suspect that's our nosy neighbor." Amanda ambled to the kitchen and pulled the door open.

Millie's face beamed as she dashed in clutching a newspaper in one hand and a foil-covered plate in the other. "Have you read what that journalist wrote about us?"

Amanda nodded. "A couple minutes ago."

"For the first time in my life, I'm an honest-to-goodness celebrity. How many people do you suppose will want our autographs or ask to have their pictures taken with us? You know a lot of films and television shows are produced in Georgia." Millie's eyes widened. "What if a famous director wants to make a documentary or a movie about us?"

Amanda gave their neighbor a droll look. "How many cups of coffee have you downed since you woke up?"

"Two. We need to paste the article in our Hilltop Inn scrapbook." Millie followed Amanda into the den and sat across from Erica. "Or better yet, frame it and display it on the wall behind our check-in desk."

Wendy meandered in from the hall. "Based on all the commotion, I assume everyone has read Gail's article."

"Which is why I brought cinnamon rolls." Millie peeled the foil off the plate, releasing mouthwatering cinnamon and vanilla scents. "To celebrate our new status as local luminaries."

Amanda tilted her mug toward Millie. "Our neighbor has assumed the role of a world-famous chef."

Millie snapped her fingers. "There's another great human-interest story. *Mildred Cunningham—From Curmudgeon's Wife to Celebrity Chef.*"

Erica burst out laughing.

Amanda nearly choked on her coffee.

Wendy rolled her eyes. "Would that make the three of us your groupies?"

Millie's brow pinched. "That depends."

"On what?"

"Your definition of a groupie."

"An overzealous fan."

"Actually, I'd rather you ladies make me one of your voting partners."

Resisting a vigorous headshake and a negative retort, Amanda rose. "I'll bring us plates and napkins."

Millie waggled her finger. "You can change the subject all you want, but one of these days you'll realize you need my vote."

"We'll let you know when and if that ever happens." Amanda spun away from the table and headed to the kitchen.

Wendy followed and poured a glass of milk. "Maybe Millie's right." Her voice was barely above a whisper.

"The three of us have enough difficulty agreeing on important issues. Adding one more person to the mix—especially one as opinionated as Millie—would make our lives that much more complicated."

"I know, but I kind of feel bad for leaving her out." Wendy pulled her phone from her pocket. "Chris texted a message to the three of us." She tapped the screen. "He says, 'Congratulations. Excellent publicity for Awesam partners and Hillside Inn.'"

A quick glance at Wendy's pinched expression made it clear how much she missed Chris. "He's right. A positive article is more effective than paid advertising." Amanda carried plates, forks, and napkins to the table. Maybe she should give their chef at least a small win. "Know what I think? We need to display a photo of the five of us on the wall behind the check-in desk."

Millie's eyes narrowed. "Does five include me or the dog?"

Amanda exchanged her best that's-why-we-don't-give-her-the-vote glance at Wendy, then faced Millie. "Make that six, including Dusty. We'll pose today and have it framed in time for our grand opening. Unless you object to the idea."

"Now you want my vote?"

"Well?" Amanda drummed her fingers. "Do you or don't you want to be included?"

Millie huffed. "When and where do you want to take the picture?"

"At the inn later today, after Abby comes home."

"Fancy or casual?"

"Given my limited wardrobe—" Wendy patted her belly. "Definitely casual."

"I'll be there, even if I'm not a voting partner." Millie scowled. "But then, neither is Abby's dog."

Amanda resisted releasing a cutting remark. After all, with opening day so close, they couldn't afford to tick off their chef.

Erica leaned forward. "You're a valuable member of our team, Millie. Which makes your influence and opinions as important as a vote."

"And you bring delicious goodies to our meetings." Wendy reached for a cinnamon bun. "My little guy's Great Grandma Millie is gonna bake his first birthday cake."

"I have the cutest pictures of Abby's first birthday." Erica grinned. "She smeared vanilla icing over half her face."

"Hold on." Millie's eyes rounded as she stared at Wendy. "You want me to be your baby's great grandmother?"

"Uh-huh. Amanda's his nana. Erica's his aunt. Abby and Morgan are cousins. And you're his great grandma. All you have to do is decide what you want my little guy to call you." Wendy bit into her bun.

Millie crossed her palms over her heart. "No one has ever invited me to be part of their family, even one as bizarre as this one."

Wendy swallowed. "So, what do you want my baby to call you?"

"Well, my granddaughter calls me Grammy." Millie lowered her hands. "My honorary grandson can call me Grammy Millie."

"Perfect."

Amanda marveled at Awesam's cheerleader and peacemaker's ability to turn a challenge into a win, even if it meant adopting cranky Millie into their family. But, including her as a voting member of Awesam's team was still out of the question.

Chapter 24

The morning before Hilltop Inn's grand opening, Erica sat on the den sofa and tapped her phone to scan the latest emails. "We have thirty-seven positive responses to Gail's article. Other than a text Sunday, I haven't heard a peep from Brad."

Amanda strode in from the kitchen. "Two weeks ago you were dead set against meeting men, and now you're worried about a guy you dated one time not calling you?"

"Don't make a big deal about my comment. I was simply wondering out loud if Gail's article scared him off."

Amanda settled in one of the club chairs. "Considering this is the last week of school, and graduation is in a few hours, the guy you don't want to make a big deal about is probably too busy to read the paper."

"According to Abby, all her friends are talking about the article. If the principal is as tuned into his students as he claims, he has at least heard about it."

"Has he canceled tomorrow night's date?"

"No."

"Well, there you go."

Erica tossed her phone on the seat beside her. "That's one more reason I didn't want to start dating again."

Wendy meandered in. "What reason?"

"I have enough going on without adding relationship complications. Anyway, today is all about Abby, not me."

Wendy plopped onto the sofa. "I didn't go to my high school graduation. I'd only been a student at that school for six months, and my foster parents were too busy to bother attending."

Erica faced Awesam's CFO. "Do you regret not going?"

"Maybe a little. Except, I was a few months away from aging out of the foster system, so I'd skipped a lot of classes to work at a fast-food restaurant. When that day came, I'd saved enough money to leave Biloxi and start a new life in Gulfport. A year later I met Kurt aka Gunter, and now I'm here with the only real family I've ever known."

Erica's heart ached for Wendy. She scooted closer and squeezed her hand. "A family who adores you."

Amanda moved to Wendy's other side and patted her knee. "A family that will never leave you."

"The day we met turned out to be the beginning of something special." Wendy pulled her hand from Erica's then removed her phone from her pocket and held it at arm's length. "Lean in close and smile big." She tapped the screen and pulled up the photo. "The blonde, the brunette, and the redhead—the exclusive wives club that became a family."

Erica peered at the picture. "A new addition to our Awesam family album?"

Wendy pocketed her phone. "Sure."

Amanda nudged Wendy. "You're not thinking about sending a copy of that picture to Gunter, are you?"

Wendy shrugged. "That would be a crazy thing to do. I'm gonna take a shower now." She padded to the hall and on to the bathroom.

"I'm curious." Erica tilted her head. "Why did you ask Wendy that question about Gunter?"

"Have you ever heard her answer any question with 'sure'?"

"That's one little word."

Amanda crossed one leg over the other. "You have to admit she's been more than a little unpredictable lately."

"True, but Wendy isn't foolish."

"Who knows what's going on in her head."

Flurries of doubt about Wendy's intentions niggled Erica. Maybe she should talk to her, or better yet do something unexpected to make her feel special. An idea took root. She texted Abby.

Footsteps striking the kitchen floor followed a single rap on the back door. Millie strode in and placed an envelope on the coffee table. "Abby's graduation gift."

"I'm glad you're going to the ceremony with us."

"Me too. Now, give me your phone."

Erica stared at their neighbor. "Why?"

"Don't act all suspicious. I want to learn how to take pictures with that newfangled gizmo."

"Well, all right then."

Two hours after Millie snapped the first photo, Erica sat between Amanda and Wendy and scanned the auditorium. The principal and five other adults dressed in graduation attire stood side by side on the stage. How different would her daughter's graduation have been if they'd remained in Asheville? Even though they had lived in the most expensive zip code, they were never part of the country-club crowd. Especially after the public notice about their home's foreclosure posted in the paper.

Amanda leaned close. "Aren't you glad you and Abby moved here?"

Erica stared at her partner's profile. How many times since they'd met had she and Amanda seemed to be on the same wavelength? "Definitely."

As the procession music began, they stood to honor the graduating class promenading into the auditorium.

Amanda nudged Erica. "There's our girl."

Erica's exuberant wave caught her daughter's attention. Abby grinned while signaling an enthusiastic thumbs-up. After the students were seated and speeches begun, memories of Abby growing up invaded Erica's thoughts. An involuntary smile played on her lips as she closed her eyes and thanked God for carrying them through the deep valleys.

She forced her attention to return to the present as the students lined up alphabetically to accept their diplomas. It would be a while before they reached the N's. She blinked when Thomas Bennett's name was called. Tommy was obviously his nickname. Were his parents sitting close by? How much did they know about his relationship with Abby? Maybe she'd have the chance to meet them today.

As more students walked across the stage, Erica marveled at how in a few months so many kids had become her daughter's friends. Thanks to Hannah. Finally, they reached the N's. Erica's lungs expanded to their fullest through deep satisfied breaths as she raised her camera to record her child. The moment Abby's name was called, Amanda and Wendy cheered while Millie released an ear-piercing, two-finger whistle. As Abby walked off the stage, Erica peered around Amanda and whispered, "That was one impressive whistle."

Millie shrugged. "One of my many talents."

Erica chuckled. At least no one could accuse their chef of suffering from timidity. While the students continued receiving their diplomas, Erica's mind shifted to tomorrow's grand opening and the last minute tasks the team needed to accomplish. Finally, the last student was called.

Wendy's fidgeting escalated as the ceremony came to an end. The moment the grads filed out of the auditorium she bolted to her feet. "I'll catch up with you outside."

Erica, Amanda, and Millie stepped into the aisle. "I'm surprised Wendy was able to wait that long."

"Another five minutes and she wouldn't have." They followed the guests outside and joined the boisterous throng of students and family members. "How will we ever find Abby in this mob?"

"Try calling her cell."

Erica pulled her phone from her purse and tapped Abby's number. The call went to voicemail. "Either she can't hear with all this noise, or her phone's still on airplane mode." Erica craned her neck and scanned the swarm. "I see her." They made their way through the crowd.

Abby waved them over.

Erica embraced then released her daughter. "I couldn't be more proud of you, sweetheart."

Amanda hugged Abby. "That makes two of us."

Millie followed with her own hug. "Three of us." She released Abby and nudged Erica. "I'm ready to take pictures now."

"All right." Erica handed over her phone.

"Hold on." Abby glanced around. "Where's Wendy?"

"Bladder break." Millie snapped mother and daughter photos. "Now just Abby."

Tommy maneuvered through the crowd and handed his phone to Millie. "Will you take pictures of Abby and me?"

"Is your phone similar to Erica's?"

"Close enough."

As Millie captured images of two young people smitten with each other, an unexpected question invaded Erica's thoughts. Was their love strong enough to sustain them through whatever lay ahead? Her chest tightened. Or would their high school romance fall apart and break her daughter's heart the first time life hurled an obstacle onto their path?

Wendy made her way through the crowd. "If ladies hadn't let me butt in line, I would never have made it. This is the most fun part of the ceremony."

"Time for official family photos." Millie took charge and snapped a series of pictures.

After Millie's last shot, Erica motioned to her. "Give Tommy your phone and come join us."

Millie's face beamed as she squeezed between Abby and Amanda.

When Tommy returned Millie's phone, Erica nudged her daughter. It was time to put their plan in place.

Abby faced Wendy. "During this past week, Morgan, Mom, and I all celebrated graduations. Our accomplishments aren't any more impressive than yours, Wendy. You've already aced two online business courses and discovered you have a talent for numbers. If you continue, you'll earn a degree. Which is why we're also celebrating your academic achievements today. Abby removed her cap and placed it on Awesam's chief financial officer.

Wendy's eyes glistened with tears as she pressed her hand to her chest.

Millie aimed her phone.

"Wait." Wendy flipped the tassel to the right. "I haven't earned a degree yet. But I will, to show my little guy that nothing's impossible when you have a family as awesome as ours." She dabbed her cheeks. "Okay, now you can take a picture."

After posing alone and with her partners, including one with Millie, Wendy returned the cap to Abby. "Thank you for sharing your special day with me."

Abby embraced her. "Heartbreak brought us together. Love and respect for each other transformed us into a family. And now you, Morgan, and I are sisters." After hugs and more pictures, Abby and Tommy bid everyone goodbye and meandered off to join their friends.

Erica linked arms with Wendy. "While they're off celebrating with their friends, the four of us are going to celebrate with our own graduation party and tomorrow's grand opening over dinner at Millie's."

Following hours of lighthearted conversation and a scrumptious meal, Wendy failed to suppress a yawn.

Amanda patted her knee. "Seems it's time to take our honorary graduate home."

Millie yawned. "It's a half hour past my new bedtime, so this is the perfect time to end our celebration."

Wendy stood. "Today has meant far more than y'all can imagine to me and my little guy." She embraced Millie. "Thank you for making me feel special, Grammy Millie."

"You're welcome, sweetie. Now scoot on home and get a good night's sleep. Tomorrow's a big day for our team."

By the time they traipsed across the yards and into their home, Wendy had made an important decision. Alone in her room, she opened her top dresser drawer and pulled out an envelope addressed to Gunter Benson. Grateful she'd postponed mailing it, she removed the selfie she'd taken days earlier along with the note she'd written. "I no longer need to prove anything to you," she said aloud. After ripping the note to shreds and releasing the pieces to the trashcan, Wendy changed into pajamas and slid between the sheets. Within minutes she drifted to a deep, satisfying sleep.

Chapter 25

Saturday morning seemed to have flown by amid a flurry of activities. With a little more than an hour before the official four o'clock check-in time, Amanda peered around the foyer. Today their reputation as innkeepers was on the line. Had they missed any important details that would expose the Awesam team as amateurs? After moving to the small antique desk beside the staircase, she opened the guestbook and stared at Mildred Cunningham's signature. Wendy and Erica had overridden her resistance to allow their chef to sign as the inn's first official guest. In their opinions keeping the peace outweighed any questionable benefit to bestowing that honor on someone who paid for their stay. At least they supported her decision to deny Millie's request to show up before tomorrow morning.

Amanda eased to the French doors opening to the turret room now serving as the inn's library, although only a couple dozen books lined the mahogany bookcase. She peered at the elaborate ceiling molding. Guests would never know the number of hours she had stood on scaffolding, adding the final step to her partners' painting projects. Thanks to a steady hand, she had mastered the art of cutwork.

She spun away from the turret room and moseyed across the foyer to the living room. Despite the damage—thanks to a broken front window—they had salvaged every piece of the original furniture except the water-soaked sofa. Fortunately, the couch from Erica's Asheville living room worked well with the other pieces. Amanda headed to the bookstand and opened the Hilltop Inn scrapbook to the first page—a photo of the home's front façade the first day Chris had driven them up the driveway. The following pages showcased the transformation from rundown eyesore to elegant bed and breakfast.

Amanda returned to the foyer and climbed up to the second story. Two chandeliers lit the central hall spanning from the windows overlooking the front lawn to those facing Millie's backyard masterpiece. Fortunately, the Harringtons had excellent taste and plenty of money to create luxurious spaces. Amanda strode to the upstairs turret room and traced her fingers on the plaque beside the door identifying the space as the Butterfly Suite. Their first visit to the Blue Ridge Inn last December had inspired Wendy to name each room.

She stepped into the room and turned in a slow circle admiring the décor. A butterfly painting their CEO had found at the local thrift store enhanced the wall behind the king-size bed. How three strangers had overcome their differences and managed to restore this house and transform their lives were nothing short of miraculous.

Amanda moseyed to the other end of the hall and walked into the Azalea Suite. On display beside a window was an enlarged framed photo of the azalea bush bursting with crimson color that had enhanced her and Preston's shotgun home's tiny front yard. At least the memory would live on in this room and in her heart. She crossed the hall and peeked into the Chattahoochee Suite. How many of today's arrivals had visited Blue Ridge before? If they were seasoned travelers, would their experience at Hilltop Inn live up to their expectations? Amanda drew in deep breaths then returned to the first floor and settled on the living room sofa to wait.

Erica sat at the built-in desk and tapped her laptop keyboard. Thus far only two guests had scheduled massages—the first for three tomorrow afternoon and the second for ten Monday morning. Would either woman suspect she was a newly-licensed therapist? Hopefully, neither would be the chatty type.

After logging off, she stepped from her private office into her workspace. Soft beige walls and dimmable lighting cast a warm glow in the transformed garage which once housed the antique Cadillac that provided the money to create the spa. Erica skirted the massage table and ambled to the dark blue accent wall lit with overhead lighting. Candles sat atop the waist-high cabinet anchored to the wall. Her CD player connected to wall-mounted speakers lay on a shelf inside the cabinet. Hopefully her clients would approve of her instructor's background-music recommendations. At least she had several good selections.

Erica turned in a slow circle, drinking in every detail. Satisfied everything was in place and ready to go, she strode into the soft green reception area. Four upholstered club chairs encircling a round coffee table created a welcoming environment. The glass-front chiller was stocked with bottles of water. She continued into the sauna room. Which guests would be the first to take advantage of this luxury?

Another mental checklist popped up as she fingered stacks of oversized white towels neatly folded on shelves in each of the two changing rooms. Thanks to Abby's help, the surfaces sparkled, and the air wafted with a spring-fresh scent. Erica read the sauna operating instructions tastefully displayed beside the door. Simple and to the point. Confident she'd checked off every item on her to-do list, she left the building then traipsed across the newly-poured patio.

Erica opened the French doors and stepped into the den. An hour ago, she'd irritated the dickens out of Amanda while insisting they check every space a third time. Awesam's president rolled her eyes and abandoned her after they inspected the downstairs guest suite. Erica smiled. Their conflicting personalities actually created a productive, albeit sometimes contentious team. Having overcome Gunter's deceptions added a powerful incentive for them to succeed despite their differences.

Erica made her way into the kitchen. Fortunately, she'd avoided a fiasco during last night's celebratory dinner. When Millie challenged their decision to keep her away from the inn today, Erica convinced their cantankerous chef that waiting until tomorrow morning would enhance her position. That plus a promise to formally introduce her to the guests and flout her talents seemed to satisfy Millie. Whatever it took to keep the peace. Erica returned to the den, turned on background music, and glanced at her watch. Five minutes after three. Which guest would arrive first?

Wendy breathed the fragrant scent of blooming roses while sauntering along Millie's English country garden's central path. She stopped beside the fountain and held her fingers under the cool water flowing from the top. The stream cascaded between her fingers and splashed onto the second tier. A shudder ripped through her. If Gunter hadn't killed that loan shark, would she be standing on her Gulfport condo balcony gazing down at the gulf's waves gently washing onto the sandy beach—still illegally married to a con man?

She pulled her hand away and headed toward the gazebo while envisioning a couple standing under the chandelier exchanging vows. After peak tourist season ended, she'd insist on promoting the inn as a wedding venue. Wendy stepped into the structure and ran her fingers along the white wrought-iron railing. If she hadn't invited Chris to Erica's birthday celebration all those months ago, would he have taken her to dinner at the Black Sheep Restaurant?

Wendy closed her eyes as vivid images bubbled up of the night Chris escorted her through the woods to the clearing behind his home. Dried leaves crunched beneath their feet. The gurgling creek welcomed them into the clearing. Brass candleholders, two Champagne flutes, and a picnic basket sat on a round table covered with a white cloth. She'd wrapped her arms around Chris's neck and whispered, "You're in love with me as much as I'm in love with you, aren't you?"

Her heart pounded against her ribs as another memory shattered the images. Chris had kissed her and claimed she made him happy. But he hadn't told her he loved her that night or any time since. Tears pooled and tracked down her cheeks. No matter how much she missed him, letting him go had been the right thing to do.

Wendy strolled to the back of the gazebo. A deer peered at her from the other side of the fence before easing back into the woods. So many wondrous discoveries lay ahead for her little guy. One of these days, she'd have to come up with a name, unless she settled for LG, short for Little Guy. Grinning at the notion, she spun away from the railing and returned to the path. As she skirted the fountain, a sportscar pulled into the driveway and continued to the parking pad. The moment their first guests climbed out, Wendy texted Amanda and stepped up her pace. She met Erica in the den. "It's time to greet our first guests." They headed to the foyer as their new doorbell chimed.

Amanda pulled the door open. "Welcome to Hilltop Inn and Spa. I'm Amanda, one of the innkeepers."

The middle-aged gentleman followed the woman into the foyer. "We're the Hamiltons."

The man's wife, dressed in what appeared to be an expensive outfit, glanced around. "I must say, the interior is even more impressive than the exterior."

"Transforming this home into an inn has been a labor of love." Amanda nodded toward her partners. "Erica and Wendy are Hilltop Inn's other innkeepers."

Mrs. Hamilton grinned. "A welcome committee. How sweet."

Amanda escorted the couple to the desk and held out a pen. "Please."

Mr. Hamilton signed the guestbook. "This is our second trip to Blue Ridge."

"We're delighted you've chosen to stay with us. The Azalea Suite has a lovely view of our backyard garden." Amanda handed their key to her partner while facing their guests. "You're welcome to leave your suitcase here while Erica shows you around."

As Erica escorted the couple into the living room and began her spiel, Wendy held up her left hand and splayed her fingers. If guests noticed she wasn't wearing a wedding ring, would they judge her?

Amanda grasped Wendy's left hand. "When you turn on your irresistible charm, our guests will love you."

Wendy stared wide-eyed at Amanda. "How'd you know what I was thinking?"

"Lucky guess."

The doorbell chimed.

Amanda squeezed Wendy's hand, then welcomed the new arrivals and introduced herself and Wendy. She followed the same routine as she had with the first guests.

Wendy glanced at the guestbook as Amanda handed her the key to the young couple's suite. Katherine and Robert Jones. Were their nicknames Kate and Bob? She summoned her best smile. "We're delighted you're staying with us." Surprised yet grateful neither asked questions during the tour, Wendy escorted them to the Rainbow Suite and unlocked the door. "This is our largest room." She pointed toward the French doors. "Those open to the patio and our English garden."

Mrs. Jones strode to the doors and opened the blinds. "I assume this was the original owner's bedroom."

Wendy smiled. "Excellent assumption. A picture of Eleanor and Warren Harrington is on the dresser."

Katherine spun around. "Did you know them?"

"No, but our chef did. You'll meet her when breakfast is served tomorrow from eight until ten in the dining room. Is there anything I can do for you before I leave?"

Mr. Jones set one of their suitcases on the luggage stand. "No thank you."

"All right then. If you need anything, please don't hesitate to call us." Wendy handed him the key then walked out, closing the door behind her.

By five-fifteen, all the guests had checked in, leaving the partners free to return to the ranch house. Wendy released a satisfied sigh as she removed a bottle of water from the fridge. "Our first official day as innkeepers is coming to an end."

Amanda pocketed the cell phone set up to respond to calls from the inn. "Hopefully none of the guests will call in the middle of the night."

"I have an idea." Wendy uncapped her water. "Let's order a couple of pizzas."

"Exactly what I was thinking."

Following a sharp rap, the back door swung open. Millie dashed in. "I brought you lasagna and a Caesar's salad."

Amanda gawked at their neighbor. "How'd you know we were here?"

Millie set the food on the table. "Have you forgotten that I can see the inn from my house?"

"And you saw us leave through the front door."

"Five minutes ago." Millie pulled out a chair. "Now that I'm here, I want to hear all about our guests."

Chapter 26

The night sky had given way to morning light by the time Erica headed up the inn's sidewalk. She climbed onto the porch and unlocked the front door. Cinnamon, vanilla, and coffee aromas wafted around her as she stepped into the foyer and peered into the living room. An older couple sat on the sofa. "Good morning." She moved closer. "I hope you enjoyed your first night with us."

The woman peered around her husband. "We had dinner downtown at our favorite restaurant, then returned to stroll through your beautiful backyard. I loved how you dedicated it to the original owner. As an avid gardener, I must say Mildred Cunningham is an excellent designer. Please extend my appreciation to her for creating such a lovely garden."

Grateful she remembered their guest's name, Erica smiled. "Mildred is also our chef, Mrs. Gilmore, so you'll meet her at breakfast."

The woman pressed her palms together. "How fun. By the way, the Dogwood Suite is lovely."

"The name was inspired by a dogwood tree that welcomed spring to my childhood neighborhood with beautiful pink flowers." *The only bright spot on the dreary street.*

"Excellent choice."

"I'm delighted you're enjoying your stay. I'll see you at breakfast." Erica slipped away and breathed deeply as she headed toward the kitchen to face day one of supervising Millie. "Good morning."

Millie removed a bowl of fruit from the fridge and set it on the island. "Do you plan to babysit me before every breakfast or just today?" Her tone hinted of irritation.

"I just spoke to one of our guests who admired your landscape talent. She's eager to meet you. To answer your question, I'm here to help before I introduce you." *But Millie wasn't far wrong.*

"You might as well admit your partners assigned you to keep an eye on me." Millie crossed her arms and tapped her foot. "You can stop worrying because I can turn on the charm as well as any of you."

Erica moved closer. "First day jitters are normal."

Millie's brow pinched. "What makes you think I'm nervous?"

"Because yesterday before our first guest arrived, my stomach turned so many flipflops I thought I might qualify for the Olympics gymnastic team."

The hint of a smile softened Millie's features. "I know I sometimes come across as somewhat unpleasant." She dropped her arms to her sides. "So, I suppose I can't blame you for showing up early."

Erica touched their chef's arm. "Our guests will love you."

"Yeah, well, I'm also a good judge of character, so whenever I notice anything suspect about a guest, you'll be the first to know." Millie pointed to a stack of plates. "Since you're here to help, you can set the table."

Pressing her lips tight to prevent the retort from rolling off her tongue, Erica lifted the plates off the counter. She entered the dining room as yesterday's first arrival ambled to the buffet. "Good morning, Mrs. Hamilton. Do you and Mr. Hamilton have a fun day planned?"

"Indeed, we do." Their guest poured a cup of coffee. "Starting with a train ride."

Should she admit she'd yet to ride the iconic attraction? Better to keep that bit of information to herself. "A perfect way to begin the day." Erica set the table while their guest returned to the living room and struck up a conversation with the Gilmores. How could she counter Millie's self-acclaimed role as the inn's private detective? Although, it would be helpful to know if she noticed something suspicious. Better to leave that subject off the table for a while. Hoping to make herself useful, Erica returned to the kitchen.

At eight o'clock mouthwatering aromas wafted from the platters of Millie's breakfast offerings they carried into the dining room. Erica summoned her warmest smile as she placed two platters in the center of the table and faced the ten of fourteen guests who had shown up. "Good morning, and welcome to Hilltop Inn's family-style breakfast prepared by our talented Chef Mildred, who also designed our English country garden."

Millie set two more platters on the table. "Today we're serving cinnamon buns, fresh fruit, quiche Lorraine, spinach and mushroom frittata, and for those who prefer a lighter breakfast, blueberry yogurt and granola."

Mr. Gilmore reached for the platter of quiche and held it for his wife. "One of your favorites, dear."

"Everything looks delicious." Mrs. Gilmore transferred a slice onto her plate. "And your garden is beautifully manicured."

Millie's face beamed with a wide smile. "Creating a country English garden to honor Eleanor Harrington was a labor of love."

"Was she the home's original owner?"

Millie nodded. "Eleanor and Warren built this home as their vacation retreat. After they passed, it made perfect sense to transform it into an inn."

A young woman reached for the fruit bowl. "My husband and I stayed in their bedroom. Why did you name it the Rainbow room?"

"I can answer your question." Erica caught the young woman's eye. "Our partner Wendy grew up believing a rainbow means God is smiling down on us."

Millie nodded. "Which is what Eleanor is doing now."

The woman spooned fruit into her bowl. "Did you know Eleanor Harrington well?"

"We were best friends."

Another guest passed the frittata to the young woman. "Her picture's in the scrapbook on the bookstand in the living room."

"There's also a picture of her and her husband in the Rainbow Suite."

"It's fun staying at an inn with fascinating history." Mrs. Hamilton handed the cinnamon buns to her husband.

He placed a bun on his plate. "Especially one that needed a total transformation."

Mrs. Gilmore swallowed a bite of quiche. "Oh my gosh, this is delicious. Your culinary skills are as amazing as your landscaping talent, Chef Mildred."

"Thank you, and my friends call me Millie."

"Well, Millie, kudos for a delicious breakfast."

Millie pressed her hands to her chest as the guests showered her with compliments. "Tomorrow morning I'll serve eggs Benedict."

When two more guests joined the group and introduced themselves, Erica motioned for Millie to follow her back to the kitchen. "You've obviously impressed everyone with your culinary and landscaping talents."

"Are you admitting that bringing me onboard was a stroke of genius?"

Erica chuckled. "I suppose I am."

Millie faced the window framing a view of the backyard. "Eleanor would be pleased with everything we've accomplished."

"She'd be especially proud of you."

"Everyone sitting around the dining room table reminds me of her dinner parties." Millie spun away from the window. "If I hadn't threatened to boycott your rezoning plans, would you and Wendy have shown up on my doorstep?"

"You're our neighbor, so of course we would have."

"But you wouldn't have asked me to be part of your team."

Erica hesitated. Should she fudge the truth?

Millie planted her hands on her hips "If you're trying to decide how to respond, I already know you wouldn't have."

"You know what, Millie?" Erica mirrored her stance. "You're right. But sometimes things just seem to work out. And lucky for us, although you were a royal pain in the backside, you happened to be the best doggone chef in Blue Ridge."

Millie burst out laughing. "Every once in a while, it pays to be a difficult neighbor." She dropped her arms to her side. "Do I still need babysitting, or do you trust me to play nice with our guests?"

"That depends. What will you do the first time someone complains about breakfast?"

"I'll give them a bran muffin and a big glass of prune juice."

Erica stifled a giggle. "I'm serious."

Millie held up her right hand. "I promise to be the most charming and hospitable chef, your honor, no matter what nonsense some jerk spouts."

"Point taken. But I still plan to show up tomorrow morning to help."

"Before you go—" Millie removed a warm platter from the oven. "Breakfast for you and the rest of the Awesam team."

"A little incentive to entice us to make you a voting partner?"

"Not a little, a boatload."

"One of these days, your ploy might win the three of us over." Erica carried the bribe to the ranch house.

Amanda looked up from her laptop. "You're back earlier than I expected. How's everything next door?"

"Breakfast is a big hit." Erica set the platter on the table. "So is our chef."

"Until one of our guests grumbles about her food."

"Millie will handle the situation like a pro."

"Yeah, well, I'll believe that when I see it."

Three hours after Erica returned to the ranch house, the Awesam partners gathered around the table to discuss the inn's budget. The moment Wendy opened her laptop, the back door swung open. Millie dashed in.

Amanda leaned back. "We heard your culinary expertise impressed our guests."

"Did you expect anything less?" Millie pulled out a chair. "Something happened a few minutes ago the three of you need to know about."

Erica exchanged glances with her partners. Had she made a mistake leaving Millie alone?

"Well?" Wendy pushed her laptop aside. "Are you gonna tell us or make us guess?"

Millie crossed her arms on the table. "I was cleaning up the kitchen when one of our guests came in and climbed onto a stool. I thought maybe she wanted to compliment me or ask for a recipe—"

"Hold on." Amanda aimed her open palm at Millie. "Which guest?"

"The young one. Her name's Katherine Jones."

"They're the couple who stayed in Eleanor and Warren's bedroom," added Wendy.

"Right. Anyway, Katherine asked all sorts of questions about the Harringtons and the inn. How did Eleanor and I become friends, and what happened to her? She also asked how the three of you ended up with her house."

Amanda's brow pinched. "What'd you tell her?"

"I simply told her that Eleanor passed away years ago and that you inherited these two houses. Don't worry, I didn't mention a word about Gunter, or that Eleanor had been married to anyone other than Warren."

Wendy's head tilted. "Did she tell you why she wanted to know?"

"She claimed fascination with the history of luxury inns. I suspect she's some sort of journalist who's looking to write a story. Except, when I asked if she'd read the article about us, she asked, 'what article?'"

"Did you tell her?"

Millie shook her head. "I changed the subject. If she's all that interested, she'll find it on her own. Anyway, I thought you three needed to know."

Erica tapped her fingers on the table. "Katherine is my three o'clock massage client. I'll let you know how that goes."

Even though no one was scheduled to check out until the next day, and four of the rooms were reserved until Wednesday, at three-thirty, Amanda strode past the empty parking pad and headed into the inn's den. She peered through the Rainbow room's open doorway. "How's everything going?"

Abby pulled the comforter and fluffed the pillows. "I'm ready to tackle the upstairs rooms."

"When you arrived, were any of the guests in here?"

"Nope." Abby grabbed the partially-filled trash bag and her supply caddy. "By now, Mom's halfway through her first professional massage."

Hopefully Erica was more enlightened about the woman who'd reserved Hilltop's most expensive room.

"I'll see you later." Abby breezed past her and headed toward the back staircase.

The team had decided that Abby only needed to clean the common rooms three days a week, and the kitchen was Millie's responsibility. Amanda ambled to the living room. The inn's scrapbook lay open on the coffee table. How many guests had flipped through the pages? She placed the Hilltop Inn's history back on the bookstand, then peered out the window. A squirrel perched on the porch railing gnawing on an acorn. How many little critters had Dusty chased up a tree since they'd moved into the ranch house?

Amanda spun away from the window and ambled to the dining room. Why had Katherine Jones asked Millie all those questions? She ran her fingers along the chair backs while circling the massive table. Had any of their guests objected to dining family-style with strangers?

She returned to the den, headed out back, and strode up the center walkway. A bird splashing in the fountain's top tier took flight. Amanda stooped to pluck a twig off the path. As she straightened, Katherine Jones strode from the spa and stepped onto the patio.

Eager to speak to their guest, Amanda approached. "How was your massage?"

The young woman halted and turned toward her. "Relaxing."

So much for useful information. "Do you and your husband have fun plans for the rest of the afternoon?"

"We do. Thanks for asking and for your hospitality." Katherine flashed a smile then headed to the French doors and disappeared inside.

Amanda hastened to the spa. She stepped into the massage room and closed the door. "Did our inquisitive guest pepper you with questions?"

"Not exactly." Erica pulled the sheet off the table. "She asked how we knew Millie, where I'm from, and how long I've been a massage therapist. After that, she didn't say a word. Before she left, she gave me a generous tip."

Amanda released a sigh. "We'll drive ourselves crazy if we react every time Millie comes running to us with some wild suspicion about a guest."

"You're right." Erica blew out a candle. "Although one of these days she might share news that actually matters."

Chapter 27

Wendy sat at the ranch house dining room table with her fingers hovering above the keyboard. As much as she wanted to disregard Millie's comments as an old lady's irrational suspicions, the possibility that Gunter had conned another reporter with lies weighed heavy on her heart. At this point all she knew about the woman who had roused their chef's misgivings was her home address. Would she violate their guest's privacy or break some sort of innkeeper-guest privilege if she searched for more information?

Dismissing the notion as ridiculous, Wendy tapped her keyboard and logged onto the internet. She typed Katherine Jones into the search bar and scrolled through the pages. Lots of results popped up, but none about the woman who'd reserved the Rainbow Suite. If their inquisitive guest didn't have such a common name, maybe she'd be easier to find. Attempts to locate her on social media proved equally useless until she appeared on one site. Nothing about her postings hinted of anything out of the ordinary. Obviously, Millie had overreacted.

Wendy clicked off the internet, then pushed away from the desk and ambled through the den to the back patio. Memories of soaking up the sun on the beach surfaced as she settled on one of the chairs she'd brought from her condo balcony. Dusty padded over, sprawled beside her, and resumed gnawing her rawhide bone. Wendy peered across the yard as the couple she'd escorted to the Bluebell Suite hauled their luggage to their car. She waved. "Did you enjoy your stay?"

The woman returned the gesture. "Immensely, which is why I posted a well-deserved, five-star review."

Wow! Their first review, and a five-star at that. Wendy grinned. "Thank you so much."

"You're welcome, and thank you for a wonderful experience. We'll be sure to recommend you to all of our friends."

The compliment warmed Wendy's heart while the sun heated her cheeks. Without a lick of innkeeping experience, she and her partners had created a vacation destination worthy of a top-notch review. If reservations continued to roll in after their grand-opening special, by fall she would earn enough salary to provide a good life for her son. A kick triggered a giggle. She wrapped her arms around her belly. "One day we'll have our own house with a big yard where you can play with your friends and a dog as sweet as Dusty." Abby's canine companion peered up at Wendy, her head cocked. She stroked the dog's muzzle, initiating an enthusiastic tail wag. "Until then, you're our favorite pet."

Mrs. Gilmore walked out of the spa and headed to the inn's patio. As far as Wendy knew, Erica's second official massage customer hadn't roused Millie's suspicions. She pulled her phone from her pocket, opened Hilltop Inn's website, and read the flattering review. If prisoners had access to the internet, would Gunter read about their success? Had anything happened this morning to rouse their chef's suspicions?

Wendy pocketed her phone then strode through the gate exiting to the side yard and headed to the patio's French doors. All was quiet inside the den. Were Katherine and Robert Jones on the other side of the Rainbow Room's closed door, or had they left for the day? Wendy hastened to the kitchen. "How did day two's breakfast go?"

Millie spritzed cleaner on the counter. "If you're curious about our inquisitive guest, she didn't ask any questions or act suspicious." She wiped the counter dry. "Everyone loved my eggs Benedict."

"Because they're delicious." Wendy removed the glass cover off a platter and reached for a cinnamon bun. "Besides these yummy buns, what's on tomorrow's menu?"

"Blueberry pancakes and scrambled eggs with cheddar."

"Are you enjoying your new job?" Wendy bit into the bun.

"It keeps me busy."

"One of our guests posted a five-star review on our website. She raved about the inn's amenities, the staff's hospitality, and the chef's delicious breakfasts."

Millie's face beamed. "So far, I haven't needed to give anyone prune juice or bran muffins."

Erica wandered in and climbed onto a stool. "That's our chef's planned response to a cantankerous guest's complaints about her menu choices."

Wendy chuckled. "Maybe we should have given her bran muffins instead of cookies the first day we knocked on her door."

"Only if they were homemade." Millie placed the bottle of cleaner under the sink. "I still say there's something odd about the guests staying in Eleanor's room, so I'll keep an eye on both of them."

Amanda strode in from the dining room. "Who are you planning to spy on now?"

"Katherine and Robert Jones."

Amanda settled beside Erica. "I thought your suspicions only applied to Katherine."

"They did until this morning." Millie stood across the counter from the Awesam board and glanced around as if she expected to find a guest lurking in the shadows. She leaned forward. "I keep the kitchen door ajar while our guests are in the dining room. Yesterday Mr. Jones didn't say a word. Today he talked a blue streak. I knew it was him because he mentioned his wife's name."

Erica folded her arms on the bar. "Eavesdropping isn't a great idea."

Millie scoffed. "How else will I hear if someone needs me? Anyway, he's a lawyer working on some big case."

Wendy licked icing off her lips, then pulled out her phone and tapped the screen. "I found him." She scrolled through his website. "Hmm." She pushed her phone toward Erica and Amanda.

Silence hung heavy while they focused on the discovery.

"Well?" Millie drummed her fingers on the island. "Are you three intentionally keeping me in suspense?"

Amanda returned the phone to Wendy. "If we show you, will you promise not to jump to irrational conclusions?"

"No matter what you think, I'm not too old to find him on my own."

"Are you kidding? You still have a flip phone."

Millie planted her hands on her hips. "Yeah, well I have one of those tablet gizmos at home."

Amanda peered at Erica then Wendy. "What do you think? Should we show her?"

Erica shrugged. "We might as well."

"Why not." Wendy sent her phone sliding across the island.

Millie leaned close, then snapped her fingers. "Aha. I knew there was something strange about that man."

"You were guessing." Erica drummed her fingers. "Besides, just because he's a personal injury lawyer, doesn't mean they're up to something."

Millie pushed the phone across the island. "Unless they fake an accident and try to sue the pants off us."

"Give it a break, Millie." Wendy turned her phone face down.

"If you ask me, we still need to keep a close eye on those two." Millie turned toward the door leading to the den.

"Hold on." Amanda aimed her open palm toward their chef. "If you're thinking about camping out in the den and playing amateur detective—"

"No need. They've already left."

"How do you know?"

Millie thrust her thumb over her shoulder. "I have a perfect view of the patio from that window. After I check Eleanor's garden for any weeds that dared to pop up overnight, I'll head home to feed my cats."

The moment their chef left, Wendy turned her phone face up and swiped her finger across the screen. "Maybe we should call Chris."

"And tell him what?" Amanda shot Wendy an incredulous look "That our chef is suspicious about a guest because he's a lawyer and his wife asked questions?"

"You're right. We'd look totally ridiculous."

"Not to mention testing the cry-wolf concept." Amanda slid off her stool. "I'm heading to the grocery store. Do either of you need to add anything to our list?"

Wendy logged off the website. "I don't."

"Neither do I."

Amanda turned the inn's private cell phone over to Wendy. "You're officially on duty until tonight." She waved over her shoulder as she headed toward the den. "I'll see you next door for supper."

Following two idle hours, Wendy greeted the first of two new arrivals. After giving them the tour and spiel, she escorted the senior couple upstairs to the Daffodil Suite and handed over the key. Thirty minutes later the second reservation arrived—a mother and daughter who visited Blue Ridge to shop. Wendy swept away the envy threatening to surface and gave them the same warm welcome she'd given the first couple. Once they were settled in their room, she returned to the ranch house and napped until the succulent aroma of tomatoes and rosemary wafted into her room. She yawned and stretched then meandered to the den and laid the inn's phone on the dining room. "So far, everything's quiet next door."

Amanda set a bowl of noodles beside the Caesar salad. "More proof our chef's suspicions are way off base."

Wendy enjoyed bantering with her Awesam family while they dined on Amanda's signature spaghetti sauce, her only culinary claim to fame. All was calm in her world. Until the inn's phone pinged a text.

Chapter 28

Alarmed by the color draining from Wendy's face, Erica dropped her fork. "What's wrong?"

"It seems Millie was right after all."

Erica's brows furrowed. "About what?"

"Them." Wendy handed the phone to Awesam's chief executive officer.

Erica's pulse pounded in her ears as her eyes focused. She read the text aloud. "My wife and I request a private meeting in the inn's dining room with Hilltop's owners one hour from now. Respectfully, Robert Jones, Attorney at Law." He copied Millie on the message."

Amanda slammed her palm on the table. "We're open for three days, and some sleazebag lawyer wants to take us down?"

"Same as Gunter," mumbled Wendy. "I need to call Chris."

"Wait." Erica swallowed against the dryness in her throat. Somehow, she had to remain calm. "If we show up with our lawyer, we'll come across as guilty before we're even accused of anything."

Amanda glared at Erica. "In my opinion, showing up without him is a huge risk."

"I agree with Amanda." Wendy's eyes flicked to Erica. "What if they hold us hostage and demand some sort of ransom?"

"Robert Jones is a lawyer, not a criminal."

"We didn't have a clue the man we knew as Kurt, Brian, and Paul was a con man. So how do we know this guy isn't dangerous?"

"Now that I think about it, Erica's right." Amanda pushed her plate aside. "If he meant us physical harm, he'd corner us here, not next door."

Wendy slumped back. "I still think we need to call Chris."

"We don't need to bother him until we find out what's going on."

The back door swung open, followed by footsteps racing across the kitchen floor. Millie dashed in and set a pistol on the table. "I'm ready."

Wendy stared wide-eyed. "Is that gun loaded?"

"I'm an old lady who lives alone with two cats. Of course, it's loaded, and I know how to shoot."

Amanda shook her head. "There's no way we're taking a firearm to a meeting."

"Well, then—" Millie pulled out a chair. "We have to come up with some sort of plan."

Erica laced her fingers. "After we hear what Mr. Jones wants, the four of us will figure out our next move. For now we need to decide how to approach the meeting."

"I agree." Amanda tapped the inn's phone. "Let's assume he has a legitimate issue—"

"Are you serious?" Millie's eyes narrowed. "Do you actually believe that an ambulance-chasing lawyer isn't up to no good?"

"What I do or don't believe is irrelevant."

"You're Awesam's president. Do you have any idea what a lawsuit would do to our reputation?"

Amanda's brows raised. "Have you heard of innocent until proven guilty?"

Millie scoffed, "You're not a lawyer."

"Give it a break, you two." A knot gripped Erica's gut. "Arguing among ourselves isn't helping the situation."

Millie crossed her arms and tapped her biceps. "It burns my buns knowing that some out-of-towner thinks he can mess with my friends."

Amanda heaved a heavy sigh. "Erica's right. We need to stop bickering and decide which one of us will take the lead."

"Only one choice makes sense." Wendy turned toward Erica. "Amanda's too quick to judge. I'm way too emotional, and our chef wants to go in packing. You're the only partner who's level-headed enough to keep the meeting from spinning out of control."

As much as she wanted to object, Erica had to admit Wendy made sense. "All right, here's what we need to do." After laying out a plan and carrying the plates to the kitchen, the foursome headed to the foyer and stopped long enough for Amanda to grab a pad of paper and a pen from the desk. Outside, they headed across the side yard and up the sidewalk to the front porch. Grateful they hadn't encountered any guests, Erica led her team straight to the dining room and pulled the double doors closed. They sat side by side facing the entrance.

Amanda set the pad of paper on the table, her pen at the ready.

Wendy chewed her fingernail.

Millie laced her fingers and tapped her thumbs. "I still think I should've brought my gun."

Three minutes passed.

"Maybe they changed their minds," whispered Wendy.

Amanda shook her head. "They want to make us squirm."

"Well, their plan's working."

Footsteps. The doors opened.

Erica pulled in a deep breath, then forced a smile and stood. "Mr. and Mrs. Jones, please close the door and have a seat."

He seated his wife then pulled out a chair and crossed his arms on the table. "Thank you for meeting with us."

As if we had a choice. Erica mirrored the man's posture. "What can we do for you?"

He glanced around the room. "Congratulations on transforming Eleanor Harrington's home into a profitable business."

Was he trying to determine if they had deep pockets? "The inn hasn't been open long enough to realize any sort of profit. We hope you're enjoying your stay."

"These past few days have been more productive than we expected."

What was he insinuating? "Blue Ridge has a lot to offer you and your lovely wife."

"I'm not here as Katherine's husband, but as her attorney."

Erica forced herself to maintain a semblance of composure. "Why does your wife need an attorney?"

"To claim her rights." He removed a folded document from his jacket pocket and pushed it across the table.

Sweat erupted on the back of Erica's neck as she unfolded and read the single sheet of paper. "Thank you for bringing this to our attention, Mr. Jones." Hoping her partners would remain calm and quiet until she had a chance to tell them what the document contained, she lifted off her seat. "We'll contact our attorney and call you to arrange another meeting. In the meantime, please enjoy your evening and close the doors as you leave." The moment their guests exited, Erica turned toward Wendy. "Do you want me to call Chris?"

She nodded, then swiped her finger across her phone and handed it over.

Erica pressed the number and put the call on speaker. Chris answered. She described what had just happened.

"I'll meet you at your house in twenty minutes. In the meantime, don't have any contact with either Mr. or Mrs. Jones." Chris ended the call.

Millie's shoulders slumped. "This is all my fault."

Amanda touched their chef's arm. "No one is to blame other than a greedy woman and her lawyer husband."

"I wouldn't blame you if you fired me."

"And lose the best chef in Blue Ridge? Not a chance."

Erica scooted to the door and peeked out. "The coast is clear." She led the way through the living room and out the front door. An hour after Chris arrived, she texted a message to Robert Jones. Thirty seconds later he replied. "They agreed to meet us at noon tomorrow."

"Good." Chris faced Millie. "If they show up for breakfast tomorrow morning, will you be able to act as if tonight's meeting never took place?"

"You can count on my discretion, and I'll leave my gun at home."

He chuckled. "Good decision. I'll see you tomorrow. And don't worry, we have the law on our side." Their attorney scooped the document off the table and headed to the front door.

"I don't know about you ladies, but it's close to my bedtime. I'll meet you here after breakfast." Millie reached for her pistol, then strode to the kitchen and out the back door.

"I'm beyond exhausted." Wendy yawned as she rose and headed straight to her room.

Erica puffed her cheeks and blew out a stream of air. "Three days as innkeepers and we already need a lawyer."

"At least we didn't choose a boring business."

"Right now, I'd take a whole lot of boring."

Chapter 29

The moment Wendy closed her bedroom door, the jumble of emotions playing havoc with her heart and mind erupted in a rush of tears. At least she could blame the momentary loss of control on raging hormones. She swiped her fingers across her cheeks then peeled out of her clothes and applied cocoa-butter lotion to her swollen belly. How long would it take to fit back into her normal clothes after her little guy was born? Hopefully not long since she was tired of her limited maternity wardrobe and couldn't afford any shopping trips for a while.

Wendy slipped into pajamas, dropped onto her bed, and leaned against her headboard. Grateful her arms could still reach around her baby bulge, she propped her laptop on her knees and opened online sudoku. Six months ago she'd had no idea she would enjoy a game involving numbers. Now it was her go-to diversion. Before she finished a puzzle, heavy eyelids forced her to set her laptop on the nightstand and turn out the light. The last mental image floating through her head before she drifted to sleep was Chris sitting across the table from her—so near and yet so far away.

Following a morning laced with dreaded anticipation, Wendy, Erica, Amanda, and Millie sat across the table from Katherine and Robert Jones in the Armstrong Law Office conference room. Millie's chocolate chip cookies seemed out of place beside bottles of water standing at attention between the two parties. Following their lawyer's advice, the four of them remained silent and avoided eye contact with their adversaries while waiting for Chris to join them. Wendy squirmed. Hopefully, she'd manage to sit through the meeting without a bladder emergency sending her racing from the room.

The door swung open. Chris, dressed in a dark suit and red tie, entered and placed a folder on the table. "Thank you for agreeing to meet us here." He lowered onto the seat of authority at the end of the table. "My name is Christopher Armstrong. I represent Hilltop Inn's owners. We'll begin by listening to what your client wants, Mr. Jones."

The man squared his shoulders and lifted his chin as if he owned the room. "Have you read the copy of the document I left with your clients, Mr. Armstrong?"

"I have."

"Then I assume you're also aware of the facts that support our case."

"What alleged facts are you referring to?"

"First, none of your clients were legally married to Gunter Benson, meaning they have no legal claim to anything he owns. Second, the man is a convicted criminal and a liar, which calls into question how he came into possession of deeds to the Harrington properties. Third, there is no record of Mrs. Harrington ever preparing a last will and testament. Based on those three facts, we claim that as her only living relative, Katherine Jones is the rightful heir to her grandmother's property. We understand and are sensitive to the current owners' predicament. Therefore, once my client takes possession, she will reimburse your clients for the money they paid to satisfy delinquent taxes. She will also allow them to live in the small house rent free until they are able to find other accommodations."

Wendy's eyes darted from Robert's smug expression to Katherine's fingers tugging on her shirt collar. Had they known all those details before they checked into Eleanor Harrington's bedroom?

Chris's expression remained neutral. "Before I respond, does Mrs. Jones have any comments to add?"

"She does not."

"Do you have any other facts to present on behalf of your client?"

Mr. Jones hesitated, as if deciding how to respond. "Not at this time."

"All right." Chris opened the folder and removed a single sheet of paper. "While none of my clients were married to the referenced gentleman, this is the only marriage relevant in this situation." Chris placed the paper on the table. "It's a legal copy of Eleanor Harrington and Gunter Benson's marriage license."

Robert Jones focused on the document, then pushed it away.

"In regard to Mr. Benson's right to the aforementioned property—" Chris removed a stapled document. "This is Eleanor Harrington's original will. If you'll note, she named her legal second husband as the sole heir to all of her property, which she had legally inherited from her deceased first husband. She stipulated should Mr. Benson precede her in death, all of her properties were to be sold and the money divided among the charities she listed on the attached page. In addition, she added a clause giving Mr. Benson the authority to use the properties in whatever manner he chose."

Katherine appeared to read the will alongside her husband as he laser focused on every page. Wendy fidgeted. Was the personal injury lawyer looking for something to discredit the will? Chris appeared relaxed, confident there was nothing to find.

When Mr. Jones finished reading, he flipped back to the first page and pushed the document aside as if dismissing it as irrelevant.

Chris removed two more papers. "These are deeds to Mrs. Harrington's properties, which you will see were legally transferred to Wendy Thomason, Erica Nelson, and Amanda Smith, and witnessed by me."

Mr. Jones perused both documents before returning them.

Chris handed over a fifth sheet of paper. "That is the document from the county tax office showing my clients paid the back taxes in full and were therefore granted legal possession." He crossed his arms on the table. "While I understand your client's interest in her maternal grandmother, she holds no legal standing to claim ownership of either the Hillside Inn or the ranch house."

Katherine's eyes remained downcast while her husband faced Chris. "I will file a civil suit on behalf of my client contesting the will based on the lack of mental capacity of an old woman duped by a man who married her for her money, and thus render her will null and void."

Chris stood. "Thank you for coming, I'll show you out."

"No need." Robert and Katherine Jones exited the office.

Chris closed the door before returning to his seat.

Amanda's eyes widened. "How long have you had all those documents?"

"Since the Las Vegas trial. I assumed sooner or later they'd come in handy."

"Smart assumption." Amanda leaned forward. "Given Gunter's history as a con artist, does Katherine Jones have a case?"

"Other than appealing to a jury or a judge's emotion, proving intent to defraud a woman who is no longer living is difficult at best."

"But not impossible."

"It's highly unlikely."

Erica uncapped a bottle of water. "It seemed to me that this whole shenanigan is Mr. Jones's idea."

"Which isn't surprising, given his wife is married to a personal-injury lawyer," added Amanda.

Millie faced Chris. "Would it help if I showed Katherine what Eleanor wrote about her mother?"

"Where are those journals?"

"At my house."

"Keep them safe. We can't allow either party to hear about or read any of Eleanor Harrington's private thoughts." Chris slid the documents in the folder. "When are Mr. and Mrs. Jones checking out?"

"Tomorrow," Erica and Amanda responded in unison.

Wendy reached for a bottle of water. "What do we do now?"

"Wait for their next move." Chris's eyes met Wendy's. "If Robert Jones is as smart as he thinks he is, he'll realize that winning a civil suit against us isn't worth his time and effort, and move on to his next case."

"You mean victim." Amanda's tone screamed of contempt.

"No kidding." Millie's focus shifted to their attorney. "Now that we know what's going on, I want to treat everyone to lunch, including you, Chris."

Wendy's muscles tensed. Would he accept or would he come up with some sort of excuse to decline the invitation?

"Thank you, Millie." Chris closed the folder. "However, my afternoon schedule is full. So, you ladies enjoy lunch, and don't worry. I've got this." He stood and carried the documents out of the room.

The tension gripping Wendy's muscles relaxed for a moment, then returned. What would happen if Robert Jones moved forward with a civil suit? What was the real reason Chris declined Millie's invitation?

Chapter 30

An hour after leaving the law office, Millie climbed into the truck's back seat. Treating her friends to lunch failed to alleviate the tension gripping her chest. If she hadn't submitted Eleanor's DNA to the ancestry database, Katherine Jones would never have discovered her grandmother's identity and threatened a lawsuit. She glanced sideways at Wendy sitting behind Amanda. Based on her demeanor during the meeting, it was obvious her relationship with Chris still suffered from a serious roadblock. When all this hullabaloo died down, she'd find out why.

Millie turned toward the side window and focused on the passing scenery during the remainder of the ride home. They all dreaded running into Katherine and Robert Jones and keeping their composure. At least Erica, and not Amanda, was scheduled to check in new arrivals this afternoon. When they turned onto their street, Millie leaned forward. "You don't need to take me home. I'll walk from your house."

"All right." Amanda eased up the driveway and parked in the carport beside Abby's car.

Millie drew in a deep breath. Somehow, she had to make amends for bringing more trouble into her partners' lives. She stepped onto the concrete and waited for Awesam's CEO to climb from the front passenger seat. "Do you need help at the inn this afternoon?"

Erica closed her door. "Thanks for asking, but no. I'll see you tomorrow morning." She turned and headed to the back door.

Millie gripped her purse and made her way to the street. Her posture hunched as she turned toward her house and trudged past the inn. Had the Jones couple returned, or were they still in town attempting to dredge up more evidence against her friends? Millie stepped up her pace.

The moment she stepped onto her driveway, she stopped dead in her tracks and gawked at the woman sitting on one of her front porch rocking chairs. Should she pretend she hadn't noticed and walk back to the ranch house? That was a coward's move, and she was no coward. Millie squared her shoulders and marched straight to the sidewalk fronting her home. Her calico cat perched on the front windowsill guarding her little kingdom from intruders. She stepped onto the porch and breathed deeply to slow her pounding pulse. "After you threatened my partners, I'm more than a little surprised you have the nerve to show up at my house."

Katherine Jones stared straight ahead. "I have a lot of questions."

"You should have asked them back in our lawyer's office."

"I couldn't."

Millie settled in the second rocker. "Why not?"

"Because they're about my grandmother."

"So is your husband's insane lawsuit."

"You don't understand."

Millie peered at the woman's profile. Had Katherine pegged her as an easy mark to fish for information to use against her friends? "Then why don't you try explaining?"

She hesitated.

Millie crossed her arms. "Do you plan to talk or keep me guessing?"

Katherine sneaked a quick glance at Millie. "Trying to steal the inn from your friends was my husband's idea, not mine."

Millie's eyes widened. Was it possible Katherine Jones was struggling with a guilty conscience? She uncrossed her arms. "If you think you're going to wheedle information out of me you can use to win a lawsuit—"

"I don't." The young woman faced Millie, her eyes pleading. "I just want to know more about my grandmother."

"Such as?"

"To begin with, what kind of person was she?"

That seemed a safe enough subject. "Eleanor Harrington was the kindest woman I have ever met."

"Kind in what ways?"

"She treated everyone with respect. I never heard her say an unkind word about anyone. And she was generous."

"I imagine she had a lot of friends."

"She did, but every week she hosted a dinner party for her favorites. My husband and I were always among her guests."

Katherine set her rocking chair in motion. "Did you spend a lot of time with her?"

"Nearly every day while they were in town. We took a lot of long walks together. I taught her how to cook."

"When did she stop coming to Blue Ridge?"

Millie hesitated. Could Katherine use that information against her partners?

"I understand if you don't want to answer. Can you at least tell me about my grandfather?"

Another safe subject. "He was also friendly, and he had a good sense of humor. He played a lot of golf, and he adored Eleanor."

Katherine fingered her wedding ring. "My mother favored her."

Millie's brow pinched. "Why did you use the past tense?"

"Mom passed away last November. Pancreatic cancer."

"I'm so sorry."

"I still miss her."

"Are you close to your father?"

"Yes, but not as close as I was to Mom." Katherine fell silent for a long moment. "Even though she'd known she was adopted almost her entire life, Mom never expressed any interest in finding her birth parents. Neither did I until a few weeks ago when Robert suggested I research them. Actually, it was more of an order than a suggestion."

Not surprising. "Is your husband interested in genealogy?"

"Only when the results lead to lucrative lawsuits."

Millie swallowed the cutting remark threatening to roll off her tongue. Time to change the subject. A chipmunk skittered across the sidewalk and disappeared under a bush. "Squirrels and chipmunks are cute but pesky little critters."

Katherine stopped rocking. "Did my grandmother tell you she'd given her daughter up for adoption?"

"Not one time during our long conversations did she ever mention having a child." At least she hadn't been forced to fib.

"I suppose she had a good reason for giving her away."

Millie struggled to keep the truth from spilling out. "Are your mother's adoptive parents good people?"

"The best. They loved Mom as much as they loved their natural child." Katherine resumed rocking. "Robert and I married during his last year in law school. I was proud he'd chosen to study law, but I had no idea he'd become a personal-injury attorney."

"Do you not approve of his practice?"

"People who suffer injury or mistreatment deserve a good defense, and he's a good lawyer. But too often he hurts innocent people, including you and your friends."

Millie's heart ached for the young woman sitting beside her. Somehow, she had to help her understand how much Eleanor loved her daughter without revealing what she'd written in her private journal. "Your sincerity reminds me of your grandmother. I know without a doubt that she would have been proud to call you her granddaughter."

"I'm sorry I never had the chance to know her."

"Do you want to come in for a while? I have fresh-baked cookies."

"I would." Katherine pulled her phone from her pocket and peered at the screen. "Except my husband is on the way back to the inn, and he doesn't know I'm here." She stilled her rocker and rose. "Thank you for telling me about my grandparents."

Millie stood. "Will I see you at breakfast tomorrow?"

Their eyes met. "I don't know."

Millie clasped the young woman's hand. "If we don't see each other again, I wish you all the best."

Katherine's eyes watered as she squeezed Millie's hand. "My grandmother was blessed to have you as a friend." She pulled away and dashed off the porch.

A lump formed in Millie's throat as her eyes followed Eleanor's granddaughter rushing across the driveway and the inn's front lawn. Would Katherine tell her husband about the visit or keep him in the dark? Either way, Millie had a duty to fulfill.

She headed inside and settled on the green velvet sofa facing the fireplace in her antique-filled living room. Her calico springing onto her lap triggered memories of the first day she'd met Wendy and Erica. Little did she know at that time the three mysterious strangers who had occupied Eleanor's properties would become her second-best friends. If she told them about Katherine's surprise visit, would they suspect she had revealed too much information?

Millie shooed her cat off her lap, then ambled to the kitchen and removed a bottle of water from the refrigerator. Following a half hour of debating her next move, she came to one undeniable conclusion. Although she'd avoided sharing anything suspect with Katherine, the three women who had welcomed her into their world deserved to know the truth. Millie lifted her phone off the ornate coffee table with a glass inlay and pressed a number.

Amanda answered.

"Something happened you need to know about."

Chapter 31

Amanda's throat constricted as she tossed her phone on the sofa beside her. "I can't believe Millie allowed our adversary to finagle information she and her lawyer husband can use against us."

Wendy pulled her feet off the coffee table. "How could Millie and Eleanor taking long walks and Warren playing golf possibly hurt us?"

"We don't know what other seemingly innocent little details Millie let slip out."

Wendy shrugged. "If you ask me, Katherine is as much a victim of her husband's greed as the three of us are."

Amanda plucked a dog hair off the sofa. "Logic dictates otherwise."

"Except emotion easily overrules logic."

"You would know."

Wendy glared at her. "What are you implying?"

"Nothing."

"You think I made a mistake breaking up with Chris, don't you?"

"That's not what I said."

"But that's what you meant."

She could tell Wendy about her conversation with their attorney at Mountain Mama's, but she had promised to keep that meeting private, and she didn't break promises. "Whatever happened between you and Chris is your business, not mine. However, if you ever want to talk about it, I'll listen."

Wendy folded her arms across her belly. "Gunter's interference in my life was the only reason I told him we needed a break, but then I realized Chris has never told me he loved me."

Amanda peered at their CFO's profile. What had Chris said about Wendy at Mountain Mama's? That he cared for her, not that he loved her. "A lot of men have a difficult time expressing their emotions."

"Are you suddenly an expert on male behavior?"

"I'm just saying sometimes things aren't what they seem."

"Such as Katherine's confession to Millie?" Wendy's tone mocked.

"That's not a valid comparison."

"The fact that Chris hasn't invited me to dinner or even bothered to call me proves I'm nothing more than his friend and client."

"You know he's never sent us a bill for his legal services."

"Because he feels sorry for us. I want to marry a man who loves me with all his heart, not one who feels obligated to rescue me from single motherhood. Which is why it's best for both Chris and me to move on with our lives."

Maybe she was right. Amanda reached across the cushion and touched Wendy's arm. "I respect your decision."

Wendy's eyes met hers. "Thank you for finally admitting I made the right move. Now, about Katherine's conversation with Millie. Unless we hear otherwise, we should assume she was honest about her intentions."

"I suppose that makes sense."

Wendy's eyes narrowed. "But you're skeptical."

"More like cautious."

Erica meandered in from the carport and settled on a club chair.

Amanda crossed her leg over her knee. "I assume our new arrivals are all checked in."

"They are." Erica leaned forward. "Something odd happened while I was showing one of the couples the den. Katherine rushed in from the front then raced to the Rainbow Suite as if she was running away from something. A couple of minutes later, her husband walked in from the backyard. What do you suppose was going on?"

"There's a logical explanation." Amanda relayed Katherine's conversation with Millie.

"Talk about an unexpected twist." Erica pulled the ringing phone from her pocket. "Someone's calling from the inn." She swiped her finger across the screen and pressed the phone to her ear. "Hello?" She listened. "Hold on." Erica tapped the screen then lowered the phone. "Katherine and Robert Jones want to meet with the four of us."

Amanda held up her open palm. "No way we're spending one second with those two unless our attorney's present."

"Understood." Erica tapped the screen again and raised the phone to her ear. "I'll call you back after I talk to my partners." She ended the call.

Amanda scooted to the dining room table. She grabbed her phone then called Chris and relayed everything that had happened following lunch.

He responded, "All right."

Amanda set her phone down. "Call Katherine and tell her we'll meet them here at six tonight while I call Millie."

The afternoon seemed to move at a snail's pace as the four women conjured up all sorts of opinions about the Jones' objective. By the time their attorney arrived, one could slice through the tension with a butter knife.

Chris gathered the women around the table. "When Mr. and Mrs. Jones arrive, I'll let them in and take control of the meeting."

Amanda clicked her fingernails on the table. "What do you suppose they're up to?"

"I have my suspicions." Chris laid a folder on the table. "However, the jury's out until we hear what they have to say." He shot Millie a bemused look. "You're not armed, are you?"

"With a gun? No. But if Katherine turns against me or my friends, I'll give her a piece of my mind."

"Only when and if I give you the go-ahead."

"Hmph."

The doorbell rang.

Amanda's muscles tensed.

Chris stood. "You ladies sit tight." He headed straight to the foyer then returned and pointed to the two empty chairs. "Please."

Unlike their arrival at Chris's office, Robert pulled out a chair for his wife before taking his seat.

Chris leaned forward and crossed his arms on the table. "What's on your mind?"

Katherine laced her fingers. "First, I want to assure you that my husband is an excellent attorney who works hard to seek justice for his clients." She paused, then eyed her husband as if granting him permission to speak.

Amanda's eyes narrowed. Was she massaging Robert's ego, or preparing to drop a bomb?

Robert mirrored Chris's posture. "Some in the law profession refer to personal-injury attorneys as ambulance chasers, which in most cases is an illegitimate description. While I'm committed to securing well-deserved and lucrative settlements for victims, every once in a while, my zeal sends me down the wrong path."

"Which is why we wanted to meet with you." Katherine laced her fingers on the table. "In addition to accepting the fact that I have no claim on my grandmother's properties, I have no desire to disrespect her or her wishes."

"What my wife is trying to say is we will not file a civil suit."

"You've made a wise decision, Mr. and Mrs. Jones." Chris removed a pen from his pocket and a sheet of paper from the folder. He pushed both across the table. "Now all we need is your signatures."

Katherine's husband chuckled as he read the document. "You ladies hired a smart attorney." He signed, then handed the pen to his wife.

She added her signature before pushing the paper back toward Chris and turning toward Millie. "Thank you for telling me about my grandparents. I want to take a picture of them home with me, if you have one to spare."

"I'll give you one at breakfast tomorrow morning." Millie eyed Chris. "Do I have permission to share something important with Eleanor's granddaughter?"

He glanced at the document then slid it back into the folder. "Go ahead."

Amanda pressed her lips into a fine line. Was Millie seconds from revealing Eleanor's private thoughts?

Millie reached for Katherine's hand. "Even though your grandmother never talked about her daughter, I know beyond the shadow of a doubt that she would never have given her up for adoption if she hadn't loved her with all her heart and wanted her to have an amazing life. While they never met here on earth, your mother and grandmother are strolling arm in arm in their eternal home."

Tears welled and tracked down Katherine's face. "Your kind words mean more to me than you can possibly imagine."

Wendy sniffled then swiped her fingers across her own cheeks.

Erica's eyes reddened.

Amanda pressed her palm to her chest. "That was beautiful, Millie."

Chris smiled. "Well said."

Robert Jones cleared his throat as he lifted off his chair. "My wife and I have dinner reservations downtown."

Katherine hugged Millie. "I'll see you tomorrow."

After escorting the couple to the front door, Chris returned. "Everything turned out for the best."

Amanda tapped her finger on the folder. "What did you have them sign?"

"An agreement to never bring a civil or criminal case against the Awesam company or any of the partners."

"Wow. You really are a smart attorney."

"Wisdom comes with experience." Chris lifted the folder off the table. "The case of Katherine Jones versus Awesam has officially come to an end." He nodded toward Amanda. "Walk me to the door."

"All right." They stepped out to the porch. "Is something wrong?"

His eyebrows drew together, and for once he seemed uncertain. "Everything's fine. I just want to know how Wendy's holding up under all the pressure."

What pressure was he referring to? "As well as the rest of us."

"Has she named her baby?"

"Not yet."

"I'll email a copy of the Jones' agreement to you."

"Thank you. One of these days, you need to charge us for your services."

Chris grinned. "I imagine I'll have plenty of future opportunity to bill you."

"I suspect you will."

He chuckled. "With that, I'll take my leave."

When Amanda returned to the den, Wendy peered at her. "What did Chris say?"

"He wanted to make sure we're all okay."

Millie faced Amanda. "In my opinion, Ms. President, this is the perfect time to make me an official partner with full voting privileges."

Amanda chuckled. "You drive a hard bargain, Chef Mildred."

Millie's brows raised. "Is that a yes?"

"Considering your role in neutralizing the Katherine and Robert drama—" Amanda peered at her partners, then extended her hand. "Welcome aboard, voting partner."

Millie's face beamed as she clasped Amanda's hand. "I promise I won't let you down."

Chapter 32

Wearied from her client's incessant stories about her seven amazing grandchildren during the deep-tissue massage, Erica escaped to her office and dropped onto her desk chair. At least the guest had rewarded her patience with a generous tip. She uncapped a bottle of water. After taking a long drink, she pulled up the inn's website to confirm her next scheduled appointment—a neck and shoulder massage tomorrow morning with her first male client. Erica closed her laptop then pocketed her phone, locked her office, and headed to her second afternoon chore.

Inside the inn, the whirring vacuum cleaner sent her straight to the living room. Erica approached Amanda.

Her partner pressed the machine's off switch. "Hey."

Erica picked up a piece the vacuum had overlooked. "When I agreed to relieve Abby for the rest of the week, I didn't expect you to pitch in."

"As soon as I discovered your one o'clock appointment was with our Chatty-Cathy guest, I figured you'd be flat worn out."

"How'd you know she'd talked a blue streak?"

"Millie told me the woman barely stopped talking long enough to take a bite of breakfast. At least she showed up a half hour after most of the other guests had already started eating. Have you heard from Abby?"

Erica nodded. "She and her girlfriends arrived in Nashville safe and sound. Do you want me to take over vacuuming duties?"

"I'm on a roll, so you start with the guest suites."

"All right, and thanks for your help."

Amanda winked. "We're family. That's what we do."

Erica gathered the cleaning supplies from the laundry room then climbed the back stairs and unlocked the first door on the left. She entered the Bluebell Suite and pulled the sheets off the bed. In a couple of hours, new guests would check into this room and enjoy their first experience at Hilltop Inn.

Her phone rang. Should she ignore it? Not as long as her daughter was out of town. Erica's pulse accelerated as she pulled the phone from her pocket and eyed Brad's name. She tapped the screen and pressed the phone to her ear. "Hey."

"It's Brad."

"I know."

"I'm sorry for canceling dinner Saturday."

"You don't need to apologize. Family always comes first. Did you enjoy your son's visit?"

"My son *and* his girlfriend. She's a champion amateur golfer, so we played every day."

A golfing family. "Sounds fun."

"Except when she outscored us twice and made us eat a little humble pie. Anyway, are you free for dinner tomorrow night?"

Erica ambled to the window and peered out at Millie's backyard masterpiece. If she said yes, would she expose her heart to disappointment? On the other hand, if she turned him down—

Brad chuckled. "I didn't realize I asked such a difficult question."

"Sorry." Erica blinked. "Abby and her friends are spending three days in Nashville, so I'm a little preoccupied."

"They're good kids. I'm sure they'll have a blast and behave themselves. Back to my question about Friday."

Erica's heart overruled her mind. "I'm available."

"Good. How about six?"

"Perfect. I'll see you then." A warm sensation washed over Erica as she slid her phone back into her pocket. At the very least, she and Brad could become good friends. She twirled around and hummed while continuing to prepare the upstairs suites for new arrivals.

With Amanda pitching in to help, they finished housekeeping duties in record time. After folding the freshly laundered sheets and stacking them in the upstairs linen closet, Erica followed Awesam's president down the front staircase. "Since you helped me, I'll stay and help check in new arrivals."

Amanda stopped at the bottom step. "While we're waiting, we need to talk about Nancy's Nuggets."

"The podcaster called you again, didn't she?"

Amanda nodded. "Two hours ago. She wants an answer today." The front doorbell rang. Amanda glanced at her watch. "Either our first check-in is early, or one of our guests left without their key." She pulled the door open. "Welcome to Hilltop Inn and Spa. I hope you had a pleasant trip."

Erica tuned out the conversation and mentally teetered between the pros and cons of accepting Nancy's offer. By the time Amanda escorted the last arriving couple to their suite and returned to the desk, Erica had come to the one conclusion that seemed to make the most sense.

"Everyone's all settled in, which means we're off duty until a guest calls." Amanda closed the guestbook. "About Nancy's Nuggets."

"In my opinion it's too big a risk. Especially since we haven't heard anything new from Gunter."

"I agree. Now all you have to do is convince our Chief Financial Officer."

"Why me?"

"Because you're in charge of strategic direction."

Erica shot Awesam's president a quizzical look as they walked out of the inn. "How exactly does a podcast invitation qualify as 'direction'?"

"It doesn't." Amanda linked arms with her. "But it's definitely strategic."

"All right. But only since you helped me with housekeeping chores." They strode across the yards to the kitchen door. Inside the den, Wendy peered up at them, then aimed the remote and turned off the television. Erica sat on the sofa and eyed an envelope lying on the cushion between her and their CFO. "We're all finished next door."

"Another letter came in today's mail."

Erica's eyes widened. "From Gunter?"

Wendy shook her head. "From that cocktail waitress."

Amanda settled on a club chair. "Have you read it?"

"That's how I know she sent it."

Erica exchanged a glance with Amanda, then reached for the envelope. "Do you mind if I read it aloud?"

Wendy shrugged. "Go ahead."

"All right." Erica removed and unfolded the single sheet of paper. "'*Dear Wendy, Erica, and Amanda. After Gunter dictated that last letter, he asked me to keep up with everything going on in Blue Ridge. I felt bad that he was behind bars for a crime he said he didn't commit, and I wanted to help him. So, I subscribed to the town's newspaper. That's how I came across that article Gail Weston wrote about you ladies. Gunter was furious when I read it to him. I've always known him as a charming, likable guy who tipped big. Which is why I was shocked when he accused me of betraying his trust. When*

I tried to defend myself, the hatred in his angry eyes frightened me. That's when I realized I had been used, and that he is guilty of murder.'

Wendy pressed her hand to her belly. "Prison is turning Gunter into a monster."

When Amanda opened her mouth, Erica feared their president was seconds from uttering a remark she'd regret, so she jabbed her palm toward her.

Amanda's lips pressed tight.

Relieved their CFO's eyes seemed laser focused on her fingernails, Erica continued reading. "'*Gunter's reaction and accusations are the reasons I'm writing, this time on my own. Although you probably already suspect, I assure you that he won't stop trying to intimidate you and steal everything you've accomplished. He knows a lot of Las Vegas cocktail waitresses, so he'll find another naïve woman to do his bidding.*

"'*I'm sorry for playing even a small role in his deception. Based on what I read in that article, you ladies are strong and smart enough to keep him from hurting you any more than he already has. Just stay vigilant and don't trust him.'*"

"She signed her first name." Erica laid the letter on the cushion. "We need to contact Chris—"

"I already called him." Wendy folded the letter and slid it back into the envelope. "He'll pick it up tonight."

Amanda crossed her leg over her knee. "When we walked in a few minutes ago, we were prepared to convince you to go along with our decision to decline that podcast interview."

"And now?"

"It's obvious one article isn't enough to counter Gunter's next move."

Erica slumped back. "I didn't consider a live interview worth the risk. Now I'm convinced that the more we tell our story, the less chance Gunter will have to con someone into spewing lies."

Wendy snapped her fingers. "Which is exactly why I decided we should accept Nancy's offer. Besides, the three of us are smart enough to handle whatever questions she fires at us." Wendy turned toward Amanda. "Especially if we go along with your idea and ask Millie to conduct a mock interview with us."

"Well then, it seems we've made a decision. Do you want to call Nancy and give her the news?"

"I already did."

Amanda stared wide-eyed at Wendy, then burst out laughing. "You assumed once we read that letter we'd change our minds, didn't you?"

"I knew *you* would." Wendy faced Erica. "And I was pretty sure we'd talk you into going along with us."

"You're right. So, when's our interview?"

"Friday afternoon at one."

"Which means our new voting partner's first official duty will be to play the role of Nancy the podcaster." The doorbell rang. Erica's eyes widened. "Did you also call Millie?"

Wendy shook her head. "Just Chris and Nancy."

Another ring.

Amanda uncrossed her legs. "One of us needs to find out who's ringing our bell."

Erica stood. "I'll go." She scooted to the foyer, opened the door, and faced two teenaged girls. The shorter teen looked vaguely familiar. "Can I help you?"

"Um..." The brown-haired girl fingered her bracelet. "Does Wendy Thomason live here?"

"She does."

"Is it okay if we talk to her?"

Erica hesitated. They seemed harmless enough. "All right. Come with me." She led them to the den. "You have visitors, Wendy."

"Who—" Their CFO's jaw went slack as she stood and looked at her visitors.

Amanda bolted to her feet and gawked at the teenagers as if they were from another planet.

Erica's gaze shifted from her partners to the visitors. Who were these girls, and how did they know Wendy?

Chapter 33

The memory of the pretty young girl breezing into the foyer and glancing into the living room before scurrying up the stairs and out of sight flashed through Wendy's brain at warp speed rendering her momentarily speechless. She swallowed the lump taking up residence in her throat. How was this girl showing up at her home even possible?

Awesam's president cleared her throat. "I'm Amanda, and these are my partners, Erica and Wendy." She aimed her palm toward the pair of club chairs facing the sofa. "Why don't you girls have a seat and introduce yourselves."

They hesitated for a moment, then complied. The girl with long brown hair crossed then uncrossed her legs. "I'm Kayla and she's Harper. She's my only friend who has a driver's license."

Wendy struggled to find her voice. "How did you find me?"

"I saw your address on the envelope."

Erica's brow pinched. "What envelope?"

"The one addressed to Wendy Thomason."

"Oh my gosh." Erica dropped beside Awesam's CFO, her eyes wide as if the light had suddenly dawned. "You're the girl in the picture Cynthia sent to her, aren't you?"

Kayla nodded. "If Mom had remembered that day was an early-release school day, she wouldn't have left the letter on the kitchen counter. She forgets a lot of stuff."

Wendy's back stiffened. *Including Cynthia's first-born child.* She stared at the teenager's blue eyes—the one feature they had in common. "Curiosity isn't the reason you drove all this way, is it?"

"Uh-uh." Kayla slumped back. "When I first read Mom's letter, I thought maybe you were a friend from her past. Until I remembered that day I saw you and Amanda sitting in our living room." Kayla's eyelids lowered. "When I came downstairs after you left, Mom was staring out the window. Her eyes were all red and teary. She told me an eyelash made her eyes water, but I knew something had upset her." A pained expression clouded Kayla's features. "She wrote you that note because she's your mother, isn't she?"

If she denied the truth, would she protect her half-sister? After coming all this way, she deserved honesty. "She is. Does your mother know you read her letter?"

Kayla shook her head.

"She doesn't know you're here either, does she?"

"No. Can we talk? Just you and me?"

Erica stood and motioned to Harper. "Let's leave these two alone for a few minutes. Why don't you come to the kitchen with Amanda and me and help us taste test the fresh baked cookies our chef brought over this morning."

Harper eyed her friend.

Kayla nodded. "Go ahead. It's okay."

After Erica, Amanda, and Harper strode from the den, Wendy patted the cushion beside her. "It'll be easier for us to talk privately if you come sit beside me."

The teenager hesitated, then ambled over.

Wendy stretched her arm across the back of the sofa—her fingers inches from the young girl's shoulders. "What's on your mind?"

Kayla picked at her fingernail. "Before you came to our house, how old were you the last time you saw my mother?"

Should she tell her? Why not? She already knew part of the story "I was five."

Kayla remained silent for a long moment while staring into space. "Do you know why she abandoned you?" Her voice quivered.

Wendy's heart ached for the young girl. How could she reveal the past without destroying Kayla's relationship with her mother? "Wait here a minute." Wendy dashed to her room. Moments later she returned clutching a book to her chest. "Here's what I know." She dropped onto the sofa. "Cynthia was a teenager when she found out she was expecting me. Even though she had choices, she was too good a person to end the pregnancy. After I was born, she wore herself out working two jobs and did the best she could to take care of the two of us."

Wendy turned toward her half-sister. "My mother wanted me to have a better life than she could give me." She handed Kayla *Sugar Snow*. "That's why she gave me this gift a few days before she left me with a neighbor."

Kayla fingered the picture of the log cabin and snow-covered ground. "If she wanted you to have a better life, why didn't she take you back after she married my dad?"

Conflicting thoughts collided in Wendy's head. She could continue to tell the truth about the woman who'd left her to grow up in seven different foster homes, or... Wendy closed her eyes and swallowed the truth threatening to roll off her tongue. *Forgive me for telling a lie.* She opened her eyes.

Kayla stared at her.

"You mother...my mother tried to find me, but a nice foster family had taken me in and moved away. After a while she gave up and moved on with her life."

Kayla's brow pinched. "I don't understand why she didn't tell us about you after you found her."

Fudging the truth didn't come easy. "Mothers do what they believe is best for their children. Besides, I have a good life here with my own family."

Kayla laid the book on the cushion between them. "Should I tell Mom I found out about you or keep it a secret?"

Wendy caught her bottom lip between her teeth. The sister she hadn't known existed a few months ago was asking for her advice. "You love your mother, don't you?"

"She's kind of clueless sometimes—"

"All teenagers think their parents are clueless."

"I suppose you're right...but yes, I love her."

"Which is why you should respect her wishes." Wendy reached across the cushion and grasped Kayla's hand. "If she wants you to know about me, she'll find the right time to tell you. For now, I believe it's best for your family if I remain a private part of her past."

"Even though I love my pesky little brothers, I've always wanted a sister. I'm glad I found you—" Tears pooled in Kayla's eyes. "Even if I have to keep you secret."

"You know what?" Wendy squeezed her sister's hand as her own eyes filled with tears. "Having each other as secret sisters makes us extra special."

"Is it okay if we stay in touch?"

Wendy released Kayla's hand and brushed the tears from her cheeks. "I wouldn't have it any other way."

Kayla sniffed. "Don't worry about Harper telling anyone about you. If her parents found out she drove me all the way here without their permission, they'd ground her for a month."

Wendy tilted her head. "Where do your parents think you are now?"

"At a party at Harper's friend's house."

"In that case, you need to head back to Nashville before you two blow your cover."

"You're a cool sister."

"Yeah, I know. Before you go—" Wendy lifted her phone off the coffee table. "We need to exchange numbers."

"Is it okay if I call or text you every once in a while?"

"Any time you want." Wendy added Kayla's number to her favorites list. "When's your birthday?"

"April third. Next year I'll turn sixteen."

Wendy recorded the date on her phone's calendar.

"When's yours, and how old are you?"

"November twelfth, I'll turn twenty-four."

"Is your baby a boy or a girl?"

"A boy."

"After he's older will you tell him he has an aunt who lives in Nashville?"

"Even better. One day before too long, I'll find a way for you and my little guy to meet in person."

Kayla reached across the cushion and embraced Wendy. "Cool. That makes me an aunt. I love you, big sister."

"I love you too, little sister."

Chapter 34

By noon Friday, Amanda's head spun from dozens of questions Millie had fired at the Awesam partners for the past hour and a half. "For someone who didn't have a clue about podcasting, you've come up with some real zingers."

Millie planted her hands on her hips. "Are you complaining or complimenting?"

"Complimenting."

Erica pushed away from the table. "You could start your own podcast and call it 'Millie's Musings.'"

"I already have a full-time job helping keep you three out of trouble." Millie lowered her hands. "Maybe I should ask for a raise."

"There's only one problem." Wendy chuckled. "You keeping us out of trouble is strictly volunteer work—until we no longer give you any reasons to keep that job."

"I've known you ladies for five months, and you've already gotten into more trouble than most people around here have in five years. I suspect what you call my volunteer job isn't about to go away any time soon, if ever."

"At least we're keeping one senior citizen plenty busy. Especially today." Amanda handed Millie the inn's phone.

"Thank you for trusting me to stand in for you."

"You don't need to hang out next door or stand guard from your front porch. Just respond if one of our guests calls."

Millie smirked. "I know the drill."

Erica tapped her watch and eyed Wendy. "We need to leave in five minutes."

"Thanks for the warning." Wendy dashed to the hall.

Millie slid the inn's phone into her slacks' pocket. "I'll listen to the podcast and cheer you on from here. Although, I'd rather go with you."

No way they'd let her anywhere near a microphone. Amanda embraced Millie. "Thanks for helping us prep."

"A hug from Awesam's president. You really were impressed."

"Yeah, well, don't let it go to your head."

"Too late." Their chef squared her shoulders and headed to the back door.

Wendy returned clutching her purse. "I'm ready."

"All right then." Amanda grabbed the keys from the kitchen bowl and led the way out to the truck. Twenty-five minutes after pulling out of the carport, she parked on the driveway beside a two-story frame house in Copperhill, Tennessee. "Let's do this." They made their way to the front porch.

A slender, middle-aged woman swung the front door open before they had a chance to ring the bell. "Welcome, I'm Nancy." She escorted them into a room off the foyer and pointed to chairs facing three of the four microphones sitting on a dining room table. Bottles of water stood within reach. A newspaper lay beside the single mike facing the three. "This is the first time I've interviewed three people at the same time."

Amanda settled on the first chair. "We appreciate your interest in the truth about our story."

Nancy took her seat across from them. "Have any of you ever participated in a live interview?"

Erica shook her head. "This is the first time for all of us."

"All you need to do is relax and treat this as a casual conversation among friends."

Wendy tilted her head. "How will we decide which one of us should answer each question?"

"I'll address my questions to you by name or eye contact. Speak directly into the mike. We'll do a quick practice round." After asking about their ages and children, Nancy completed a mike check. "We go live in ten seconds." She counted down on her fingers, then leaned close to the microphone. "Good afternoon, friends, and welcome to Nancy's Nuggets. Today I'm fortunate to have Amanda Smith, Erica Nelson, and Wendy Thomason joining me in the studio. Some of you have already read about them. For those who haven't, I'll read the recent article my friend Gail Weston wrote."

Nancy pulled the newspaper close and read the entire piece. "Now you know why I wanted to talk to these ladies. Given the difference in your ages and lifestyles, how did you become friends in the span of three days, Erica?"

"Being stranded alone in a blizzard gave us a lot of time to become acquainted and talk about our lives. Wendy and I discovered we had learned a lot about people when we worked as waitresses."

"Amanda, considering Wendy's only two years older than your daughter, what did you discover you had in common with Wendy?"

"We both grew up on the Gulf Coast fewer than ninety miles apart. Which is why neither of us had ever experienced snow before our trip to Blue Ridge."

Nancy smiled. "And your first experience was a once-in-a-century blizzard. What did you learn about the two women who became your friends, Wendy?"

"Well, Erica's favorite wine is chardonnay, and Amanda is careful with her money. She refused to buy a warm coat because she wouldn't need it back in New Orleans. Both Amanda and Erica thought I was an incurable shopaholic. They were right about the shopaholic part, but I wasn't incurable. Anyway, neither of them judged me when my credit card was denied during our first shopping trip together."

Amanda stole a quick glance at Wendy. Six months ago she wouldn't have had the courage to share that incident.

"The three of you obviously learned to respect each other. Amanda, what was your first reaction when you discovered the man known as Gunter had deceived you?"

Grateful Millie had asked a similar question, Amanda leaned close to the microphone. "Shock, then disbelief followed closely by anger."

"What was your first reaction, Erica?"

"Mostly I felt disbelief and hurt."

"What about you, Wendy?"

"Total denial. Until my new friends helped me accept the truth."

"After you discovered everything that had been taken from you, how did you find the courage to start a new life hundreds of miles from your hometown, Amanda?"

"My first inclination was to play it safe and go back to the job I'd had years earlier as a New Orleans tour guide. Until my daughter, Morgan, asked me about my goals."

"Which are?"

"Financial independence and controlling my own destiny. I couldn't have achieved either without taking a big risk."

"What about you, Wendy?"

"Morgan asked me that same question. I told her I'd always imagined being a businesswoman people looked up to. That's when I started thinking about my future. I didn't want to go back to waitressing, so I enrolled in an online business course. It didn't take long to realize that I'm good with financial stuff."

"Which is why Wendy is our company's chief financial officer," added Amanda.

"Erica, what gave you the courage to move to Blue Ridge?"

"Amanda and Wendy's vision of the future, and my daughter Abby's faith in me."

Nancy's eyes remained trained on Erica. "How, in a few short months, were you and your partners able to transform a home in poor repair into a luxury inn?"

"With a lot of hard work and more than a little divine intervention."

Nancy's focus shifted to Wendy. "What experiences enabled you to tackle such a big project?"

"Years ago, Amanda helped turn a rundown, shotgun house into her family's dream home. Even though we didn't always agree and still don't, we worked as a team. Including our partner, Mildred Cunningham."

"You've obviously accomplished something extraordinary. What bits of wisdom do you want to share with our female listeners? Starting with you, Amanda."

"Sometimes life presents seemingly unsurmountable challenges. When that happens, find the courage to tackle whatever stands in your way with a positive attitude."

"Excellent advice. What do you want to add, Erica?"

"Pay attention when God puts people in your path who want to make your life better."

"So true. You're pregnant with your first child, Wendy. What advice do you have?"

"Well, courage is like a little acorn. If it falls on the sidewalk or if a squirrel eats it, nothing happens. But if it is planted and watered, it will sprout and grow into a giant tree. So, no matter what happens, take whatever little bit of courage you have and nourish it until it grows into something beautiful."

"Thank you, ladies, for enlightening our audience with words of wisdom. Today we've been blessed to hear from three women who serve as an inspiration to all of us. Be sure to visit their Hilltop Inn and Spa website. On tomorrow's podcast you'll hear from a gentleman who saved a child from drowning. Until then, stay safe and take time to hug your loved ones." Nancy switched off the microphones. "That was terrific, especially since this was your first experience with a live interview."

Wendy scooted away from the table. "Our partner, Millie, helped us with a mock interview."

"Tell her thank you for doing such a good job. If you don't mind, I'll interview you again next year, and be sure and bring Millie along."

Amanda extended her hand to Nancy. "Thank you for inviting us."

"You're welcome. Considering the number of listeners I have, your interview should prevent other influencers from believing Gunter Benson's lies about you ladies."

"There's always hope."

Chapter 35

Following a jubilant drive from Copperhill and a stop at the Sweet Shoppe for cupcakes, Erica spent the remainder of the afternoon in her bedroom. With a half hour before Brad was due to arrive, she stared at a photo of her and Abby taken the day they moved into the ranch house. Since that fateful day in December when her world turned upside down, she'd struggled through heart-wrenching chaos. Now for the first time in six months, she had settled into a comfortable routine that offered a secure future. The last thing she needed was a romantic relationship to play havoc with her emotions. And yet she had enjoyed her first dinner with Brad. Was it possible for a man and a woman to enjoy a close friendship without romance?

Erica placed the photo back on her nightstand then dressed in white pants, a bright pink tunic, and sandals. She had never thought of Jack or Gunter as friends. Brad seemed different. He was obviously comfortable engaging in casual conversation. Besides, other than helping her climb out of his Corvette, he hadn't held her hand or kissed her, which made fretting over his intentions more than a little premature.

The doorbell rang.

Erica grabbed her purse and sunglasses, then headed straight to the foyer. Summoning what she hoped would come across as a howdy-friend expression, she opened the front door. "Hey."

"Hi." He nodded toward his Corvette as they strode toward the driveway. "I'll put the top up if you prefer."

Erica donned her sunglasses. "Down is more fun."

"I agree." He opened the passenger door. "One of Jan's caps is in the glovebox."

Obviously, Jan was his wife. "Thanks. I'm fine without a hat." During the drive to East Main Street, the breeze tousled her hair while the late afternoon sun warmed her cheeks. After Brad circled the block twice, a spot opened up across from Harvest on Main.

Erica's pulse quickened as they crossed the street. The one other time she'd been inside the restaurant was the day Chris met them in its private room and gave her, Amanda, and Wendy keys to Gunter's secret post-office boxes. She cringed at the memory of emptying the Asheville box and discovering months of unopened bills and foreclosure notices on her home.

At the foot of the stairs leading to the front porch, Brad touched her arm. "Are you okay?"

Erica blinked. "I'm fine. Really. Is this one of your favorite restaurants?"

"There are a lot of great places to eat in Blue Ridge, so I don't really have a favorite. Although this was one of Jan's."

He'd mentioned his wife twice in fifteen minutes. How long before her name came up again?

Inside the rustic building, the hostess seated them at a table for two beside a window. After they ordered glasses of chardonnay, Brad set his menu aside. "How did Hilltop Inn's Grand Opening week go?"

"A lot differently than we expected." Erica relayed the Katherine and Robert Jones saga.

"And I thought managing a high school was challenging."

"Thanks to Chris and Millie Cunningham, everything ended on a positive note." Erica's focus returned to the menu.

"I read the article about you and your partners. The challenges you overcame make everything you accomplished with the inn that much more impressive."

"Those challenges brought the three of us together and made us stronger."

He nodded. "In addition to beautiful and kind, my wife was also a strong woman."

Erica's focus returned to the menu. Make that three times he'd mentioned her.

Their waiter returned with their wine. After they ordered, Brad wrapped his fingers around the stem of his wine glass and seemed to stare at the golden liquid. "Before Jan lost her battle with cancer, she poured every ounce of energy into comforting our boys and encouraging the three of us to live our lives to the fullest."

"She must have been an amazing wife and mother."

"Jan was also my best friend. Sometimes we'd talk for hours about our boys. Our hopes for the future. Our work. She was a high school chemistry teacher. The kids all loved her." Brad sipped his wine. "Enough about my life. What about you? Are you divorced or widowed?"

"First, I hope you know how fortunate Jan was to have a husband who enjoys conversation. Some women never experience that sort of relationship with a man."

"Including you?"

"My first husband..." Erica broke eye contact. Why did she say first? Would he notice and expect an explanation? "Jack was a police officer who couldn't control his fists. Which is why I divorced him."

Brad's jaw clenched. "Any man who uses a woman as his punching bag belongs behind bars." He studied her. "You called Jack your first husband."

He'd noticed.

"I assume you married again."

"Not exactly." How much should she reveal? Could she trust the man sitting across from her?

Brad folded his forearms on the table. "Anything you say will remain between the two of us."

Erica took a sip of wine, her eyes trained on his. Something in his eyes gave her the courage to divulge the truth. She leaned forward. "Turns out the second man I married already had a wife."

"He's the guy who deceived you and your partners, isn't he?"

Erica nodded. "I knew him as Brian Parker. His real name is Gunter Benson. He's a serial bigamist, a con artist, and a convicted murderer."

Brad stared at her for a long moment. "You're one of the two bravest women I've ever had the privilege to know."

"Gunter also illegally married Amanda and Wendy."

"Make that four of the bravest women."

"Bravest? More like desperation that gave the three of us the strength to take control of our lives."

"After your experiences with those two men, I'm lucky you accepted my dinner invitations."

"I assumed I could trust a high school principal, especially in a small town." Would he take offense if she revealed her reluctance to begin another relationship? Didn't he deserve to know the truth? "I know this is only our second dinner and I enjoy your company...it's just..."

"I understand. Truth is, neither one of us is ready for any sort of relationship beyond friendship."

Erica gazed into his eyes. "I've never had a male friend."

"And I've only had one female friend." Brad lifted his wine glass. "To the beginning of a special friendship."

Relieved and to her surprise, a little disappointed, Erica tapped her glass to his. "Do you mind if our next dinner as friends is my treat?"

He grinned. "You pick the place and time, and I'll be there."

Chapter 36

Waiting for one more new arrival, Wendy settled on one of the inn's front-porch rockers and set the chair in motion. A smile played on her lips as her little guy responded to the gentle movement. She wrapped her arms around her belly. "This time next month, I'll cradle you in my arms and rock you to sleep on this porch." She closed her eyes and imagined the ranch house living room transformed into a proper room for a baby boy. Pale blue walls. Stars painted on the ceiling.

A car engine's soft whir nudged Wendy's eyes open. A white sports car eased up the driveway and parked on the concrete pad between the inn and ranch house. Eager to welcome today's last check-in, Wendy lifted off the chair, pressed her fingers to her back, and ambled to the steps as the senior couple pulled suitcases along the front sidewalk and up the stairs. "Welcome to Hilltop Inn and Spa, Mr. and Mrs. Webster. I'm Wendy." Grateful she remembered the note on their reservation, she smiled at the woman. "And happy birthday."

"Thank you." Mrs. Webster held up an Owl's Nest shopping bag. "My first birthday purchase."

Her husband chuckled. "But not her last."

His wife's eyes drifted to Wendy's baby bulge. "You'll soon celebrate a very special birthday. Your first child?"

"Yes." Wendy unlocked the front door.

The woman stepped inside. "Do you know the sex?"

Wendy nodded. "A healthy baby boy."

"We have two sons, a daughter, and seven grandchildren." Her eyes took in the lobby. "What a lovely inn."

"Is this your first trip to Blue Ridge?"

"Our third." Mr. Webster pulled their luggage into the foyer.

"We're delighted you're staying with us this time." Wendy held out a pen. "Who wants to sign our guestbook?"

Mrs. Webster reached for the pen. "I will."

Wendy plucked their key off the desk, then escorted the couple into the living room. "This house has undergone a major transformation during the past five months, thanks in part to our partner Amanda's fixer-upper experience." She shared the home's history, then aimed her palm toward the bookstand. "We recorded the progress in that scrapbook."

Mr. Webster ambled over and leafed through the first few pages. "Impressive."

"Thank you. Have either of you scheduled a massage?"

His wife nodded. "I have for tomorrow at four."

"Our massage therapist is also one of our partners." Wendy motioned toward the dining room. "Every morning between eight and ten, Chef Millie serves delicious breakfasts. The menu changes every day, except for her cinnamon buns. We have a full house, so tomorrow you'll meet twelve other guests."

"Meeting new friends is one reason we enjoy staying in B and Bs."

"Coffee is available in the dining room at six. If you're early risers, you can enjoy your coffee while viewing the sunrise in our backyard garden, which our chef designed."

Mr. Webster closed the scrapbook. "You and your partners are a talented group of women."

"We complement each other." Wendy escorted the couple through the foyer and into the den. "You reserved our largest suite." She unlocked the Rainbow Suite and pushed the door open. "This was the original owners' room."

Mrs. Webster headed to the French doors. "Your chef created a beautiful garden. Has anyone reserved it for a wedding or other special occasion?"

"Not yet." Wendy moved beside their guest. "Another advantage of the Rainbow Suite is the short walk to the spa."

"We've obviously reserved the suite with the best view."

"Yes, you have." Wendy handed her the key. "Our number is on the nightstand. Don't hesitate to call if there's anything you need."

"We will, and if I don't see you again, I wish you and your son all the best."

Had their guest noticed she wasn't wearing a wedding ring? Did it matter one way or the other? "Thank you, and I hope you and your husband have a wonderful stay with us." Wendy walked out, pulling the door closed behind her. After returning to the foyer and pocketing the inn's phone, she stepped onto the porch. A squirrel scampered across the railing while a hawk soared overhead and landed on a branch.

Wendy gripped the hand railing, eased down the steps, and moseyed along the sidewalk fronting the inn. Next year she'd take her little guy to a beach so he could play in the surf, build sandcastles, and watch seagulls dive for their dinner. After making her way through the empty carport, she walked through the kitchen to the den. Grateful to have the place to herself, she set the inn's phone on the coffee table then curled up on the sofa and drifted to sleep.

A bell nudged her eyes open. Wendy blinked. Maybe she'd been dreaming. She closed her eyes. The bell rang again. Were they expecting someone?

She pushed off the sofa and padded to the foyer. Her heart jumped to her throat as she pulled the door open and faced Chris.

"I hope I didn't interrupt something important."

"A nap, that's all. Did Gunter send you a nasty letter, or did another guest file a lawsuit?"

"I'm not here to deliver bad news. We need to talk."

Wendy's brows pinched then released. "If you're here about Awesam, Amanda and Erica aren't home."

"I'm not."

Wendy swallowed against the dryness in her throat. If he wasn't acting as their business attorney—

"Do you mind if I come in?" Chris grinned. "Or we could talk on the porch."

"Sorry, I'm still half asleep." Wendy stepped aside then led the way to the table. "Can I bring you something to drink?"

He pulled out a chair. "No thanks."

She sat across from him and brushed hair away from her cheek. "What's on your mind?"

Chris's eyes met hers. "Mom called an hour ago." He paused. "She found your father."

"Oh my gosh." Wendy fanned her fingers across her chest. "Where does he live? What does he do? Does he have a family?"

"One question at a time. His name is Douglas Hewitt. He lives in Hilton Head and is a partner in his family's real-estate development company. He's married and has two teenaged sons."

"And a daughter he doesn't know exists." Wendy lowered her hand. "I never expected her to find him. Now that she has, what should I do?"

Chris leaned forward and crossed his arms on the table. "You have the same three choices you had when Vincent found your mother. One, you can ignore the news and move on. Two, I can contact him and find out if he wants to meet you. Or three, you can surprise him with a visit."

Wendy slumped back. If Chris contacted him, would he refuse to meet her? If she pretended Linda hadn't found him, would curiosity drive her crazy? Only one response made sense. "I want to surprise him."

"That's what I thought you'd say. Which is why I've arranged to drive you to Hilton Head tomorrow afternoon."

"What? I mean why, since I can fly to Hilton Head on my own or drive by myself."

"First of all, there are no direct flights, which means dealing with three airports. Secondly, in your condition you have no business driving alone for six hours."

Wendy scoffed. "I'm pregnant, not disabled."

"And thirdly, you need your attorney present."

She had finally accepted moving on without Chris. How could she possibly spend hours alone in a car with him? "Don't you have meetings with clients?"

"Dad's covering for me for the next three days."

Wendy's brow furrowed. "Why three?"

"I can't leave until tomorrow afternoon, which will put us in Hilton Head late. I reserved two rooms for three nights."

Wendy's chest tightened. "Why three?"

"I don't know how long it will take to connect with your father. Anyway, all you need to do is pack a bag and enjoy the ride."

With the man she still loved with all her heart. "All right."

"Good." Chris stood. "I'll see you tomorrow."

Fearing her knees might buckle if she attempted to stand, Wendy remained seated while her attorney walked out. The moment the front door closed, tears erupted and tracked down her cheeks. How would her father react to seeing her for the first time? Would spending three days alone with Chris break her heart all over again?

Moments after a vehicle pulled into the carport, Amanda and Wendy walked into the kitchen. "Anything exciting happen while we were gone?"

Wendy swiped her fingers across her cheeks. "Chris left a few minutes ago."

"A personal or professional visit?"

"Linda found my father."

"I'd call that exciting." Amanda dropped keys into the bowl. "What's your next move?"

"Chris is driving me to Hilton Head tomorrow for a surprise visit the next day. I'll be gone for four days."

Erica laid shopping bags on the kitchen counter then sat beside Wendy. "Are you okay?"

"At least Cynthia knew she had a daughter. Douglas Hewitt doesn't have a clue."

Erica reached for Wendy's hand. "No matter what happens, you'll thrive as the brave, brilliant woman we know and love."

Wendy sniffed. "No one ever called me brilliant before."

Amanda settled on the other side of Wendy. "Only because no one knows you as well as we do."

"Can one of you drive me to Hilton Head?"

Erica exchanged a glance with Amanda. "I have massages scheduled."

"And I have check-in duty tomorrow. Besides, it's best to have your lawyer with you when you step into an unknown situation."

"I know...it's just...spending all that time alone with Chris..."

Amanda patted Wendy's arm. "Sometimes, things work out exactly the way they're supposed to, honey."

Chapter 37

Following hours of idle conversation interrupted by long stretches of awkward silence, four bathroom breaks, and a nap, Chris pulled up to the beachside resort. After he removed their bags from the trunk and turned his car over to a valet, Wendy followed him inside. While her attorney checked in, she glanced around the fancy lobby. Had he picked an expensive hotel to impress her or to cushion the blow if her father rejected her? A twinge of guilt pricked her conscience. Chris had spent countless hours acting as her attorney and spending his own money without sending her a single bill. As soon as she started earning a salary, she'd find a way to pay him back.

"We're all set."

Wendy spun around and faced Chris. "Are we staying on the same floor?"

"I'm one floor below you."

She walked beside him as they made their way to the elevators. A door yawned open. They stepped into the empty space. Chris pressed a button.

"The top floor. Did you reserve the penthouse?"

"Close."

"I was kidding."

"So was I."

Wendy's eyes focused on the passing floors. "You know, I could've pulled my own suitcase."

"Why don't you pretend I'm your bellman."

"Are you expecting a generous tip?"

He chuckled. "I'll put it on your tab." The elevator doors eased open. Chris pulled their bags to the end of the hall and unlocked a door. "This is your room."

Wendy's brow pinched as she stepped into the spacious two-room suite. "Why didn't you reserve a regular room?"

"This is tourist season in a tourist town. Last-minute options were limited."

She ran her fingers over the sofa's white upholstery. "Are you also staying in a suite?"

"No." He pulled her suitcase into the bedroom.

Wendy stood in the doorway. "Since you're paying, you should stay here and give me the single room."

"Not a chance." Chris lifted her bag onto the bed.

Wendy's chest tightened as she moved away from the bedroom and ambled to the living room doors leading to the balcony. Her eyes drifted to waves breaking onto the shore. Even from here they appeared bigger than those in the Gulf—except when storms churned the water into surf-worthy swells.

Chris moved to her side. "Are you up to dinner out?"

Her heart urged her to say yes. Her weary body screamed no. "I'm really tired. Do you mind if I stay here and order room service?"

"Not at all."

His arm brushed her shoulder, sending a tingling sensation cascading through her. She inched away. "Thank you for understanding."

"You're welcome. Call me in the morning so we can meet for breakfast and discuss our next steps." He set the room key on the small round dining room table. "Good night, Wendy."

"Good night, Chris."

He turned away and walked out.

Fighting the urge to rush after him, Wendy tossed her purse onto the sofa and searched for a room service menu. After ordering, she dropped onto the sofa and called Amanda.

"How was your trip?"

"Uneventful." *Except for sitting beside the man I love for six plus hours.* "Is anything happening back home?"

"Nothing out of the ordinary. Erica and I are praying for a good outcome tomorrow."

"So am I." A sudden wave of exhaustion released an audible yawn.

"Sounds as if you need a good-night's sleep."

"I'll open the balcony door and let the ocean lull me to sleep." Just as she had the last night she'd spent in her Gulfport condo. "I'll call you tomorrow." Wendy ended the call then headed to the bedroom and opened the deck door. She breathed in the salty sea air. Did Chris's room also face the ocean? Was he disappointed she didn't agree to go out to dinner?

Wendy spun away from the glass and peered around the room awash in white, soft grey, and pale blue. The last time she'd slept in a hotel suite, she and her partners were waiting to testify in Gunter's murder trial. Now she was facing another unpredictable outcome. She might as well settle in for the night. After unpacking her suitcase and setting her toiletries on the bathroom counter, she traipsed to the living room, collapsed on the sofa, and propped her feet on the coffee table.

Chris had been right about her not driving alone. She'd never have made it without falling asleep. As much as she didn't want to admit it, she needed him—at least for the next three days. Wendy aimed the television remote and flipped mindlessly through the channels. She stopped on a music channel. Somehow, she had to stay awake until her order arrived.

Wendy tossed the remote on the cushion beside her then moseyed to the balcony doors. If she woke up early enough, she could watch the sun rise. Not tomorrow. Maybe the second morning. She spun toward a buzzer resonating through the room and scurried to open the door.

The young man holding a tray smiled. "Room service, ma'am."

She stepped aside.

He walked in and set a tray on the dining room table.

How much should she tip him? "Wait here." Wendy dashed to the bedroom, removed her wallet from her purse, and pulled out a bill. Was it too much? She was staying in an expensive suite, for goodness' sake. The guy probably expected an even bigger tip.

Wendy returned and handed over a five-dollar bill.

He smiled. "Thank you, ma'am. Enjoy your dinner."

The moment he left her alone, Wendy carried her cheeseburger and lemonade out to the balcony and settled on a chair facing the railing. Did her father live near the beach? Where had he lived when he met Cynthia? Would he even remember her mother? She bit into her sandwich while focusing on dark clouds forming on the horizon. Were they moving away from or toward the beach? By the time she finished eating, the threatening clouds had drifted closer to shore. Maybe a storm tonight meant clear skies tomorrow.

A flash of lightning followed by a distant roll of thunder sent Wendy back inside. She turned off the living room lights, padded into the bedroom, and changed into pajamas. Had Chris gone out to eat, or had he ordered room service?

Another lightning flash followed by loud thunder—this time much closer. Wendy darkened the room and opened the drapes. Within minutes, the smattering of raindrops escalating to a full-blow storm sent a shiver cascading down her spine. Would facing her father turn into a huge mistake she'd live to regret?

Chapter 38

Sunlight streaming into the bedroom along with her little guy pressing on her bladder awakened Wendy. She glanced at the bedside clock. Seven-fifteen. So much for experiencing the sunrise. Was it too early to call Chris? Not according to her stomach grumbles. She unplugged her phone and typed a message. Breakfast in forty minutes? Meet where?

"Carolina Room."

Thumbs-up. While showering and drying her hair, Wendy's emotions teetered between anticipation and dread. She had survived her mother's second rejection without falling apart. Would the same hold true if her father also rejected her? Her mental roller coaster continued as she dressed then made her way to the restaurant.

Chris met her at the entrance. They followed the hostess to a table beside a window. Chris seated Wendy, then sat across from her. "Were you able to rest?"

She lifted her menu off the table. "Well enough. What about you?"

"Eight hours straight, after the storm passed."

What kind of storm would they experience when they confronted her father? "Speaking of storms, what's your plan for today?"

"We'll attempt to connect at the Hewitts' home first."

"Why not where he works?"

"His home is more personal."

Their waiter approached, filled one cup with coffee, and took their orders. When he left, Chris eyed Wendy while stirring sugar into his morning brew. "Discovering he has a daughter will come as quite a shock to your father, so don't let his first reaction affect you."

Wendy fidgeted. "He might refuse to see me a second time."

"If he does, he'll miss out on a relationship with an amazing woman and his grandson."

"No matter what happens, I'm glad you're here with me."

Chris smiled. "So am I."

By the time they finished breakfast and climbed into Chris's car, Wendy's confidence had moved up a notch, until they arrived at the destination. She gawked at the grand home surrounded by lush landscaping. "Douglas Hewitt is obviously successful."

"Real-estate developing is a lucrative business."

"What if he thinks I'm after his money, especially since I brought my attorney?"

"We'll make your intentions clear." Chris opened his door. "Are you ready to meet your father?"

Wendy breathed deeply, then slowly released the air. "I am now." She clung to Chris's arm as they made their way up the driveway and onto the front porch. Wendy pushed her sunglasses to the top of her head. Was her father short or tall? Was he clean-shaven or did he have a beard?

Chris pressed the doorbell.

Seconds passed.

A woman who appeared to be in her fifties pulled the door open. "May I help you?"

"Good morning, ma'am. My name is Christopher Armstrong. Is Mr. Hewitt available?"

The woman's eyes shifted to Wendy then back to Chris. "The Hewitts are out of town."

Wendy's shoulders slumped. Had they come all this way for nothing? "Are you a relative?"

"No ma'am. I'm the family's housekeeper."

Chris fished a business card from his jacket pocket. "When do you expect them to return?"

"Mr. Hewitt is coming home tonight. The rest of the family is staying at their mountain home for another week."

Wendy's eyes widened. How many homes did he own?

Chris handed over his card. "Please tell him Ms. Thomason and I will return tomorrow morning at nine."

She glanced at the card. "You're an attorney?"

"I am."

"What reason should I give Mr. Hewitt for your visit?"

"Tell him there's a woman from his past he'll want to meet."

The housekeeper's eyes shifted from Chris to Wendy then back to Chris. "Yes, sir, I'll tell him." She stepped back and closed the door.

Wendy spun around. "Do you suppose she'll remember to tell him?"

"We'll find out tomorrow morning. Now that we have the rest of the day free, what do you want to do?"

Chris's arm brushing Wendy's shoulder as they climbed off the porch sent a tingling sensation rippling through her limbs. She caught her bottom lip between her teeth. Maybe she should spend the day alone on her balcony, peering down at tourists. Except Chris was paying a lot of money to stay in a luxury hotel on the beach instead of a cheap motel on some highway.

Chris nudged her arm. "I didn't realize I asked such a difficult question."

Wendy blinked. "Sorry. I have a lot on my mind."

"All the more reason to do something fun."

"How about walking barefoot in the surf?"

Chris opened the passenger door. "Barefoot beats wearing shoes in the water."

Wendy slid onto the seat. "Do you want to join me? As my friend, not my attorney."

"I can't think of a better way to enjoy the rest of the morning than with a pal." He closed the door, then rounded the front of the car and climbed in beside her.

During the ride, Wendy stared unseeing out the side window. How could she spend the entire day pretending she wasn't deeply in love with the man who called her his pal? She swallowed against the dryness in her throat and forced her brain to focus on the passing scenery. By the time they arrived at the hotel, her palms were moist. As they headed to the elevators, she found her voice. "I'll change and meet you back down here in twenty minutes."

"Deal." Chris fell silent until the elevator stopped on his floor. "I'll see you in twenty."

Wendy glanced sideways at the female passenger remaining onboard. What was she thinking? "He's my attorney, not my husband."

The woman shrugged.

Wendy pressed her damp palms on her thighs. Why hadn't she resisted the urge to explain?

The elevator moved up to Wendy's floor. The woman stepped out. "Have a nice day."

"You too." Grateful, the woman turned left, Wendy turned right and made her way to her suite. Inside, she changed into shorts and slathered sunscreen on her bare skin then pulled her hair into a ponytail. With ten minutes to spare, she stepped out to the balcony and peered at the pool below. She'd spent hours walking on the beach fronting her Gulfport condo while waiting for the father of her child to return from his long stretches away from home. Weeks he'd spent with his other illegal wives and at countless casinos.

Wendy's jaw clenched. Forget Gunter Benson. She spun away from the railing and stepped back inside. Today she'd enjoy the surf and sun in the company of a man she wished had been her baby's father. She propped her sunglasses on her head then donned a pair of flip-flops and made her way to the lobby.

Chris stood beside the stairs leading down to the pool level. Dressed in shorts and a tee-shirt and sporting a pair of sunglasses, he looked more like a college guy on spring break than a lawyer. "You're right on time." He held her arm as they descended the steps. "Is this your first trip to the east coast?"

"It is." Wendy lowered her sunglasses. "What about you?"

"When Allison and I were kids, our family spent a lot of summer vacations at the beach."

"Including Hilton Head?"

"One time."

They strolled through the pool area, down the ramp to the beach, and across the hot sand. At the water's edge, they stepped out of their flip-flops. Wendy breathed in the salty sea air as the last remnants of a wave rolled across her feet before receding. "I remember spending a day at the beach with my mother. We built sandcastles and ate peanut butter and jelly sandwiches."

"Every child should have the chance to build sandcastles and play in the surf."

"I agree." They ambled along the cool sand at the water's edge. "Do you have a favorite childhood memory?"

"There are so many; however..." Chris paused as if stalling or weighing the impact of his next words. He bent down and plucked a shell off the sand, then straightened. "My fondest memories are going to Georgia football games with Dad. That's how I learned to love the sport."

Wendy brushed a stray hair off her cheek. Why did she ask that question and open herself up to the pain of raising a fatherless child? "Did your mom and sister ever go with you?"

"Every once in a while."

People they passed smiled and spoke to them. They obviously thought she and Chris were a couple. "When did you start playing football?"

"Mom didn't allow me to play until I turned ten."

"Because she didn't want you to get hurt?"

"All those years I played, I never suffered anything more serious than bruises, a few minor cuts, and damaged pride every time I missed the ball."

A tiny crab skittered across the wet sand and disappeared down a hole. "Did you miss often?"

"One miss a game is too often."

"Do you know Brad Barkley?"

"He was my high school coach, and a doggone good one. It's a shame he lost his wife at such a young age."

"Erica's gone to dinner with him twice—as a friend."

Chris tossed the shell into the surf. "Some friendships turn into amazing marriages."

"What do you mean?"

He shrugged. "I'm simply stating the facts."

"As an attorney?"

He adjusted his sunglasses. "As a friend." Two young children stood knee-deep in the water splashing each other. "Allison and I loved boogie-board surfing. You should try it one day."

"Maybe when my belly isn't the size of a ten-pound bowling ball."

"Is your little guy enjoying the walk?"

"Oh yeah. He's also the reason I shouldn't stray too far from the hotel."

"Understood." They walked another fifty feet, then turned around.

A flock of seagulls soared above the water. "Have you ever flown a kite?"

"Nope. Have you?"

"Uh-uh. I imagine it would be fun, especially on a beach." They continued chatting about beach activities as they strolled back to the hotel. "What do you say we sit on the side of the pool and cool off our feet?"

"Good idea."

After spending the afternoon snacking, relaxing by the pool, and chatting with other guests, they dined in an outdoor restaurant overlooking the pool. By the time they finished eating, Wendy could no longer control her yawns. "Sorry."

"We have a big day tomorrow, so we both need to get plenty of rest." After Chris paid the bill, he escorted her to her room. As she pulled the key card from her pocket and opened the door, he touched her arm. "Thank you for a fun day."

Wendy turned toward him. Their eyes met. "I'm glad we're friends."

His eyes lingered on hers. "So am I. Good night, Wendy."

She summoned every ounce of will power to resist telling him how much she loved him. "Good night, Chris."

Chapter 39

Following a restless night riddled with anxiety-driven dreams, Wendy sat across from Chris in the Carolina Room and swallowed her last bite of scrambled eggs.

"Do you want to go over our approach one more time before we leave?"

Wendy shook her head. "If his housekeeper shared what you told her, at the very least, my father will be curious enough to talk to us."

"Which is why I phrased our intentions that way."

"You're a smart lawyer."

Chris chuckled as he signaled to their waiter. "Are you just now figuring that out?"

Wendy shrugged. "I've known all along." After Chris signed the bill, they made their way through the lobby and out the front entrance. His car waited for them under the canopy.

The valet rushed from his stand and opened the passenger door. "Good morning, ma'am."

Wendy responded then slid onto the smooth leather seat while Chris circled to the driver side. As they eased away from the entrance, Wendy glimpsed the low-hanging clouds hinting of rain. Did the weather foreshadow today's outcome? What if the housekeeper hadn't passed on Chris's message? No matter what happened, she had to control her emotions. During the drive, Wendy closed her eyes and mentally rehearsed what she'd say if they came face-to-face with her father.

"We're here."

Wendy opened her eyes the moment Chris turned onto the Hewitts' driveway. He cut the engine, then reached across the console and touched her arm. "Are you ready?"

Wendy filled her lungs then slowly released the air. "I am now." She climbed out before Chris opened his door and rounded to her side. He gripped her elbow while they made their way to the front porch. The door opened moments after he pressed the bell.

A distinguished, blue-eyed man sporting a neatly-trimmed beard pulled the door open.

"Good morning, Mr. Hewitt. I'm Chris Armstrong. We'd like a few minutes of your time."

"I'll give you five." He led them through a grand foyer and into a formal living room, then aimed his palm toward a white sofa facing a stone fireplace. "Please."

Wendy lowered onto the sofa while glancing around the space. The contemporary décor was similar to Gunter's Gulfport condo.

Her father sat on a love seat catercorner to the sofa. "What mystery from my past has brought you to Hilton Head?"

Chris settled beside Wendy. "Before my client explains, you need to know that her only objective is to meet you."

"I see." Douglas Hewitt's eyes shifted to Wendy. "I'm listening."

Here goes. She squared her shoulders. "My name is Wendy Thomason. Do you remember this woman?" Wendy handed him the family photo her mother had sent her a few weeks earlier. "Her name is Cynthia."

His brow pinched as he eyed the photo. "Who is she, and what makes you think I should know her?"

"She's my mother." Wendy paused long enough to decide her next move. "Twenty-four years ago, did you live in Biloxi, or were you visiting?"

His eyes remained trained on Wendy as he returned the picture. "My frat buddies and I spent one spring break in that town. Why are you asking?"

"Because...that's where you met her."

A hint of understanding hardened his expression. "What's the real reason you're here?"

Wendy swallowed against the dryness in her throat. "My mother abandoned me when I was five-years-old. A few months ago, I met with her for the first time in eighteen years. She has no idea who my father is, and neither did I...until two days ago."

Chris removed a folded sheet of paper from his jacket pocket and handed it to her father.

He stared at the document for a long moment before tossing it onto the coffee table. "What do you want from me?"

"Nothing. I just wanted to meet you and find out what kind of relationship you had with my mother."

"What relationship? Best as I can remember, she was a one-night stand, and I was a dumb college kid who'd had too much to drink." Her father folded his arms across his chest. "My wife and I have been married for twenty-two years, and we have two sons. You need to know that I'll do whatever it takes to protect my family and my business from any sort of scandal, including giving you a check."

"I don't want your money." Wendy's shoulders stiffened. "The only reason I'm here is to learn what kind of man you are, and to find out if you want your only daughter—at least the one you now know about—in your life." Wendy regretted the cutting words seconds after they rolled off her tongue. "I'm sorry. I didn't mean to make such a harsh remark."

Douglas Hewitt stared at her for a long moment. "You seem like an intelligent young woman." He unfolded his arms. "I'm sure you understand my position. Twenty minutes ago, I had no idea you existed, and now you're expecting to be part of my life?"

Wendy stared at the man who had fathered her. How should she respond? With grace and maturity, that's how. "My only expectation is that one day I can tell my son about his grandfather, without any strings attached." She removed a business card from her purse and laid it on the coffee table. "I can tell you're a decent man, and I understand you never expected a woman claiming to be your daughter to show up at your door."

He picked up the card. "Chief Financial Officer?"

"Business success is obviously in my genes. Now that I've satisfied my curiosity, I won't bother you again. Unless you decide having a daughter in your life isn't such a bad thing after all." Wendy retrieved the document identifying Douglas Hewitt as her father.

The hint of a grin softened his features. "You're an impressive young woman."

"What else would you expect from your daughter?" She rose.

The men followed her lead.

Wendy extended her hand. "It's been a pleasure to meet you, Mr. Hewitt."

His eyes remained laser focused on hers as he grasped her hand. "Ms. Thomason." He released his grip.

"Thank you for seeing us, Mr. Hewitt. We'll show ourselves out." Chris led the way to the foyer and out the front door. "You were incredible."

Wendy glanced over her shoulder. No one stood watching from the living room window as her mother had when she and Amanda left her Nashville home. "Do you suppose he'll ever reach out to me?"

"I'd say there's at least a fifty-fifty chance he will."

As Wendy settled on the passenger seat, the emotions she'd managed to control threatened to come unhinged. Moments after they pulled out of the circular driveway, tears erupted and spilled down her cheeks.

Chris pulled to the curb, then slid his arm around her shoulders and drew her close.

Wendy sniffled. "I promised myself I wouldn't cry." She swiped her fingers across her cheeks. "I'm okay now."

"You're way more than okay."

"I'm glad you came with me."

"So am I."

Moments after Chris pulled away from the curb, a smattering of raindrops splashed onto the windshield. By the time they arrived at the hotel, a downpour pelted the canopy covering the entrance. As Wendy stepped from the car, wind whipping through the space sent a chill racing through her limbs. Inside the lobby they headed straight to the elevators. While waiting for one to arrive on the lobby floor, she folded her arms across her chest and massaged her chill-bumped skin. "I didn't sleep much last night. Do you mind if I spend the next couple of hours resting in my room?"

"I'll give you all the time you need."

Chris had uttered those same words the day she told him they needed to stop dating.

"In fact, since it's forecast to rain a good part of the day, and I have some work to take care of, why don't we meet in your suite at five and order room service?"

Too exhausted to resist, Wendy nodded as an elevator door slid open. She stepped into the empty space, turned, and leaned against the back wall. When they reached Chris's floor, he nudged her. "I'll see you at five."

Too tired to utter a response, she nodded. Back in her suite, Wendy kicked off her shoes and collapsed onto the bed. Would her father tell his family she existed or keep his one-night fling a secret? She closed her eyes and let the rain lull her to sleep.

Chapter 40

Sunlight streaming into the bedroom nudged Wendy awake. She rolled over and glanced at the clock. Her mouth fell open. How was that possible? She swung her legs over the side of the bed, then dashed to the bathroom and peered at her disheveled hair and smudged mascara. Five o'clock was twenty minutes away, and she looked a mess.

After washing her face, reapplying her makeup, and smoothing her hair, Wendy changed into white pants and a red top. Should she wear fragrance? Why not. She spritzed perfume behind her ears then padded to the living room and opened the drapes. How long had the sun been shining?

Wendy's pulse accelerated as she spun toward the buzzing sound. She rushed across the room and pulled the door open. "Come on in."

Chris stepped inside and handed her a box of chocolate truffles. "A gift for one of my most intriguing clients."

What did he mean by intriguing? "How'd you know truffles are my favorite?"

"Amanda told me." He held up two bottles. "One cabernet for me and one non-alcoholic red for my expectant dinner partner." Chris carried the bottles to the table. "Were you able to rest?"

"Would you believe I slept six straight hours?" Wendy set the candy box on the end table. "What about you? Did you finish your work?"

"Yup. I hope you're hungry."

"I'm starving."

"Good, because I ordered chateaubriand for two—rare, but not cold in the middle."

"With mashed potatoes?"

"And grilled asparagus. The rain ushered in a cool front. If you'd like, we can open the balcony door and dine alfresco with the ocean as our background music."

Wendy slid the door open. "You sound more like a restaurant maître d' than my lawyer."

"At your service, ma'am." Chris moved to the kitchenette then returned with two wineglasses and a corkscrew. After opening both bottles, he poured then handed Wendy a glass.

She sipped. "In six or seven months, when I finish nursing my little guy, I'll be able to try the real stuff."

"Do you like wine?"

She nodded.

Responding to the buzzer, Chris set down his glass and headed straight to the door.

"Good evening, sir." The waiter pushed a cart across the room. After setting the table, he transferred two plates and lifted off the silver domes. "Would you like to make sure the steak is prepared to order?"

Chris cut into the meat. "It's perfect." He fished a bill from his pocket and handed it to the waiter.

"Thank you, sir." The young man pushed the cart aside then let himself out.

After seating Wendy and blessing their meal, Chris took a bite. "Delicious, but not quite as good as my filets."

Wendy tasted her steak. "You're right." She pointed her fork at Chris. "However, your sister deserves the credit for her marinade."

"True, but I mastered the grilling technique."

"Good point." Wendy dipped her fork into the potatoes. "What's your impression of my father?"

"He seems like a decent guy, and he's obviously successful."

"I wonder... If he's been married for twenty-two years, do you suppose he knew his wife when he had the one-night stand with my mother?"

"He claimed he'd been a dumb college kid, so possibly."

Wendy swallowed a bite of potatoes. "When you were in college, did you and your buddies go on wild spring breaks?"

"Are you asking if I ever drank too much and slept with a stranger?"

"Not that it's any of my business, but yeah."

"The answer is never. In fact, I've only been on one spring-break trip."

"So, you weren't one of those wild college guys who spent more time partying than studying?"

Chris chuckled. "Are you cross examining me, Counselor?"

"Hey, you're my lawyer. I need to know if you have a scandalous past."

"Well then, Ms. Thomason, you can rest assured that your attorney has never done anything that would land him in jail. He's only pulled a few shenanigans he can't reveal to his mother, which shall remain closely-guarded secrets." Chris winked. "I imagine you were involved in your share of mischief when you were a teenager."

"Now you're cross-examining me?"

"Hey, you're my client. I need to know if there are secrets lurking in your past."

Wendy smiled. "A few, which are also safely-guarded."

"One of these days, we should compare notes."

As their playful banter continued through dinner, Wendy's emotions teetered between pleasure and pain. On the one hand, she was relieved their breakup hadn't destroyed their friendship. On the other, his playfulness made her love him that much more. She swallowed her last bite of steak and pushed her plate aside. "Compliments to your menu selection, Mr. Armstrong. All I need now is one truffle for dessert."

"At your service, Ms. Thomason." Chris retrieved the box and set it in front of Wendy, then removed the lid.

"Dark chocolate. Perfect." She bit into a candy and savored the rich semi-sweet taste. "You have to try one." Wendy pushed the box to Chris.

He tasted. "Now I understand why truffles are your favorite. They're almost as satisfying as a kiss."

Wendy blinked. Did he make that comment to confuse or to mock her? She broke eye contact and lifted off her chair. "What do you say we enjoy the view from the balcony?"

"Great idea." Chris followed her out to the railing and stood beside her.

His arm brushed her shoulder, sending a tingle racing through her limbs. She breathed in the fresh air. "There's something magical about the ocean—the way it spans as far as the eye can see and thousands of miles beyond. Have you ever been on the other side?"

"One time when my family spent two weeks touring Europe."

"Someday I want to take my little guy over there and show him the rest of the world."

"Why haven't you decided what to name your baby?"

"It's a big decision."

Chris remained silent for a long moment. "I have a confession."

"That you really were a wild college guy?"

He pivoted toward her. "Supporting you as your attorney is one reason I insisted on accompanying you on this trip. The other was to discover the truth about us."

Wendy caught her bottom lip between her teeth. Was he seconds from telling her she'd made the right decision about breaking up? Afraid to make eye contact, she stared straight ahead.

"That day in my office when you told me you wanted to stop dating, I was torn between begging you to change your mind and letting you go."

"Why didn't you follow me?"

"Because I was still grappling over my feelings for you."

That's the reason he never told her he loved her—because he didn't.

"The longer we were apart, the more I realized how much I care for you. I kept my distance to give you time to sort out your own feelings." Chris gently turned her shoulders toward him.

Her eyes met his.

"Yesterday and again this morning, I saw the truth in your eyes, Wendy. You're as much in love with me as I am with you." Chris touched her belly the exact moment her baby moved. A smile covered his face. "You need to know that I love this child inside you as if he was my own flesh and blood. I want nothing more than to spend the rest of my life loving and caring for you and our son. Which is why I spent the afternoon on an important mission." Chris withdrew a small black box from his pocket and dropped to one knee.

Wendy's heart beat wildly in her chest. Was she dreaming, or was this really happening?

He opened the box revealing a sparkling diamond ring. "I love you with all my heart, Wendy. Will you marry me and make me the happiest man alive?"

Tears pooled and spilled down her cheek. "My heart is so full of love for you it might burst. Yes, Chris, I'll marry you and spend the rest of my life making you happy."

He lifted off his knees and slid the ring onto her finger then gently wiped away her tears. "I believe it's time to test my theory."

Her eyes remained locked on his. "What theory?"

"That kisses are a far more delicious dessert than truffles." Chris gathered her in his arms and kissed her deeply. When their lips parted, he gazed into her eyes. "One day I'll show you and our son the world."

A smile she could not contain spread across her face. "Even if we never set foot out of Blue Ridge, I'll be the happiest woman alive."

Chapter 41

The morning after the newly engaged couple returned from Hilton Head, Amanda leaned on Wendy's bedroom doorframe. "The day I met you I never thought I'd say this, but I'm going to miss having you around."

Wendy smiled. "You pegged me as a childish shopaholic, and I thought you were stubborn and judgmental."

Amanda laughed. "At least *I* was wrong."

"And I discovered that even though you always want to do things your way—"

"Not always—"

"Most of the time. Anyway, as I was gonna say, it turned out you're the most kind-hearted woman I know, except for Awesam's CEO and Abby. And you're gonna be one amazing nana to my little guy."

Amanda scoffed. "You need to give that child a name."

Wendy patted Amanda's cheek. "I know."

Erica ambled over. "Are you two reminiscing, or is this true-confession time?"

"A little of both." Wendy donned a red tunic and white sandals. "Who's driving?"

"I am." Abby joined them. "That way the rest of you can enjoy a glass of wine and not worry about getting behind the wheel."

Erica slid her arm around her daughter's shoulder as the partners strode to the den. "Since the day Abby was ticketed for blowing through a stop sign, she's been the most cautious driver in town."

"I don't ever want to face another judge, at least not in a courtroom."

"Or end up in an accident," added Erica.

Abby nodded. "That too."

Millie breezed in from the back door. "Thank you again for inviting me to join you."

Wendy looped arms with their neighbor. "There's no way we'd exclude our little guy's Grammy Millie."

"As long as the Armstrongs don't mind."

"They're hosting dinner for our families to become acquainted, and you're part of our Awesam family."

"You mean awesome."

Wendy grinned. "That too."

"Okay, you guys. It's time to go." Abby led the way out to the truck and slid behind the wheel. Ten minutes after backing down the driveway, the five women walked into Grace Prime Steakhouse. The hostess led them to a private room.

After welcoming them and introducing them to the rest of their family, Chris's mother, Linda, strategically seated the guests with the two families intermingling. She settled at one end of the table with Abby to her right and Millie to her left. Amanda sat beside Keith at the other end. Wendy was sandwiched between her fiancé and his grandmother Susan.

While Keith blessed the meal and prayed for the engaged couple, Amanda's heart swelled with admiration. The daughter she had brought into this world as well as the daughter she'd unofficially adopted had both fallen in love with men from extraordinary families. No one deserved that blessing more than Wendy.

When Keith ended the prayer, their waiter offered the choice of red or white wine, then filled Wendy and Abby's glasses with non-alcoholic white liquid. After everyone ordered, Keith reached for his glass. "One wish I've always had for my children is that they would experience relationships as wonderful as mine and their mother's. And now with Wendy and Chris's wedding days away, my wish has been fulfilled." He lifted his glass. "To the love of my son's life and our precious grandson."

Amanda's mouth curved into a satisfying smile. Even if Wendy never saw her father again, her baby would experience the joy of a loving grandfather.

Following the toast, the two families engaged in lively conversation about weddings and favorite foods. Abby shared her plans to continue working at the crisis center while taking child-psychology courses. During dinner, Millie and Susan, Chris's grandmother, seemed to hit it off as they imparted bits of wisdom from their years of experiences. Allison, Keith, and Chris told fun stories about growing up in Blue Ridge. Amanda and Erica shared tidbits about Hilltop Inn.

Moments after the waiter cleared the plates off the table, Chris tapped his spoon on his glass. "Now that we've enjoyed our first meal together as a family, my beautiful fiancée and I have two announcements. First, our wedding will take place next Saturday in the Hilltop Inn's gazebo, with our family, a couple of close friends, and any inn guests who want to join us. Afterwards, we'll have a reception in the inn's living and dining rooms. Millie, we'd like you and Grandmother Susan to prepare the food."

"We'd be delighted, right, Susan?"

"Absolutely."

"Excellent." Chris reached for Wendy's hand. "The love of my life will share the most important news."

A radiant smile lit Wendy's face. "Since the day Allison confirmed my sonogram's accuracy, I've called my baby 'little guy.' My family thought I hesitated to name him because I had only picked out girls' names, which was true at first. But then, I couldn't come up with a name that seemed to fit. Until a few days ago on a Hilton Head balcony."

Wendy turned toward Linda. "You and Keith named your son Christopher Ryan. To honor you both as well as the man who will be the most amazing daddy, our little guy's birth certificate will read Ryan Christopher, son of Christopher and Wendy Armstrong."

Linda pressed her palms together. "What a beautiful way to blend our families."

Keith nodded. "Excellent choice."

Allison signaled a thumbs-up. "Way to go, guys."

Erica smiled. "Well done."

Abby pulled her phone from her pocket and tapped the screen. "Did you know Ryan means little king?"

Amanda chuckled. "The perfect choice for the first boy in our unique, little family."

Susan rose. "And this is also the perfect time for the traditional Armstrong celebration dessert." She moved an intricately iced cake from the sideboard to the table in front of the engaged couple. "Lemon chiffon with buttercream frosting." Susan pointed to the words scribed in yellow. "Congratulations, Wendy and Chris." She handed Wendy a silver cake knife. "Your first wedding gift."

"Which I'll treasure forever." Wendy cut a slice and passed it across the table to Allison. "For my sister-in-law who will also deliver our families' first grandbaby. Maybe our second will be a girl."

Allison's glowing smile hinted that she and Mark were privately relishing their own bit of exciting news.

Wendy served cake to the rest of the guests.

Millie tasted, her eyes appraising. "Did you bake this scrumlicious cake?"

Susan grinned. "I did. Is 'scrumlicious' some sort of newfangled word?"

"I borrowed it from Abby—scrumptious and delicious. Anyway, since we're both master bakers, you need to bake the bride's wedding cake, and I'll bake the groom's."

"Excellent idea. Together we'll prepare the most delicious appetizers for our grandchildren's wedding."

One glance at Millie's expression made it clear that Susan was fast becoming her second best friend.

After dessert and another hour of family bonding, Linda pulled Amanda aside. "Does she suspect anything?"

"She doesn't have a clue." Amanda embraced Linda. "Thank you for tonight."

"This has been one of our most enjoyable family dinners we've ever had."

"The next one will be our treat to celebrate the arrival of our grandson."

Chapter 42

Still floating on cloud nine, Wendy sauntered into the kitchen humming a favorite tune then set her phone on the counter and poured a glass of orange juice.

Erica closed the dishwasher and pressed the start button. "You're extra cheery this morning."

"A short engagement has its advantages. On a balcony in Hilton Head, I said, 'yes I'll marry you,' and two weeks later I'll say, 'I do.' There's no time to waste a ton of money planning a big fancy wedding."

Amanda ambled in. "The same sentiments Morgan expressed."

"Which also proves we're both smart and practical." Wendy swallowed a sip of juice. "Are Morgan and Keith gonna be here for our wedding?"

Amanda nodded. "They'll drive up Saturday morning."

"They can stay in my room that night. Except for the cradle, I'm leaving all my bedroom furniture here. A final break from every physical reminder of my life with Gunter." Wendy grabbed her phone and tapped the screen.

"Who are you texting?"

"Kayla to bring her up-to-date."

"Your secret penpal sister." Amanda laughed. "We definitely have a unique family."

"A family that began as a bizarre wives club." Erica faced Wendy. "What's on your agenda for today?"

"My handsome fiancé and I are going to plan little...I mean, our baby's room, then go to lunch." Wendy patted her belly. "I still want to call Ryan little guy." The soft whir of a car engine sounded in Abby's parking spot. "He's here. I'll see y'all tonight." Wendy stuffed her phone into her purse then dashed out the back door.

Chris climbed out and wrapped his arms around her. "Good morning, angel."

Wendy breathed in the musky scent of his cologne. "I love that pet name."

"Have you decided what to call me other than Chris?"

"Hmm. I'm thinking either Counselor or Darling Prince Charming—"

"Everyone calls me Counselor, and the other's a mouthful."

Wendy patted his cheek. "Which is why I'm abandoning the first and shortening the second to darling."

Chris grinned "Now that we have those two important decisions made, it's time to move on to the next." He released her then opened the passenger door.

Wendy slid onto the smooth leather seat. "One item we definitely need to buy is a baby car seat."

"We'll find one after lunch." Chris closed the door then scooted to the driver's side. "I have some good news. There was a cancellation at the Blue Ridge Inn next Saturday."

Wendy's eyes widened. "Does that mean we'll spend our wedding night at the inn where we first met?"

He nodded. "In the Rose Room making new memories."

Wendy buckled her seatbelt and imagined spending their first night together as husband and wife. "Not that I'm bragging, but I was pretty sexy before my belly grew to the size of a watermelon."

A smile lit Chris's face as he reached across the console and pressed his hand on her baby bulge. "There's nothing sexier than a beautiful woman carrying a precious new life inside her body."

Wendy's eyes met his. "How do you always know the right thing to say?"

"Truth comes easy."

"You really are my Prince Charming."

He patted her belly. "And Daddy to our little king." Chris winked then gripped the steering wheel and backed onto the street. Ten minutes later he turned onto his driveway. cut through a wooded lot, and parked in front of the single-story, log cabin. "I have a surprise for you." He pressed a button above the rearview mirror opening the garage door.

Wendy's mouth fell open as she gawked at a white SUV adorned with a giant blue ribbon. "You bought me a car?"

"After next weekend, sharing a truck with Amanda and Erica will be more than a little inconvenient."

"You spent all that money, and I've never paid you a dime for all your legal services."

Chris grinned. "At least now you're eligible for the family discount. C'mon and take a look."

After relaying key features of her new ride, Chris held Wendy's hand as they walked across the porch and into the house whose smooth-walled contemporary interior stood in stark contrast to the rustic façade.

Duke greeted them with an enthusiastic tail wag.

Wendy stooped to reward the black lab with a head rub. "Have you managed to catch any squirrels?"

The dog responded with a muffled bark.

Wendy laughed. "I'll take that as a no."

"Good assumption." Chris set his keys on the granite counter separating the upscale kitchen from the dining area on the left and the great room anchored by a stone fireplace stretching to the top of the vaulted ceiling.

Wendy set her purse beside the keys then ambled to the door off the great room and peered into the main bedroom suite.

Chris joined her and slid his arm around her shoulders. "Our room obviously needs a few feminine touches."

"Actually, I love your taste. Although…" Wendy tapped her finger to her chin. "Half a dozen fancy throw pillows will add just the right amount of Wendy flair to our bed. And a pretty painting on that blank wall."

"Anything you want, angel."

Wendy leaned into him. "You know, sometimes I can be a little devilish."

Chris squeezed her shoulder. "I'm counting on it. Back to décor, at least Ryan's room is a blank canvas."

"Speaking of—" Wendy headed to the kitchen counter and removed paint swatches from her purse. "I picked these up yesterday." She scurried to the hall off the dining room which led to two more bedrooms and a bathroom. The bedroom on the right was set up as an office. Wendy stepped into the empty bedroom on the left facing the backyard. "This is the perfect view for a little boy who will one day play in those woods."

"I agree."

"What was your room like when you were growing up?"

Chris joined her. "Chaotic, but colorful."

"I have no idea how to decorate a little boy's room." Wendy handed Chris the swatches. "Which is why I want you to select the colors."

"Are you sure?"

"Positive."

Chris flipped through the choices. "How about these two?"

"Perfect. Now all we need to do is decide how to furnish his room." Two hours after browsing websites, they'd ordered everything they'd need to furnish their baby's nursery. Wendy's stomach grumbled. "All these big decisions have worked up an appetite."

"This is a good time to head out to lunch." Chris plucked his keys off the counter. "On the way, I need to stop by my parents' house and pick up a client file."

During the drive, a smile bloomed as Wendy closed her eyes and pictured Ryan's room with stuffed animals and a comfy chair where she could rock her baby to sleep.

"What happy thoughts are floating around in your brilliant mind?"

"Our babies will grow up in a happy home with a mom and dad who will never abandon them, and an extended family that loves them uncon-ditionally. A blessing I'll never take for granted."

Chris stole a quick glance at Wendy. "Have I told you how much I love you today?"

"One more time than I've told you."

"You can catch up later." Chris pulled the car to the curb and cut the engine in front of the Armstrongs' two-story, stone-and-brick home overlooking downtown Blue Ridge. "Hold on a second." He tapped his phone. "This might take a few minutes, so come in with me."

"All right." They headed up the sidewalk to the front porch, then into the foyer. The moment they passed the formal dining and living rooms and stepped into the combination kitchen family room, a dozen voices shouted surprise amid enthusiastic applause.

Wendy gasped as her hand went to her chest.

Linda approached. "Welcome to your combination wedding and baby shower."

"How did you pull this off without me having a clue?" Wendy's eyes shifted to Amanda, Erica, and Millie. "The entire Awesam team is here. Who's gonna welcome today's Hilltop arrivals?"

"I'm heading to the inn to assume innkeeper duties while the rest of the team celebrates." Chris kissed Wendy's cheek, then headed out.

"Oh my gosh." Wendy's focus shifted to Morgan standing beside Abby. "You drove up from Atlanta?"

"My new job doesn't start until next week. Besides, I wouldn't miss my sister's surprise party. Kevin will drive up and join me Saturday morning."

Faith, Blue Ridge Inn's assistant innkeeper, stood beside her daughter and Abby's best friend, Hannah. "I hear you're spending your honeymoon at our inn."

Wendy pressed her hand to her belly. "Chris and I figured we need to stay close to home and to my doctor."

Allison signaled a thumbs-up. "Smart decision."

Britany joined them. "Chris chose the right woman, after all." She held up her left hand displaying a diamond ring. "I hear you're giving your baby the same name as my fiancé."

Wendy's brows raised. "You and Ryan are engaged?"

Her face beamed. "As of two weeks ago.

"That's awesome." Wendy hugged Chris's high school girlfriend. "It's ironic how my baby will have the same name as the guy who won your heart. Especially since I once considered you my rival."

Linda slid her arm around her daughter's shoulders. "You and Britany both ended up with the right men."

Britany nodded. "Mom's right."

Susan looped her arm around Wendy's elbow. "As our guest of honor, who's only a few weeks away from giving birth, you need to give your feet a break and take the seat of honor." She led Wendy to a recliner angled toward the L-shaped, sectional sofa. "Before you open your presents, we'll enjoy a lovely lunch of delectable finger foods."

Wendy's eyes teared up as she peered at a baby car seat surrounded by dozens of wrapped gifts stacked around the floor-to-ceiling stone fireplace. "My whole life...no one has ever given me such a special party."

Susan gently dabbed Wendy's tears. "Today is the first of many special celebrations, honey."

Chapter 43

Sunshine illuminated the cloudless sky as Erica, Linda, and Abby wrapped a garland of flowers around the gazebo railing, and Morgan and Kevin draped loops of sheer white fabric between the pillars. "How appropriate that our first wedding celebration is for one of Hilltop's owners."

Amanda attached the end of the garland to the railing. "Especially since the wedding-venue concept began with Wendy's vision."

Morgan stepped back from the ladder. "Outdoor weddings are magical."

"I agree. Which is why one day, Tommy and I will have our wedding right here."

Morgan stared at Abby. "Are you making some sort of announcement?"

She shook her head. "We want to wait until we can afford our own place."

Erica stole a quick glance at her daughter. *Hopefully until they're both in their twenties.*

Millie and Susan headed up the walkway. "The dining room is ready for the reception."

"It's time for Amanda and me to tend to the bride." Erica waved over her shoulder as she headed down the garden path. Back at the ranch house, she carried a bottle of chilled non-alcoholic cider and flutes to Wendy's room and closed the door. "This is a special moment for the three of us."

Amanda secured Wendy's long blonde hair behind one ear with the elegant pearl-and-rhinestone floral clasp Morgan had worn for her wedding. "The day you first breezed into the Blue Ridge Inn dining room and introduced yourself, none of us in our wildest imaginations could have predicted today. Although, you did flirt with Chris a couple of times before we left town."

"Hey, I was simply being friendly."

"Sure you were."

Wendy lifted *Sugar Snow* off the dresser and traced her finger over the log cabin pictured on the cover. "It's ironic how this little book represented the perfect family to me, and now the love of my life and I will raise our babies in a real log cabin. With my amazing family minutes away." She set the book down. "I love you both so much."

"A mutual feeling that calls for a pre-wedding toast for our exclusive little wives club." Erica twisted the cap off the bottle and filled the flutes. "During the past six months, the three of us have walked through the deepest valleys and emerged triumphant."

Amanda tapped her glass to Erica's then to Wendy's. "To our beautiful bride and brilliant chief financial officer." She sipped the golden liquid. "Every time I open our freezer, I remember the day you persuaded Erica and me to help you create a miniature snow family on Blue Ridge Inn's front porch railing."

Awesam's CEO grinned. "With pretzel-stick limbs and raisin eyes."

"Think of all the fun you two would have missed if you'd ignored me and stayed inside."

"We couldn't resist your powers of persuasion." Amanda swallowed another sip. "I can't imagine what Faith thought when she first laid eyes on our creation."

Erica nodded. "Especially when those fist-sized snowballs began to melt and drip all over the porch. One of these days we'll laugh about our own guests and Millie's crazy antics."

Awesam's partners continued to reminisce until Abby peeked in. "The guests are all here. Y'all need to be ready in ten minutes."

"We're on it." The moment the door closed, Wendy's partners helped her step into the lacy white maternity wedding gown they'd found online.

Erica stepped back. "You're radiant and beautiful."

Amanda placed her hands on Wendy's shoulders. "Are you ready to meet your groom?"

"Almost." Wendy donned the diamond earrings Chris had given her the day after the surprise shower. "Now I'm ready."

Wendy held the bouquet Millie had created from her own garden and stepped onto the inn's patio while Erica and Amanda joined the guests lined up along the path leading to the gazebo.

Her father-in-law held out his arm. "Our son is eagerly waiting to become one with his beautiful bride."

Wendy slid her hand around his bicep. "I love Chris with all my heart."

Keith squeezed her hand. "You two young people are blessed to have found each other."

A recorded version of the bridal march signaled the guests to turn toward the inn. Wendy's heart drummed in her chest as her father-in-law escorted her along the stone path toward her groom wearing a white tuxedo with a gold lapel. Her eyes met Chris's the moment she stepped into the gazebo.

The family's pastor faced the couple. "Who gives this woman's hand in marriage?"

"I do." Keith placed her hand in his son's.

Following a few rehearsed words, the pastor faced Chris. "You may share the vows you've prepared now."

Chris's gaze met Wendy's. "When I met you, I was intrigued by the girl with beautiful eyes, a warm smile, and playful nature. I fell in love with the woman whose heart is tender and whose mind is sharp. A woman who possesses the strength of a lioness and the gentleness of a lamb. I choose to spend eternity with you without pause, without doubt. I promise to laugh with you during times of joy and comfort you during times of sorrow. To love you unconditionally and passionately. To protect and honor you. I will cherish you and our family as a loving husband and father. Your beautiful face is the one I want to see every morning when I awaken and every evening before I fall asleep. You are my best friend, my inspiration, and my one true love."

Wendy's heart beat wildly in her chest as she gazed deep into her groom's eyes. She summoned a breath. "You are my dream come true. I promise to love you with every fiber of my being and to stand beside you as your partner and your lover. I promise to dream with you, to celebrate every precious moment of our lives with you, and to walk hand in hand with you through every valley and across every mountaintop. I want to wake up to your arms wrapped around me every morning and every night until the end of time. You are my rock. You are my best friend. You are my one true love."

The pastor's next words were but a blur as Wendy connected with her groom on a spiritual level that lifted her spirits higher than she'd ever experienced. The moment Chris drew her into his arms and kissed her as his wife, she understood beyond a shadow of a doubt that God had brought them together.

Family, close friends, and six Hilltop guests cheered and applauded as the newlywed couple strolled hand in hand down the English country garden path and into the inn. Wendy's heart overflowed with joy during the cheerful reception catered by Millie and Susan.

Three hours after stepping into the gazebo as Miss Thomason, Wendy clung to Chris's arm as Faith welcomed them to the Blue Ridge Inn and escorted them to the Rose Room across from the parlor. Wendy entered the Victorian-inspired space and drew her fingers across the four-poster canopy king bed's soft comforter. "This is the inn's most romantic room."

"The perfect setting for the world's most beautiful bride." Chris pushed the door closed. "I have a gift for you."

Wendy laced her fingers around her husband's neck. "You already surprised me with a car and diamond earrings."

"I know, but this gift is extra special." Chris gently pulled away then removed a folded document from his suitcase and handed it to her.

Tears of unspeakable joy spilled as Wendy focused on the adoption paper.

Chris gently dabbed her cheeks. "I am now and forever Ryan Christoper Armstrong's legal father."

"Oh my gosh. How did you pull that off with Gunter?"

"I'm an attorney, with the power of persuasion."

Understanding that mere words would fail to express the depth of her love, Wendy melted into her groom's arms and kissed him with heart-pounding passion.

Chapter 44

Wendy settled into her new life with ease, savoring every moment with Chris before he returned to work. Reluctant to drive anywhere alone, she fulfilled her CFO duties from their home office and called Millie a half-dozen times for cooking advice. Duke kept her company while Chris was away from home. At least one family member visited every day as she counted down to her due date.

Twelve days after spending their first night together as a married couple, Wendy sat on the leather sofa in their great room, gripped Chris's hand, and counted the length of the tenth contraction in fifty minutes. The moment it subsided, Chris grabbed his phone. He pressed Allison's number and gave her an update.

"It's time. I'll meet you at the hospital."

Chris pocketed his phone then helped Wendy to her feet. "How's your pain level?"

"Still tolerable." She clung to his arm as they made their way to the garage. The moment she slid onto her SUV's passenger seat, another contraction hit. When it subsided, Wendy pulled her phone from her purse and pressed Amanda's number.

She answered before the first ring ended.

"We're leaving for the hospital now."

"Erica and I are on our way."

Chris backed out of the garage, then turned the car around and headed down the driveway.

Wendy grimaced as a third contraction erupted—this one the most intense yet. "You might need to speed up a bit. It seems this little guy is eager to meet his mommy and daddy face-to-face."

"Especially now that we've given him a name."

"The perfect name, mind you."

During the remainder of the drive, Wendy hummed her favorite tune while focusing on the passing scenery—until another painful contraction confronted her.

Chris pulled onto the hospital driveway.

Allison waited for them at the entrance. She opened the passenger door and helped Wendy step out. The moment her feet touched the pavement, her water broke, depositing a puddle between her new car and a wheel-chair.

Allison helped her patient step around the puddle and lower onto the chair. "I have a feeling you're one of those fortunate first-time mothers who delivers her baby in record time." After giving Chris instructions, she wheeled her patient straight to a birthing room.

Wendy changed into a hospital gown amid a flurry of activity and es-calating contractions. Chris rushed in and held her hand. Moments later Amanda and Erica joined them. In between contractions, they took turns pressing cold cloths to Wendy's forehead while Chris stroked her fingers and whispered words of encouragement.

Before another hour passed, Ryan Christopher Armstrong pushed his way into the world, took his first breath, and announced his arrival with a hardy cry.

Chris pushed a strand of damp hair off Wendy's cheek the moment Allison laid his son on his mother's bare chest. "You were amazing, angel, and our son is perfect."

Wendy gazed into her little guy's blue eyes and fell deeply in love. "He's beautiful."

The moment Chris touched Ryan's open palm, his son wrapped his tiny fingers around his daddy's forefinger. Tears spilled from Chris's eyes. "I love you and your amazing mother more than mere words can convey."

Wendy's heart swelled with joy as she gently kissed her son and whispered, "This is the first of a lifetime of happy moments you'll share with the most wonderful family this side of heaven."

"Beginning with my big announcement." Allison swaddled her nephew and placed him in her brother's arms.

Wendy peered at her sister-in-law's glowing smile. "Oh my gosh, you're pregnant, aren't you?"

Alison grasped Wendy's hand. "In November, Ryan's cousin will enter this world as our family's first granddaughter."

Wendy squeezed her sister-in-law's hand. "We'll need to plan a big family Christmas celebration at Hilltop Inn."

"Perfect."

Thank you for reading The Wedding. Click here to preorder book four, Christmas at Hilltop Inn: https://www.amazon.com/dp/B0DD52Z3BP? ref

More Blue Ridge Series titles will follow in 2025. Keep up with the progress in my newsletter. If you aren't receiving my newsletters click here: https://www.subscribepage.com/pat-nichols-newsletterand I'll send you a link to a free standalone novel.

Want to learn more about my books and my author journey? Check out my website: https://patnicholsauthor.blog

Acknowledgements

Continuing to write books for the Blue Ridge series is a so much fun. The reception from Blue Ridge residents has been heartwarming—especially from John Lavin, owner of the real Blue Ridge Inn and Jennifer Sullivan, owner of Owl's Nest. If you visit Blue Ridge, both the inn and store are wonderful.

I appreciate and value all who are joining me on my writing journey. To my editor and dear friend, Sherri Stewart for her ability to take my work to a new level. To my cover designer, Elaina Lee for her artistic genius.

To my beta readers, Pat Davis, Bev Feldkamp, Carlene Dunn, Kitty Metzger, and Kathy Warner for providing feedback and suggestions. To my launch team and all who post reviews for your support. To my newsletter friends and readers for your loyalty.

A special thank you to my family for encouraging me and helping me prove it's never too late to follow your dreams.

Above all, I'm grateful to God for His amazing grace and the gift of eternal life through Jesus.